ANDREI VIRZO

Salt in the Fifth House

CanvasForum

Salt in the Fifth House

FIFTH HOUSE

Andrei Virzo

For Ed, may this remind you daily how worthy you are of love and how much your mother, cousins, aunts, uncles, and I love you.

You are more than words on paper.
You are our cosita linda. Your story is
still being written, hermanito bello.

Andrei Virzo

Contents

Foreword

There is a lot of discourse over the use of AI in writing. I have never been a person who favors lying, so I am going to own up and be honest about my use of AI in this project.

There is an artist out there who is currently receiving rewards for taking my brother's painful story, without consent, knowing how he was struggling with addiction, and publishing his work.

This story destroyed my family emotionally. Multiple lawyers said we had grounds to sue because this person absolutely broke the law, and we had proof right in their copyrighted "art".

Since we couldn't sue, because my brother was not in a good place to do so, my mother and I decided to write and publish our ACTUAL family's story in the name of our family. Salt in the Fifth House is that story.

I have PTSD and ADHD, and the combination of those made me not sleep until I published this story. I paid ghostwriters who scammed me and did not finish the work "on time." I needed the story of my family to be out before that "artist" decided to franchise my brother's painful memories any further.

I used AI to help me edit. I used Sudowrite trained on my own manuscript, outline, and wording. I also trained my own AI model on my own manuscript to help me finish the ghostwriting that the scammers, to whom I lost thousands of dollars, did not complete.

I will NOT be using AI for my next series, which I have already started writing on paper. I am a new author writing from a place of pain and have made many first-time self-publishing mistakes. I have edited and rewritten and re-published this book many times since I found out the effect that AI has on the writing community to remove any AI assistance. However, I still want to be transparent about the history here.

I'm very open about this. Thank you for reading my family's story.

Love,

Andrei Virzo

Preface

If you've picked up this book and you're struggling—with meth, with pills, with booze, or with the long, sleepless nights that come when you try to outrun your own mind—pause here.

There is no shame in the aching. No sin in seeking refuge.

If you are hurting, if you are using, if you are barely holding the pieces of yourself together: please, reach out. You are not alone. You are never alone. There are even strangers who will meet you in your darkest hour and call you by your name, not your mistakes.

Here are some lifelines to start with:

- **SAMHSA's National Helpline**: 1-800-662-HELP (4357)
  – Free, confidential, 24/7 assistance for individuals facing substance use disorders.
- **The Trevor Project**: 1-866-488-7386 / thetrevorproject.org
  – 24/7 crisis support for LGBTQ+ youth.
- **National Runaway Safeline**: 1-800-RUNAWAY (786-2929) / 1800runaway.org – Support for youth in crisis, including those experiencing homelessness.
- **True Colors United**: truecolorsunited.org – Resources

and support for LGBTQ+ youth experiencing homeless-ness.

- **Ali Forney Center**: aliforneycenter.org – Housing and support services for LGBTQ+ youth in New York City.
- **New Alternatives**: newalternativesnyc.org – Support services for LGBTQ+ homeless youth in New York City
- **Gloria Casarez Residence**: projecthome.org/gloria-casarez-residence – LGBTQ-friendly affordable housing for young adults in Philadelphia.

If you've been told God stopped loving you when you came out or when you came undone, know this: love does not abandon its children.

Local **Episcopal churches** across the U.S. welcome LGBTQIA+ people not as a charity, but as family. Many offer housing aid, food, warm showers, and even just a quiet pew to sit and breathe.

To find an Episcopal church near you, visit:

- **Episcopal Church Directory**: episcopalchurch.org/find-a-church
- **Episcopal Diocese of New Jersey**: dioceseofnj.org/map-of-the-diocese-list-of-churchesEpiscopal Diocese of New Jersey

This book was written from the scars of addiction, the ache of being queer in a world too cruel, and the healing that can grow from broken places. If you see yourself in these pages, I hope you'll stay. I hope you'll fight. I hope you'll find your way to a warm meal, a soft bed, and a love that feels like home.

You are not alone. Not now. Not ever.

With love,
Andrei Virzo

One

WHAT THE FUCK!

There are moments when the ground beneath you doesn't crack open dramatically but shifts in a nearly imperceptible, devastating way, like a breath held too long or a note sung just out of tune after you've paid way too much to see a live opera you don't quite understand. You hear that note, look around, and think, Why on earth did I spend $982 on this ticket, and Why does my stomach feel like there's a hole in it?

Perhaps not everyone feels these moments of deep regret when it comes to their spending habits. Maybe it's something else that makes you feel breathless. Everyone remembers a moment that hits you so deeply in your core that you feel guilty, dizzy, and gross. You think so many things at once, and even though you live in a part of the world with slim chances of an earthquake, you ask yourself, Is this an earthquake? You're left reeling, not because of an actual earthquake, but because the ground rearranged itself into something unrecognizable.

That's what this felt like.

Some people float through life with carefully polished personas, wrapping themselves in artistry and nostalgia. They craft elegant soundbites about others' suffering as if borrowed pain is a language they're fluent in. They speak with reverence, but the reverence is hollow. They mistake proximity for a connection that is deep enough to understand someone truly.

And sometimes, they mistake someone's deepest wounds for inspiration.

That's how I felt when I found out about the exhibit. It was like something sacred had been taken—not an object or a memory, but a person—my brother.

Luca isn't a theme. He's not a motif or a cautionary tale rendered in pastels, oils, and glitter. He's real. Complex. Messy. Brilliant. Alive.

When I found out, so many memories rushed through my head—memories of his real canvas: his sweet smile, his giggles in the mornings before school, his fear when we heard shattering at home, his reliance on holding my hand or looking for my eyes during the darkest moments of our childhood.

But none of that made it into the exhibit.

Instead, someone who once claimed to love him decided to paint his suffering. To shape his trauma into a spectacle. To pin it to pristine white walls and let strangers gawk, praise, and theorize as if his life were a thesis. As if his pain belonged to them.

His fractured spirit wasn't like some part of an art installation. It is an art installation—a beacon for all to see and know.

Let me walk you through that cold Philly morning. That morning I can never forget. It was bone-chilling, clinging to

2

your jeans even after you'd come inside, wet pavement, bus exhaust smells in the air, and gray skies with a tint of brightness you have to earn. The kitchen window had icy fog, and my coffee had already gone lukewarm because I'd been pacing for half an hour.

My thumb hovered over Luca's name, that tiny contact photo of him from three Thanksgivings ago, where he's smiling, but his eyes aren't.

Calling him is like casting a line into a stormy ocean. You wait. Sometimes he bites. He often disappears beneath the incandescent roaring ocean waves, grazed by lightning.

But disappearing is his coping mechanism. Mine is insistence.

So I called him again. And again, and just as I'm about to try for the seventh time, the line clicks.

"Heyyy," he says, soft and syrupy, like chamomile tea spiked with a fifth of Jameson.

I exhale. "Hey, you! How are you? Where are you?" I ask it lightly, like I didn't just rehearse that exact tone fifteen times. Don't spook him. Don't sound desperate.

"Ehh, I'm alright."

Ehh.

That one syllable hit me like a paintball. Three soft pellets that sting on impact. I know that "ehh." I've known it since we were kids, when he'd come home from school with a bruised lip and a silent story. It's the same sound he made after our dad's funeral, sitting at the edge of the couch in a too-small suit, biting the inside of his cheek.

"What's going on?" I ask in my usual tone.

He laughs, an ambiguous laugh with his voice half bracing. "You're not gonna believe this," he says, warily.

My chest tightens. It's never good when he says that. I know it

3

better than anyone. That phrase has preceded everything from manic episodes to losing jobs to breakups he claimed "weren't that deep," but left him crying on my couch for three days.

"Tell me," I say, steady but soft.

Then he drops it.

"It's Bjorn," he says, still clenching.

Bjorn, that emotionally manipulative, pastel-turtleneck-wearing devil in designer shoes, had always had a way of piercing Luca's soft spots. I exhale, anxiously waiting for the full tea.

What did Bjorn do this time? Sometimes, I wish I could erase Bjorn from my brother's life. I understand the fixation, as someone who often fixates on things, I get it. Also, as a person with eyes, I get it. Bjorn was beyond handsome. He was a walking, talking Viking statue with a copper-wired beard that could grow down to his chest. His hair formed shiny, foamy waves made of silk. His eyes were a piercing hazel, like a fish-eye freshly printed photograph of a sunset on a lake.

Bjorn naturally drew everyone's eyes in the room right to his sun-soaked eyes. When my brother started dating him, Bjorn had boy features; he was younger, slimmer, and looked less like a statue and more like a nerdy blonde kid. But in his late twenties, he grew into a three-dimensional Viking that everyone was drawn to.

I always see my brother's lovers as sweet boys who can eventually ride away with my brother into the sunset on a horse with the words "happily ever after" hovering over them. Until they hurt him, that is. Then I see them for what they are, and Bjorn, well, Bjorn was a Viking in distress hiding behind his success as an artist. He looked like the sun, but when you kept eye contact with him, you could see the empty narcissism of a supernova. A man who hurt too much to love anyone outside of the minuscule torn scraps of love for himself he could muster daily.

"He… He created a thirty-piece art exhibit related to… about… me," Luca says, his words barely more than a whisper.

I blink, unsure if I'd heard him right. "What do you mean about you?" I hoped it wasn't what I thought it was. I waited and noticed the involuntary tapping of my foot.

"Me," he says. "The art exhibition is me… the worst parts of me anyway."

Luca? I try to comprehend. An art exhibit about my little Luca?

The worst part of him, meaning the art, was not about his success but about his pain. About his trauma. Luca. My baby brother. The boy who once buried a bird in the backyard and cried until I rode my bicycle to the Dollar Store to get him a stuffed bird plush that we named "Bird." The man who saved every letter I ever sent him from college and cataloged them by mood, the person who still completely breaks down if someone places a mirror in front of him—was now a fucking art exhibit.

Can anyone imagine the irony in it? He laughed when he told me this. It was a brittle, fragmented laugh. It rattled in his throat and came out sounding like a scream in a nice suit—the kind that's all sharp edges, no softness left.

I couldn't find words. I couldn't relate to the anguish my brother was feeling. So I did what any sibling would do. I summoned the righteous fury of our bloodline and said:

"WHAT THE FUCK?!"

He laughs again, the pitch a little too high to be authentic. If you weren't listening, you'd think he is okay, just brushing it off. But I could tell. That laugh was falling apart.

We talk a little more, and he tells me about some of the paintings on his wall.

"So, what do they look like?" I ask quietly.

He exhales like he's about to read his autopsy report.

"One of them," he says, "is me. Kind of. Except I'm... melting. Like a pile of regret caught in a microwave. Real classy." He pauses. "My eyes are purple in it. Not, like, lavender-romantic, more 'possessed by every bad decision I ever made.'"

"Chic," I say. "Demonic despair is very in right now."

"There's another one," he says. "It's harder to explain. I look... different. Technically, I'm a rat. Like, small. Insignificant. Vermin-chic."

"A rat?" I echo, because subtlety has never been my strength.

"Yeah. But not a gross one," he insists. "Like, a cute one if that makes sense?... Lost in what I think is supposed to be Canada? There are pine trees. Snow. Existential dread. You know it's me."

"I mean, if I saw a sad little rat in flannel having a crisis in the Yukon, I'd assume it was you," I offer.

He hums like that's the nicest thing anyone's said to him all week.

For a moment, he almost says something more. Instead, his voice softens. "There's one with our childhood bed sheet. The red one. With the white stars."

I swallow bile. "He used that?"

"Hmm," he says. "Right in the middle. Like it was a flag for... a war, lost or something."

I was infuriated, words catching in my throat. "Was... was Mom painted, too?"

He hesitates, then answers, "He painted the bald spot. The one you'd only see if you were there that night. In the kitchen."

My eyes sting. "How did Bjorn know?"

He doesn't answer.

Then, a long silence.

We drift into safer subjects from there on, current events, almost instinctively.

"So... what else is new?" I ask, voice thin.

He tries to sound normal. "Not much. There's this cafe I go to now. It's quiet."

"That sounds nice," I say.

"There's a dog that sleeps by the window," he adds, almost absentmindedly. "I met him at the park, and he follows me around sometimes."

I smile a little, though it feels far away. "I wish I could see it."

Luca has been quiet for a while. "I miss you," I say, and the words barely make it out.

"I miss you, too," he says. I appreciate that he always tells me he misses me, too. He always states it clearly, with no periods or pauses.

When we hang up, I do what I always do.

I Google it.

Two hours.

Two endless hours scrolling through high-res JPEGs of my brother's pain. Beautiful lighting. Stark backgrounds. Quotes from gallery attendees describing the work as "UNAPOLO-GETICALLY RAW," "A TRIUMPH OF VULNERABILITY," "A LOVE LETTER TO THOSE WE LOSE."

A love letter? To those we lose? Luca wasn't gone. We didn't lose him, he's right here. His light is still there. What the fuck is wrong with people? Every wound, every heartbreak, every relapse, every time he flinched when someone raised their voice was painted, abstracted, and sold.

7

Thirty paintings. Thirty. And that wasn't even counting the "mixed media" installations, which sounded like someone ran our childhood through a paper shredder, dipped it in glitter and resin, then slapped a $15,000 price tag on it.

Oh, and the Washington Post covered it.

And then, there it was.

Me.

In one of the paintings. I think. Not my face, but the outline. My shape, blurred and static. I was in the background of his story, watching, not saving. And there was our mom. Her scalp was exposed under harsh lighting. And there was that red bed sheet, twisted into a crumpled noose.

How did Bjorn get all these things so right and so wrong at the same time?

I couldn't breathe.

I grab my coat and walk speedily. Down the block. Around the corner. Past the bakery that still sells our favorite empanadas. Past the train station where Luca used to wait with headphones in his ears, quietly taking the day in.

I walk and walk, doing all the CBT breathing exercises I learned in therapy, whispering things like "change your environment" and "disrupt the spiral" until the world stops tilting under my feet.

I finally come back inside my home, where I find my husband standing in the kitchen, sleeves rolled up, quietly moving around the stove. He is making eggs, scrambled just the way I like, a little overcooked because he knows I can't stand them runny. Toast is already cooling on the counter. The familiar scent of butter and coffee fills the room, trying its best to soothe whatever storm I walk in with.

He hands me a plate without a word, just that soft, steady

look he always gives me when he knows something's wrong but won't push. He sits across from me at the little kitchen table, elbows on the worn wood, hands wrapped around his mug. He waits, letting the silence settle between us, patient in a way that makes me feel safe and a little seen.

I poke at my eggs, but the words get stuck in my throat when I finally say it out loud, banging the fork, "My brother's ex-boyfriend made a thirty-piece art exhibit about every addiction my brother's ever had. Can you believe it?!"

He stops, mid-sip. Blinks. For a second, I thought he hadn't heard me. Slowly, his eyebrows shooting up, "WHAT THE FUCK."

Exactly. He is my soulmate.

Two

LION

꧁ꙮ꧂

Luca was born in late July, with the kind of fiery air only the stars could design—a Leo, sun-drenched and lion-hearted, reigning from the fifth house like it was his divine inheritance. It all makes sense in retrospect: the quiet yet unforgettable print he left in every room, like a curtain call, was inevitable; the relentless pursuit of joy, love, and applause, not out of vanity but out of a deep, almost childlike need to shine brightly enough to guide someone else home. His passions weren't hobbies—they were epics. His crushes are operas. Even his pain had a spotlight and a soliloquy. The fifth house, the cosmic playground of creativity, pleasure, and self-expression, had carved its initials into his rib cage. He didn't just feel things—he lived them out loud, in color, in fire. And maybe that's why he cooked the way he did. Perhaps that's why he loved with the same desperate, blazing sincerity that could light up a city or burn it to the ground.

"Baby Luca has arrived!"

I hear my aunt's voice bursting through the hallway, breathless, high-pitched with joy, trembling like a bell struck too hard. "We have to go!" she announces, her footsteps quick and uneven as she enters the room. Her hands flutter at her sides, searching for keys or a purse or something else she's already holding. Her eyes shine like she's seen heaven. She turns to me and smiles that soft, grown-up smile that only adults seem to know how to do. She brushes a curl away from my face, her touch feather-light.

"Come on, beautiful," she whispers, her voice suddenly humble. "Your brother is here."

We pile into the car like we're chasing something ephemeral… Maybe we are. A new life has just begun, and we're racing to stand at its threshold.

The hospital in Argentina is loud and full of movement, humming machines, nurses calling to one another in clipped Spanish, footsteps tapping against linoleum like a fast heartbeat. There's a sharp, sterile scent, bleach and metal, and something faintly floral, like someone tried to make the place smell kind.

I remember the floors, impossibly shiny and bold blue, like we're walking through the shallow end of a pool. The elevator is a giant, metallic box, vast and echoing. It groans and hums as it swallows us whole. My entire family is there: Tito, Palo, Me-Lina, and Sacha.

Sacha, or "Sa-chi-ta," as Grandma always blurts out like it's one long, musical word. She never quite nails the syllables. We joke that she makes names up on the spot, borrowing bits from soap operas or American movies. Honestly, considering some of the names floating around in our family, it's not that far-fetched.

We rush down the hallway. We know the room is on the left, the big one, and we push through the door just as I hear it.

"Hijaaa."

That word hits me like warm water, like something ancient and intimate. "Hija." It's my name, but softer. My name wrapped in lullabies, prayers, and soft hands that pull the blanket up to my chin at night. Only Mami says it like that. With pride. With tenderness.

And then I see her—my mami.

My mother was lying in the hospital bed, a loose gown draped over her shoulders, her hair curling and frizzing in that stubborn way it always does when she's tired. Her face is flushed and glowing, despite the purple hollows blooming beneath her eyes. Her hands, always moving, always doing something, are still now. They cradle around something so small, so quiet, it takes me a second to understand.

My mami was born to be a mother. Not just mine. Not just Luca's, but everyone around us. She became a mother to my ex, and my brother's ex, and even Bjorn; yes, that Bjorn. That two-faced motherfucker.

She lifts her gaze to me, her voice soft and steady. "Hija, conoce a tu hermano, Luca." It meant, 'Daughter, meet your brother, Luca.'

And there he was… my little brother. Wrapped in a pale-yellow blanket, tiny beyond belief, his skin flushed like a peach, soft as petals. His eyes flutter open, then close again, like he's deciding whether this world is worth seeing yet. He makes a tiny whimper, so close to a cry, but gentler, more like a sigh or a question.

He doesn't look real. He looks like something borrowed from another world.

I lean in closer, my breath catching. And suddenly, something inside me stretches wide, a kind of awe I've never felt before. It quickly tightens. Something else creeps in behind the wonder.

Wait.

Is he Mom's only baby now?

What about me?

I'm the cutest, aren't I?

But why is baby Luca so, so, so fucking cute!

I don't think that exact phrase. I'm still too little for the glamorous poly-functional four-letter word. But was jealousy creeping in? It was there, right? A realization that maybe I'm not the sun anymore, just one more star in Mami's sky.

But then Luca moves.

One tiny hand slips from the blanket and brushes against mine. His fingers, impossibly small, curl around my pinky finger like they've done it a hundred times. Like he knows me already. Like he's saying, you, too. You are here. And just like that, something melts. Something revered and ancient and wild. I'm not just a daughter anymore. I'm a sister. Luca's sister....

I recall the jealousy that lingered with me in the initial months that followed. It was this looming shadow that stretched behind me when Mami bent down to kiss Luca's cheeks, or when she hummed a lullaby I used to think was mine. But slowly, something shifted. What stays with me, more than anything, is how deeply lovable Luca is.

His dimples, two of them, appear like little exclamation points when he smiles. And he smiles like sunshine. He smiles with his ears, his ears would wiggle while the exclamation points lit up his cheeks. His whole face lights up like he's got a secret, but only he's got the answers, the keys, and like it's all so silly to be a secret anyway. He's warm. Quiet. Gentle. That's my Luca.

My little sweetie pie.

No matter what version of himself he wears for the world, distant, sharp, moody, I still see that boy with syrupy giggles and peanut butter hands. The one who clung to me like a shadow. The one who trusted the world because he trusted me. That's the Luca imprinted inside my heart.

When Mami went back to work, her hands were always full, and her feet were always tired. It was I who stayed home with him. I became the one to take his temperature when his fevers spiked. The one to sit beside him and count his breaths when his chest wheezed like an old accordion. I read over his homework, even when I didn't understand a word. I reheated the food Mami made; it was always simple and always good.

And somewhere along the way, I start to think: I'm his mom, too.

And I like it. I like being the one who knows.

I like being the one who loves.

I've always wanted to be like Mami. The kind of woman who anticipates needs before anyone speaks them. The kind who listens through actions, who says I love you through packed lunches and the smell of eggs frying before school.

I remember her meals, always healthy, always real. No candies, no neon snack cakes like the other kids brought in. Just what our little bodies needed: bright salads, soft proteins, warm pastas, eggs in a hundred variations. Mami showed love in her details. In the effort. In the simplicity of little moments.

We didn't have much. But everything we had, we loved.

Luca and I had the whole day together. Especially when we were little. One of our favorite games was playing radio hosts. We'd crawl under the blanket fort and pretend we were on the air. We'd press the big red "record" button on an old tape

14

recorder. The mic was a wooden spoon. Our voices filled the space.

"Hello, hello, hello, Radio Baba Land here," I'd announce, trying not to giggle.

I'd nudge him. "Say holaaa, Luca."

He'd grin, his dimples deep and sweet. "Hola Luca," he'd chirp, proud of himself.

I'd burst out laughing. "Nooo! Just say hola! Not Hola Luca!"

He'd giggle uncontrollably. "Oh, thorry!" he'd lisp, the S's sliding out like honey. And we'd laugh until the blanket fort shook.

My little Luca. My co-host. My world.

People don't see the sweet little radio host in him. People see the torn leather jacket. Completely missing his essence. It feels like people don't get him. Sometimes, it feels like he doesn't even get himself.

When strangers look at him now, with his tired eyes and quiet intensity, they invent stories. They think he's a tragedy and didn't get enough love. That his sadness is a bruise formed from neglect, but they're wrong.

Luca was loved. He is loved.

He doesn't speak that language in the way others expect. He's never been good at explaining feelings. But neither are most people, if we're honest. Anyone who's ever been in love knows that silence can be its language. You don't need grand speeches to be worthy of care. You don't need to bleed publicly to prove your pain is real. Luca's love is in his actions. In the way he used to crawl into my lap when I was sad, without saying a word. In the way he'd gently tug at my sleeve to show me something he made. In the way he listens, closely, even when you think he's not. In the way he remembers.

15

That's my Luca.

Not a mystery. Not a tragedy.

Just a boy who was deeply, wildly, unequivocally loved.

And still is.

Luca has always been loved. Not just loved, adored. By our mother, first and forever. By me. By his father, in his own fractured, distant way. By every lover he's ever had, even the ones who didn't know how to love him right. It's impossible not to love Luca. He walks into a room, and people soften, their edges blur. Something in his face, open, curious, already aching, invites you to ask questions. Makes you want to reach for him, even if you don't know why.

Loving Luca didn't always feel easy. Not for me. Being someone's guardian when I was still a child was strange. Seven. Eight. Nine. Ten. Fourteen. Seventeen. At times, I hated it. Bitterly.

I hated how it stole my freedom and made me the serious one, the caretaker, when I just wanted to be the silly sister. The one with inside jokes and dance routines, not who made doctor appointments and packed school lunches. Other times, I wore the role like armor, with pride. I told myself, This is who I'm meant to be. I was his protector, his defender. I was his first safe place. I called him my baby before I knew what raising one meant. But I also told myself, in the quiet hours, in the gaps between arguments, I failed him, especially at ten.

I was ten years old, trying to carry a toddler's universe on my back, and when I inevitably stumbled, I blamed myself for the crash. "My therapist says ten-year-olds shouldn't be guardians," I mention now, half-laughing when I say it. But the guilt doesn't laugh back. It just lingers, soft, heavy, unshakable.

By the time I reached my teens, resentment had taken root—

a slow-brewing ache that turned into irritation, guilt, and distance. I resented being his parent. And he, in turn, resented me. We didn't talk about it much, but one day, when the air between us felt especially tight, he turned to me and said it, quietly, but sharp enough to cut.

"All I ever wanted was for you to be my sister."

That sentence still echoes. But what he didn't know was that I was his sister. Fiercely. That was my version of sisterhood, protecting him at all costs. That's how I understood love back then: as a form of defense. As a sacrifice. As a duty.

It wasn't always pretty, but it was always love. Luca is so much like Mami, almost painfully so. He loves hard. Without hesitation. With this deep, practically ancient tenderness that feels rare in someone so young. He always knows just what to say. He's the one you call when you need truth, not bullshit, when you need someone to see you. He's everything good in our bloodline, distilled. He is the sweetest boy I've ever met.

Luca was loved. He is loved.

He just needed more. So much more than most people ever will. He needed galaxies. Solar systems of attention. A sky full of constellations made just for him. And what he got instead was our world. Small. Busy. Fractured. Loving, yes, but imperfect in all the ways that mattered most.

He was born from love. The purest kind. The kind that lives in mami's bones, the kind that cooks you breakfast while the rent is overdue, that stitches your costumes by hand, that remembers your favorite bedtime song long after you've stopped asking for it. But it wasn't enough, not for Luca. He needed two present parents. He needed older siblings who weren't half-parents themselves. Cousins who showed up. A partner who waited for him to grow before asking him to carry everything.

He needed someone to teach him how to pour all that endless need that black hole of wanting back into himself. And none of us knew how. We were all still trying to learn that lesson for ourselves, clawing toward it like a finish line that kept moving.

We didn't honestly know how to love ourselves, let alone teach Luca how to love himself. Sometimes, we apologize to him now.

"I'm sorry," we say.

"I wish I had known."

"I wish I could've done it differently."

However, the truth is, I'm not sure we even know what we're apologizing for, because Luca was born into a family amid evolution. A family still shedding old skins, still learning what love meant without the sharp edges. And he needed that love immediately. And we, especially the Bjorns of this world, didn't know how to offer it to him.

Wrong time. Wrong tools. Perfect soul. That's the unbearable part.

We don't all get what we need in this life. Not when we need it most.

Luca didn't get the galaxy of real-time love he needed, which would have nurtured that luminous seed inside his heart. The one that made him so bright, so tender, so good.

Instead, he got us. Our version. Our world.

We tried. God, we tried.

But sometimes, trying isn't enough when the soul before you asks for the universe.

Three

OUR MAMI

~❧~

Some women are made of fire, while others are made of earth. My mother is made of earth, the type of soil that holds up cities, the kind you have to break through with a pickax to plant a seed that might grow.

Mami was built of grit and stone and memory. Her body carried the scent of cumin, detergent, and the soft musk of exhaustion. Her hands always smelled like onions, even when she wasn't cooking. And her silence had a sound to it, like the echo of a bong tapped for the celebration of a new moment.

Our mother carried the weight of two countries on her back and two children in her soul. You could see it in her shoulders, hunched not from poor posture but from years of lifting a family into being. Her eyes told stories she never spoke aloud, deep, dark brown like bitter coffee left too long on the stove. They were always alert, always watching, as if she were the lookout for dangers no one else could see. They had memories of long flights, missed birthdays, and late nights translating bills she couldn't read. She never cried in front of us. Never. Not once. If tears ever came, they came alone in the laundry room or maybe into the pillow, long after we were asleep.

I remember her most vividly in the quiet hours. The nights I would come into the kitchen for water, I would find her sitting at the table, folding laundry with one hand while scribbling in her green notebook with the other. It was a small thing, frayed at the edges and full of underlined numbers, due dates, and to-do lists written in tight, sharp cursive. She treated that notebook like a holy book, underlining total amounts twice as if the extra ink might protect us from overdraft fees. But the moment that sticks with me more than any other is how she looked at my brother, Luca.

She called him mi niño lindo, my beautiful boy. She always knew he had an otherworldly softness that didn't belong in a world like ours. He moved through life like someone meant to fly but was handed a manual for crawling. He confused her. Not because of who he was, Mami never recoiled from his gentleness. No, what baffled her was the world he would have to survive in. She didn't fear him. She feared for him.

She would say to me, late at night, when Luca had gone to bed, "¿Cómo voy a protegerlo si el mundo no quiere que viva como él es?" How do I protect him if the world doesn't want him to live as he is? She didn't have the answer. None of us did.

So she did what most immigrant mothers do when love meets terror: she built a fortress, not of stone and steel, but of habits, routines, and silences. The rules were simple. Luca could bring anyone he felt safe with home; he had to call to tell her he was okay every night. And above all, what happened in the house stayed in the house, not out of shame, but survival. She cooked safety into every meal, folded it into the corners of our sheets. She tried to speak freedom into us while holding tight to the parts of us that might get us killed.

And we tried. We did.

But safety sometimes looked like confinement. Her love, enormous and unwavering, could also be suffocating. We weren't allowed to fall apart in front of other people. We weren't allowed to name things we didn't understand yet. There were no tantrums, no explanations of queerness or sadness. Everything was coded, implied, whispered. And the walls got higher.

Luca and I learned how to read each other in silence. We knew what a slammed door meant, what it meant when he lingered too long in his room, what it meant when I spent too much time outside the house. We interpreted our mother's fortress differently.

For him, it became a prison of unspoken needs. A place where he couldn't name his desires, so they became layered, secret, endless. He learned to smile through his aching. He learned to nod and say, "Yes, Mami," even when he was breaking inside. He learned to make himself smaller. Kinder. More palatable.

For me, it became a chamber with no air. I choked on the silence. I rebelled early, slamming doors, arguing, and leaving the house for hours at a time. I dreamed of escape as if it were a button I could build and press one day. I made lists in my head of what I would do the moment I left: dye my hair, get piercings, and sleep in past noon. I wasn't angry at her. I was furious at the limits. At the fear. The way love, in our house, sometimes felt like a cage with golden bars.

It's not fair to call it a prison. Not really. She was trying to keep us alive. And when Luca fell, and he did fall, over and over, it wasn't because he wasn't loved. It was because he needed galaxies of love, but he only got a world. He needed patience, endless time, and freedom to stumble. He needed someone to say, "You don't have to be anyone but yourself." And even though Mami loved him fiercely, she didn't always have the words.

None of us did.

We all apologized to him in different ways—Mami with the food. I did it with overprotection, Papá, with gifts. But none of us knew what we were apologizing for. We were all just learning how to love in real time and stretch our arms wide enough to hold a boy whose heart demanded infinite space.

And Luca's heart, God, that heart. It was enormous. Soft. Terrifying. He loved everyone. He called people "mi amor" without irony. He gave away sweaters, shared his last bite, and left voicemails with full-blown love letters. And the world broke him anyway.

Sometimes he'd come home with his face tired in ways I couldn't fix.

"You okay?" I'd ask.

"Just tired," he'd say, trying to smile.

But tired was code. Tired meant someone said something cruel. Tired meant he'd swallowed pain all day and didn't want to add to the pile.

Mami would ask, "¡Comiste? Ven, te hice algo." Did you eat? Come, I made you something.

It was the only way she knew how to hold him. And maybe that's enough. Maybe showing up with chicken soup and humble eyes is its kind of peace and healing.

As I grew older, I began to see the architecture of our lives more clearly—the blueprints, the scaffolding of the fortress, the

22

rooms Mami had sealed off within herself to make space for ours. And I realized, with a kind of aching gratitude, that we were never alone. We were never unloved.

The fortress might have been cold sometimes, but it was always full.

Mami didn't get everything right. She yelled. She broke plates once. She locked herself in the bathroom when she couldn't take it anymore. But she never stopped showing up. And that's the thing. Her love was a verb. Messy. Active. Imperfect. And I still want to be like her. Not in the bone-deep exhaustion. Not in the loneliness she never admitted. But in the way she held space. The way she gave love felt like an action. In the way she showed up, even when she had nothing left. I want to build a home like hers. Kitchen. Fortress. Sanctuary. Because Luca needed it. I needed it. Even though we felt trapped sometimes, that house, and fortress, kept us from falling completely apart.

Mami, I understand now. I know why you built the walls and why you double-checked the locks, why you didn't always have the words. And I forgive the silence. Because beneath it, you were humming and holding the soil together and holding us together. And even though we didn't say it enough back then, thank you. We heard your silent dedication. We still do. And in every soft thing I make room for, in every friend I welcome, in every meal I cook, in every late-night phone call I answer, I carry you. I have the best parts of you. I take the fortress, but now with windows. I accept the silence, but now with language. I carry Luca, too.

He still calls me when the world feels like too much. And I don't always have the answers. But I always pick up. I say, "You okay?" And he says, "I'm tired." And I say, "I'm sorry… I'm making soup."

That's the legacy, not perfection, not understanding every-thing, but showing up, being there, and holding steady. And when I become a mother, if I become a mother, I hope I will be made of the same earth, not the soft kind, the kind that remembers every footprint.

Four

PAPAOUTAI

Luca's dad was a wildly successful Argentine salesman, a man built from charisma and contradictions. His name was Javier. He could sell anything, not just products but dreams, apologies, even silence. His slow, honeyed accent matched eyes lit up like streetlamps just before night. But beneath that warmth, something erratic flickered in his gaze, like a bird ready to fly through a closed window.

"Your father is passionate," Mami used to say, always with a cautious smile that never reached her eyes. "Passion is a dangerous gift when you don't know how to carry it."

He was, arguably, psychotic in the way only a man completely consumed by love or ego can be. He was madly in love with Luca and I's mother. There's no neat word for what he was to me. Stepdad is technically correct, but that label feels flimsy, like trying to call a hurricane "a bit of rain."

Mami's name is Sallay, a gift from Abuela, who wanted to

name her Sally but couldn't quite let go of the poetic flair of a single misplaced vowel. She was a stunning woman, a walking legacy of mixed heritage: West African roots braided into her Spanish lilt, with high cheekbones and a spine like an iron rod. She moved through the world as if she were used to being worshipped, and perhaps she was. She'd only had two men in her life, Luca's father and my father, and I'm told each loved her with a kind of all-consuming awe. I think Mami and Luca share that inherited magnetism. There's something in the way people orbit them, particularly men. Men who become drunk on proximity. Obsession disguised as love. I didn't inherit that flair. That could be for the best. Watching the way it scorches everything it touches has made me wary of love that arrives like wildfire.

Javier wasn't all bad. That's the first truth I have to offer. He loved us. Not in the consistent, responsible, tuck-you-in-at-night way, but in the scattered moments that made you think, maybe, this time he'll stay.

He used to bring home candy for Luca and call him "mi campeón." Sometimes he'd ruffle my hair and tell me I was "muy inteligente," like he meant it. Once, he even helped me build a science fair volcano. We burned the carpet with baking soda lava, and Mami was furious, but I remember him laughing so hard he cried. That laugh, when it came, could fill a room.

But here's the second truth: he hurt us.

He disappeared for days, sometimes weeks, without warning. He yelled when the world didn't bend to his will. He punched walls and broke things we couldn't afford to replace. He had this way of weaponizing silence, of making absence feel like punishment. We'd wait for him like people wait for rain in a drought—desperate, hopeful, and eventually resigned.

My therapist, God bless her, once told me, "Two truths can exist simultaneously. Love and pain often hold hands."

She deserves a TED Talk. So here's how I live with it:

He loved us in his broken, chaotic way.

He caused us pain that we're still unraveling.

Those truths don't cancel each other out. They exist side by side, like siblings who share a room but can't stand each other.

Luca's father left echoes, not just in memory but also in our habits, bodies, and voices.

You could hear him in the stomp of Luca's footsteps when he was angry, a mimicry so unconscious it scared me. You'd listen to his charm like Luca would lean in just a little when he talked, his voice softening with that same easy grin his father had, like every word was meant just for you. And I felt him in myself, in the way I snapped at people I loved most, like love was a burden I needed to protect myself from.

When I was twelve, I asked Mami if I could attend a friend's party. She said no; we didn't have the money for a gift, and that was that. I screamed at her. Told her she didn't care about my life. I slammed the door so hard that a picture fell from the wall. It wasn't until later that I realized I wasn't angry about the party. I was furious that she had to be both mother and father. I was angry at the man who left us and didn't take the weight he should have carried.

Mami didn't cry. She sat quietly on the couch, picking up the broken frame. She never tried to be our father. She was too busy trying to keep us from falling apart. She wore every hat: financial planner, disciplinarian, chef, therapist, homework tutor, referee, and, when necessary, the wall we leaned against when we didn't know how to stand alone.

She had this saying when things got too hard: "We don't have the luxury of unraveling."

I wanted a dad who thought I was cool. I wanted someone to validate my weird mix of nerdy and queer, someone who didn't wince at my softness, who said "I'm proud of you" without sounding like it was a favor. I wanted someone whose admiration wasn't contingent on my grades or being my mother's daughter. I wanted someone to see me, just me, without proof that I mattered. An objective stamp of existential coolness…just once.

Luca wanted something else, too. He wanted a dad to throw a baseball with, to teach him how to shave, how to flirt without sounding desperate, how to use condoms, and how to be the kind of man who makes it through this world without losing his backbone or his heart.

What we got were men who saw love as a gendered task, one they were either too proud or too broken to fulfill.

"I just wanted someone to show me how to fix a fucking tire," Luca muttered once, while we were stuck on the side of the highway in his beat-up Civic. "Like, I know how to Google it…I mean…"

I nodded and picked up his words from the ground. "You wanted someone to hand you a wrench and say, 'I got you.'"

He didn't respond; he looked down at his dirt-covered fingers and muttered, "Yeah."

We tried patching the holes with therapy, laughter, sarcasm, and avoidance. We tried, but it's hard to fix something without the original instructions manual. Sometimes, I wonder if absence has shaped us more than presence ever could have.

In the hours between school and work, Luca turned to tinkering with electronics, taking things apart and putting them back together like they meant something. He doesn't speak about our father, not out loud, but in between circuits and solder, I see the same boy quietly saving space in systems that were always meant to short-circuit. You can feel it in how he carefully rebuilds each piece, leaving just enough distance and ensuring nothing fully connects.

I turned to writing. Trying to name the ache and trying to make sense of the shapeless grief that comes from mourning someone who's still alive.

Our father? He lives somewhere else now. A tidy little apartment in Queens, or maybe back in Buenos Aires. He sends the occasional Facebook message. Thumbs-up emojis. A photo of a dog. Once, he messaged: "Miss you, champ." I left it on read.

He got to leave. To start over. Untouched by the mess he helped create. Meanwhile, we stayed, trying to sweep up the shards without cutting ourselves open.

Forgiveness is tricky. Sometimes it feels like weakness. Like saying "what you did was okay," even when it wasn't. But sometimes, it feels like a strategy, a necessary detour on the path to peace.

I've forgiven parts of him, not for his sake, but for mine, because carrying hate is exhausting. Because I have enough baggage without packing his guilt in with my grief. Because healing, I've learned, isn't about justice. It's about liberation.

Mami told me once, during one of our late-night tea talks: "Forgiveness doesn't mean you invite them back in. It just means you're done bleeding for their absence."

I've tried. I'm still trying.

Luca?

He never says much. But I watch him in his studio, dirt smudged on his face like war paint. I watch how he draws fathers who look like shadows and sons who look like questions. And I know, even in his silence, he's still reaching.

Five

SOY YO

⚜

I left. I left Miami with a suitcase filled with guilt and a scholarship in hand. Mathematics at a university far enough from home to make my absence feel like a strategy instead of an escape. I told myself I was pursuing ambition, chasing light. But the truth was more straightforward: I couldn't watch myself disappear one soft layer at a time. I couldn't hold the weight of being another tragic girl from Sofla.

Florida has a way of pulling you into the deep swamp of the Everglades and leaving you wet, green, and monstrous. It may be the suffocating humidity, or the snakes, reptiles, and frogs that lift a poisonous air into the atmosphere. Maybe it's the ports or the history of importing drugs that make Florida the most dangerous place for a growing, thirsty soul. Florida pulled me in, deep into the warm green moss. Snakes of desire and over-consumption wrapped tightly around my neck. I was a zombie waiting to morph. I fell into the dark potholes, just like

Luca and everyone we knew, but the second half of me, the one that craves progress and stability, managed to pull me out.

There was this terrible sinkhole within me that came with a voice in my twenties that told me to leave. Get out of the swamp. The poisonous swamp. Florida is the land where dinosaurs never went extinct. Instead, they shrunk through radiation and poisoned the oceans and lakes with narcotics. Everyone who lives on the coast of Florida is covered in poisonous vines trying to escape. Especially those that seem like they're having the most fun.

After failing to get the snake's grip from my neck for years, the adrenaline fueled by the fear that I'd be forgotten, that I'd be a tragic portrait motivated me to fill out an application to a school far far away to pursue any dream, any dream of being a person free of snakes with a credentialed education.

No one tells you that leaving doesn't make the pain lighter. It just changes the address. The reality of the suffocating, murderous, poisonous snakes keeping us all trapped in the little suburban towns in Florida felt even more real up North. Everyone was so different. The air felt clear and poison-free, cold and refreshing like the oysters. The oysters were cold, not warm, and full of sand. People didn't have snakes around their necks. Instead, they had scarves. I mourned for the people I left behind in Florida. It's silly to think a location could feel so treacherous, but it felt genuine to me then. The pain of leaving Luca and Mami behind consumed me with a deep sadness that would linger throughout my days. I kept my eyes forward in classrooms and labs, and my heart tethered to voicemail messages from our mother. She'd call and tell me she and Luca were okay, but it felt less accurate every day. She'd call and tell me he was painting again, which meant he wasn't OK at all.

I spent years working on myself. I spent eight years away from home, prioritizing my value in the world over theirs, and figuring out how to love others while loving myself. It was a hellish ride.

As the seasons passed, I remembered the beautiful memories Luca, Mami, and I shared. I remembered how, no matter what tornado storm we were a part of, two events were always so blissful and happy: church on Sundays and Christmas. I searched for churches, but I couldn't figure out why. I would buy a tiny Christmas tree every year and put a Santa hat on my kitty cat. Like a squirrel, I was gathering the best nuggets and nuts from my childhood and storing them for the winter.

I thought of Luca daily. I felt guilty leaving him behind. I was so desperate for bliss and peace. I needed it as much as I needed my next breath, which meant wearing my metaphorical airplane mask before thinking about putting masks on them.

I went to school and controlled my homegrown reptile demons in the evening. I worked hard in my multiple jobs, learning how folks in the north produced goods and staying motivated. On weekends, I sought peace in parks and sometimes in churches.

I visited many churches, but ultimately I could not feel comfortable in a church that wouldn't accept my brother exactly as he is. I would walk out as soon as I heard this "only man and woman" nonsense.

Churches and society get this wrong: the battle of choice. I lived it and witnessed it. Those of us with LGBTQIA+ families know this: we are born this way. The book I read at church when I was little was about love. It accepted and embraced people who were born every way. The made-up ideologies these churches were spewing went against the book's teachings, which I greatly respected. Everything my mother taught me about love, these places, supposed sanctuaries, were bungling.

My brother was born perfectly prepared to love, regardless of outer factors. He was always Luca. No amount of pain, pushing away, praying, or a "programmed" version of a scripture that should preach openness can change that. This indoctrination of hate, the antithesis of the scripture, all it does is drill the hole of self-hate deeper and deeper into beautiful, perfect souls to the point of exhaustion and deterioration.

I would not accept it. I would continue looking for churches until I found one that actually... read.

I spent many years figuring out who I was. The echoes of my father and stepfather created an impossibly hardened brick wall that my lovers and friends could not get through.

It got to the point where I was utterly alone. That solitude burned me. I could not bear it.

I looked in the mirror and cried and cried. Then I called the nearest tattoo shop:

"Hey, I need a tattoo tonight. Can you do it?"

"Sure, what are you thinking?"

"Amazing, uh, a game controller with the cord spelling out self."

"Neat, come on by, I'll be here."

"Sweet."

I was convinced after months of mourning that my habits and learned behavior pushed every human I attempted to connect with far away from me, that a tattoo would remind me to stop being such a see you next Tuesday.

To my surprise, that is not how human behavior works, despite our collective wish that it did. Instead, I had another not-so-thought-out tattoo on my arm that was cute, with the same shitty behaviors as my companions to go to sleep with.

When I met Darius, everything changed. Darius was the second sweetest man I'd ever met. I knew immediately I never wanted to be too far away from him. I loved his beautiful, round green eyes and subtle, shy smile. He was the light that shone on the mirror I held in front of myself. That light gave me the courage to undergo the complex process of accepting my flaws and seeking professional guidance on adopting new behaviors.

Darius held my hand the first time he saw my darkness and trauma. Holding it back tightly, I said, "I'll go to therapy, I'll work on all of it, I'll do it for me, and I'll do it in hopes that you can keep holding my hand."

It was hard, painful, and impossible, but we made it to that gorgeous day by the water. Dressed like a princess, I told him, in front of everyone we loved, that I would be my best self and persevere in our love every day.

I built a life so far away from Miami, it felt like my two beautiful angels were on another ocean. I called them every day and checked in. Come live with me in paradise, where there is therapy, fulfilling work, and temptation is harder to find. There are no reptiles here, at least not out in the open. Bring a scarf!

They both grew stranger, my mother and Luca. They became stranger and stranger, and the pain, even through the phone, was too much to bear at times, especially from paradise.

It wasn't until Bjorn's exhibit, yes, the exhibit, the public crucifixion disguised as art, that I stopped pretending my distance was harmless. There he was: my brother, dissected in oil and canvas. A body of work, a work of body. Every ache, relapse, and prayer we said together was painted in bold strokes. He didn't even attempt to conceal his vulnerability. He signed it.

I cried for two days. Not because I was surprised. But because part of me always knew Luca's pain would be consumed. He was too beautiful, tender, and unfiltered to be ignored forever. And the world, well, the world, loves a wounded prophet.

Six

THE ROOM THAT HELD HIM

Our mother cooked many meals a day, as if it were an act of survival, perhaps because it was for Luca, for me, and herself. She flipped pancakes at sunrise while answering emails for a job that didn't pay enough. She packed sandwiches with trembling hands, worry tucked between slices of cheese. She stirred rice and beans in the evening with the same determination as she stirred hope into our tired bodies. Hope that somehow this country won't eat us alive.

In between all that, she was trying to save her daughter from herself and raise her son in a world that wouldn't love him the way she did. She was trying to figure out how to make a three-person salary stretch across a one-bedroom apartment, one income, and no degrees. Love, in our house, was a verb. And amid the noise, the late rent, the unspoken fears, there was one piece of sanctuary: Luca's room.

That room was a paradox. A contradiction in every corner.

It smelled like incense, burnt circuit boards, and sometimes, a faint hint of betrayal. Like a secret kept too long. The door, always slightly ajar during the day, glowed at night like it held a universe behind it. And in many ways, it did.

Luca's room was the sanctuary of a young man who had survived too much to be still called young. But everything about it betrayed that truth; boyhood clung to the space like dust in the corners. Stacks of half-used sketchbooks lay like sacred scripture on his desk. Pages torn out and pinned to the walls, held up by peeling tape and stubborn hope. A stuffed monkey was sitting in the far corner, slumped and one-eyed. He swore it wasn't his. "It came with the apartment," he said once with a shrug, though neither of us believed that.

Above his bed, photographs were taped in a constellation only he understood: friends, art, childhood Halloween costumes, crooked smiles. One of the pictures was of me when I was five, my front tooth missing and my face sticky with chocolate. Another way of Mami, straightening her hair in front of the mirror, completely unaware she was being seen.

Our mother always knocked twice before entering, not out of fear of what she'd find, but out of respect. That room wasn't just Luca's; it was his refuge, his mirror, and his museum of becoming. A fragile ecosystem where he could breathe, unfold, and break without consequence.

The unspoken agreement in our home was simple: Luca could be whoever he needed to be behind that door. He could paint until three in the morning with jazz buzzing softly through his headphones. He could cry in the middle of the day and laugh too loudly at midnight. He could have had partners over, and though he never mentioned them later, their presence lingered like perfume.

He could love in the shadows and mourn in the daylight. He could fall apart and stitch himself back together, one bolt at a time.

I remember once walking past his door and hearing music swell from inside. Fiona Apple, maybe. Or Björk. Something strange and sharp and beautiful. And underneath it, the sound of him laughing with someone. A kind of laugh I hadn't heard in months. Carefree. Full-bodied. Alive.

I wanted to knock. I tried to laugh with him.

But I wasn't allowed in Luca's room. That was the rule, unspoken, but absolute. Maybe it was rebellion. Perhaps it was payback for the years I kept my door closed during those brittle, early-teen stretches when I was too incredible, too private, too fragile to let anyone in, least of all my little brother.

Now the roles had reversed. His door stayed shut. And even when it wasn't just slightly ajar, light spilled like an invitation. I knew better. I wasn't welcome.

Sometimes I hovered, pretending I needed something from the hallway closet, hoping for a glimpse and hoping to catch him being himself. Not because I wanted to interrupt, but because I missed him. Because I wanted to witness him as he learned to witness himself.

But that room wasn't mine to enter. Not anymore. And he had every right to keep it that way.

Mami knew. She didn't say much, but she knew. She learned when Luca was eight and asked if boys could marry each other. I think she knew when she found the crumpled note from another boy in his jeans pocket, scrawled with "I like you. Like, like-like."

But she also knew she couldn't teach him how to be someone who loves men. She was still figuring out what that meant for

39

herself, as a woman. She didn't know how to teach us how to love men, only how to survive them. For men, in her worldview, it was a matter of survival. Learning to survive people rather than love them can be the opposite of a skill. It becomes a weapon. Our Abuela gave her a sword to use for love, and like a great mother, she sharpened those swords and passed them down to her children. My brother and I brought a sword to every love encounter.

Swords aside, she understood this much: the world outside our apartment, outside of love encounters, would bruise him for being soft, so she ensured he had a place to stay smooth. Her quiet rebellion created a pocket of safety in a universe of risk. If she couldn't protect him everywhere, she'd at least protect him there.

Luca's room was not tidy. It was not curated like the bedrooms in catalogs or teen dramas. It was chaotic, layered, and lived in. It was a mood board of trauma and tenderness, a living, breathing diary.

On the walls, he had nothing. Just the dusty Grey-white walls of a small apartment complex. Nothing obvious to give away how he felt or who he truly was. A mystery of electronics, clean laundry, and hints of dandruff. Another family gift we shared.

His desk was littered with pens, broken earbuds, crusted paint jars, and notebooks, pages half-filled with poems he refused to claim. Beneath the bed were shoe-boxes of memories: some collected, some burned, some rewritten until the paper gave up.

Sometimes, late at night, I would sit on the floor of his room while he was at work. It was my way of trying to connect with him. The room had its own language. It hummed and sighed, buzzing with the frequency of healing.

He would bless me once or twice a year with an invitation into his sanctuary. We sat quietly and intensely discussed our feelings while he painted or tinkered.

"What do you think it means," he asked once, while flicking blue onto canvas, "when people say they're finding themselves?"

I shrugged. "Maybe it means they're tired of being who the world told them to be."

He paused. "Yeah," he said. "But what if who I'm finding isn't safe outside this room?"

That landed like a stone in my chest.

"Then you bring the room with you," I said softly. "Build pieces of it wherever you go."

He smiled, but it didn't reach his eyes.

Another night, maybe a year later, he said, "Sometimes I feel like I'm undergoing a metamorphosis. Like I'm in that book… what's it called? The one with the bug?"

"Kafka?"

"Yeah, that one. Except it's not my body turning. It's everything else, my mind, my heart, my identity… all of it shedding layers no one taught me how to peel."

I sat with that for a moment.

"And this room?" I asked.

He looked around.

"This room is both my cocoon and my cage."

That hit me so hard that I remained quiet the rest of our time in his room, a rare occurrence for me in our family home. Because he was right, that room had cradled him. It had allowed him to bloom, but it also reminded him of why he needed a sanctuary in the first place.

A beautiful, soft boy should not have to feel safe in only one room. He should be secure in the whole world.

41

Like everyone else.

Like anyone else.

Sometimes I wonder what would've happened if he hadn't had that room. Would he have grown wings at all? Would he have found art? Would he have found pieces of himself buried beneath paint and dust and silence?

Maybe the room wasn't magic. But it gave him a place to remember who he was when the world tried to make him forget. It gave him silence when the noise became too cruel. It gave him mirrors that didn't distort his softness.

That room was a lighthouse in a house held together by borrowed light, shame, and broken lineage. A rebellion. A prayer.

Years later, I helped him move out. He was twenty-eight and ready to leave the city. We packed his electronics, sketchbooks, shoe-boxes, and even the monkey he still pretended wasn't his. As we were taping up the last box, he looked around the empty room.

"You know," he said, "I used to think this room was the only place I could be fully myself."

"And now?" I asked.

He looked at me, and something in his face, his jawline, and the set of his eyes looked older. Stronger.

"Now I think it was the first place. Not the only one."

He handed me a box, and we left.

But I never forgot that room.

I still dream about it sometimes, walls painted with longing, incense smoke curling like ghosts in the corners, and a boy learning how to take up space in a world that taught him to shrink.

Seven

FRAMED

Luca didn't understand why he was central to Bjorn's paintings. Years had passed since their paths parted, silent as an old wound. Yet somehow, Bjorn had quietly nurtured an obsession, collecting fragments of Luca's existence like stray threads, weaving them into an exhibition Luca hadn't consented to. Three years of painting him, each stroke a silent whisper, an intrusive glance into secrets he had hoped were buried.

He confided in friends, seeking logic or comfort, but their answers fell short. They offered theories: love, obsession, artistic madness, but none soothed the ache of being dissected publicly, displayed as an artful ruin. He felt reduced to a caricature: a tragic lover, a cautionary tale splayed on white walls for strangers' consumption.

Grief has colors, and for Luca, it was red.

It wasn't the soft red of petals or romantic sunsets. This

was fierce, primal, and scalding, humming like an angry wasp trapped near his ear, furious at exploiting his humanity. It was the violent crimson rage of seeing your private pain brushed onto canvases, your scars glossed with varnish, and presented as something brave or profound.

When the exhibition opened, Luca withdrew into isolation. Three days behind his bedroom door, he ignored hunger pangs and grappled with a cruel paradox: healing wounds someone else had forcibly reopened. His phone became a tool of self-torment, the screen flickering incessantly with notifications, admiration, scorn, and intrusive fascination.

"Luca's hot, but what a mess."

"Hot and messy. Tell me more."

These words cut deep. He scrolled relentlessly, searching desperately for compassion, for one voice that understood his outrage, someone brave enough to say, "What about the subject?"

But silence echoed louder than empathy.

He wept in defiance. He wept because the progress he painstakingly fought for had been hijacked, commercialized into something grotesque and voyeuristic. The world applauded Bjorn, but Luca felt robbed of his privacy, his healing, commodified, each tear a protest against exploitation.

Luca refused to be a mere canvas, a martyr, or Bjorn's stepping stone to artistic fame. He was Luca. He was honest, tangible, and actively living his story.

That evening, after closing his shift at the restaurant early, Luca drove home with newfound resolve. He methodically packed his belongings: a stack of favorite books, toiletries, his worn yellow hoodie, and a small photo of himself with Meow, his steadfast feline companion. The image was creased and faded, capturing a rare moment of uncomplicated peace. Cradling Meow, he whispered his intentions.

"Ninety days in rehab. Think that'll do it?"

Meow's presence is comforting as always. Luca once admitted to one of our cousins that Meow was the only living thing that understood him. He told Meow every secret, every decision. Meow was Luca's most loyal companion, never judging, always around, purring and ready for those five seconds of affection before the day was done.

"I'm going to miss you terribly," Luca confessed, feeling the heavy weight of his decision. "But this… this might be how I find myself again."

The next morning, he left silently, telling only me. Our conversation was brief but profound.

"You know how proud I am of you, right?" I assured him.

He paused, the words holding him for a moment before he responded, "I'm just exhausted."

Luca stepped away from the world that had defined him unfairly, into a space of quiet reconstruction. His journey would be challenging, undoubtedly filled with introspection and hardship, but it was his choice. It was a reclamation.

Eight

BROCCOLI REHAB

Rehab was not a romantic word. It was not a place people dreamed of going. It was where people went when all other lights had gone out. But for Luca, rehab became a kind of wilderness. And sometimes, wilderness is where healing begins.

For the first three days, he barely spoke. His throat hurt from detoxing, and his thoughts were too tangled to unravel. The air smelled like antiseptic and overcooked vegetables. The mattress felt like regret. He kept his eyes low, his hands in his pockets, his heartbeat erratic. Everything inside him wanted to leave. But somewhere even deeper, a quieter voice told him to stay.

He had survived a public unraveling. And now, behind locked doors and beige walls, he had to learn how to live again.

At first, healing came in whispers.

The schedule was rigid: wake up at 6:30, meditate at 7:00, attend group therapy at 8:00, complete chores, eat meals, take steps, journal, and go to bed at 10:00. It was mechanical, yet mercy lay beneath the repetition. For the first time in a long time, someone else was helping him carry the day.

Dana was his counselor. Dana wore Doc Martens and spoke like she'd seen every version of rock bottom and taken notes. She didn't coddle. She asked him questions that made him want to disappear and stay in the room at the same time.

"What do you think your pain protects you from?"

"I don't know."

"What would happen if you didn't perform being okay?"

"I don't KNOW."

"Hmm. Then maybe that's where we begin."

Luca began a dance of hatred and love with Dana. He could not stand how she smelled like ham sandwiches every day at noon. He hated that she always wore a collared shirt. The worst one was the bright green shirt. It was too big for her figure and the most annoying shade of green. It wasn't neon, but neither was it light or dark. What an ugly shirt, he thought. Dana suggested journaling during one of their sessions together. What a sappy, cliché of a woman, he thought. He often wondered where she became credentialed. Was it an online degree? Did she even have a degree? Dana is literally...

"Hey buddy!" she interrupted with her usual calm joy.

"Hey Dana..." Luca responded quietly.

"Looking forward to today's session!"

"I'm sure you are, Dana..."

"Oh hey, make sure you pick up your composition book from the cubbies," she said as she hurried past him.

"Can't wait," said Luca, with his typical wit and charm fit for a Tuesday morning in Hope Los Angeles Rehabilitation Center of Florida.

After fighting Dana internally for weeks over the unnecessary and uselessness of journaling, Luca finally broke down and started journaling. His first entry read, "This is stupid."

He smirked and went back to his room for a nap.

As the days passed, he decided to keep writing, despite the first entry having made him smile in defiance. Sometimes, he would write, "I hate it here." Each day, he would loosen up the entries, writing less in spite and more in honest curiosity.

"Hey Luca-Tuca!" cheered Dana.

"Can you not, um, call me that please?" Luca responded in absolute disdain for this moment and this woman.

"Sorry, I get overzealous sometimes. Ah, well, how are you doing, Luca? How's the journaling?"

"Dana, can I be honest with you?"

"It's all I've ever hoped for, Luca."

"I think a lot of the things we do here are, fucking, stupid. I try it out anyway, like the journaling thing. It's OK, fine even, but I don't understand the point. What is the point of writing in an empty book? Who cares about some stupid line I write?" Luca ranted but felt relieved.

"Hmm. I hear you on that. Do you care about things you write in the journal?"

"No, Dana, I just told you I don't."

"Right. How about this, Lukes—sorry, Luca," she chuckled nervously and cleared her throat before continuing. "How about you try writing a letter to all the people you think wouldn't give a shit about what you write," she said confidently.

"Wow, you said shit. Didn't think you had it in ya," Luca said playfully.

"I'm not all bad, Luca, there's… Every day, there's a reason we are all here, a reason I'm here, and our reasons may have a lot

48

more common ground than any of us would care to admit," she said authentically.

Luca appreciated her candor; he needed that realness from her today.

It took him a few days, but without even thinking about it, he started writing letters he would later discard. He wrote them to everyone who doesn't care, like Bjorn, his father, and his fifteen-year-old self.

He participated in art therapy. He painted silently for hours, creating vivid, strange images, like trees with skulls etched on their ancient bark. The cafes he frequented were melting. An upside-down bird hanging with one mighty leg, gripping an open cage. One day, he painted a cracked window with the word "try" in red. Dana asked what it meant.

He shrugged. "I don't know. But it's mine."

Each week, the layers slowly and carefully peeled back like old wallpaper in a house where no one thought beauty was beneath the mold. He learned terms such as "cognitive distortion" and "re-parenting." He knew how trauma stored itself not only in memory but also in posture. He was aware of brain health and the concept of building new neural pathways through targeted therapy techniques.

They practiced grounding exercises, including HALT, 5-4-3-2-1, and breathing into the belly instead of the chest. He found comfort in structure, even if it irritated him. He learned to sit with discomfort instead of racing it to numbness.

As the weeks passed, he felt the migraines growing stronger. With confusion. With silence. No one knew his name except for Dana, the nurse, who would make his head throb with her enthusiasm. He didn't speak in a group. He didn't smile at jokes. He walked with his shoulders hunched forward, as if he were apologizing to gravity.

His weekend therapist, Jamal, was young, Black, and whip-smart, a former user himself; he quoted research during sessions like scripture. "Meth suppresses dopamine receptors in the brain. For users like you, that means basic pleasures won't register the same. We have to retrain your brain to feel joy again. It's science. Not weakness."

Luca nodded. It felt like mercy, like being told that the darkness wasn't moral failure, just biology. Luca understood biology. He loved it. Whenever Jamal hit him with a scientific explanation, he remembered the basics of food science and chemistry. He would remember the joy he felt in Graduate School.

Each day, he scribbled in his notebook: snippets of dialogue, images, the smell of bleach and boiled carrots, and the names of the other residents: Malik, who cried in his sleep; Dena, who wore angel pins; and Zoe, whose laugh felt like a wave of hope.

He noticed the small things. He noticed when a new guy came in, shaking and sobbing, and he handed him his extra blanket. He noticed when the cafeteria served plantains, and one man wept because it reminded him of home.

He slowly began painting again; at first, he used only pencils. Then charcoal. Then pastels. He refused oil, not after Bjorn.

One night in creative therapy, the counselor played music and asked the participants to draw a memory they hadn't shared before. Luca drew Meow, not as a cat, but as a small star sitting in the corner of a room, blinking, and glowing.

He was healing.

Outside, Isabella, his best friend, kept Mami updated and wrestled with her anger. At night, she read articles: Methamphetamine Use Disorder: A Review of Pharmacologic Interventions. She learned about cognitive-behavioral relapse prevention, community reinforcement approaches, and matrix models. She understood for the first time that rehab wasn't punishment. It was science. It was care. It was love, with charts.

When Luca called three weeks in, his voice was unmistakable.

"I miss the restaurant," he said.

"It misses you back."

"I think I'm getting better. I... laughed today."

She cried but didn't let him hear it.

Meanwhile, Darius wrote handwritten letters with stickers, dried flowers, and affirmations like "You are not your worst day." Luca kept them under his pillow. He never really liked his brother-in-law, but seeing him send letters of support softened him. He started to see what I loved so much about him.

He was learning the architecture of resilience, one frame at a time.

In family therapy, he cried.

He said, "I don't want to be seen as broken."

I said: "You're not broken. You're rebuilding."

He told Mami, "I'm sorry I shut you out."

She said, "You never had to apologize for surviving."

It wasn't perfect. He had urges. He had days when he didn't speak. Nights when he dreamt of overdosing and woke up in a sweat. But he didn't leave. Not on day 30. Not on day 60. Not even on day 65, when everything inside him screamed that he had done enough.

He stayed. And in staying, something cracked open.

On day 78, he laughed a full, throat-deep laugh. Someone told a joke in the group about trying to flirt at AA and calling it Alco-Tinder. Luca lost it. He laughed so hard he had to step outside. And outside, he looked up at the sky and whispered: "I forgot I could feel like this."

Luca talked to me this time around in rehab. He thinks I'm a real pain in the ass, but I am nothing if not persistent.

"I finally found it!"

"Found what?" He humored me.

"I found a church where you would be embraced. Like, their thing is everyone's interpretation of the book is their own, and all they encourage is for you to choose Love and pray either alone or together."

"Oh," he said plainly.

I was elated to have my little brother back. My brother is a quiet man when he's sober.

"Yeah! I sent you a Book of Common Prayer from the Episcopal Church. Go to the daily devotions and say one prayer each day, then tell me how you feel."

"I don't have faith like that," he shared honestly.

"Come on, just try it."

"Doesn't the church hate me, us, whatever?" He asked, completely ignoring my first elevator pitch.

"Not this church, most Episcopalian churches even have gay priests."

"Mm. I'll believe it when I see it, I guess."

Luca didn't expect the Book of Common Prayer to mean anything to him. He had always thought churches were places people went to hide. He had grown up with fire-and-brimstone preaching that assured him people like him were an abomination.

Suddenly, all of those bad memories of church rushed through him, and he felt like throwing up. He hoped Dana was around so she could say something annoyingly optimistic that he could roll his eyes at and shift his focus to. He remembered the masses in Spanish. The heteronormative preaching of it all. He remembered feeling like this place, the Church, was NOT safe for him. Luca didn't ever acknowledge his attraction to running away, fiercely from big feelings. Still, this whirlpool of memories, the desire to run was a punch to the stomach, making his empty feelings sink deeper. Church wasn't a sweet, happy memory for Luca. It was something to run far away from.

He could feel the burning red of angst and anger in his chest swelling now. He resented me for a moment. What a bitch, he thought. I always assume that what I need is what he needs. Then, Dana's voice in his head now, "Remember to breathe, buddy! From the belly, right where it hurts." He rolled his eyes and practiced H.A.L.T. He used the breathing techniques he had been practicing.

When he started to breathe clearly, he went to his room and took a notebook and colored pencils. He scribbled and drew abstract hands in bright colors. It reminded him of the art he used to paint when he was younger. He must've passed by that place a hundred times, assuming the flag was performative. Luca didn't expect the Book of Common Prayer to mean anything to him. He had grown up in churches that had made him feel like a sinner, a mistake in the eyes of God. He had walked by the local catholic church a hundred times, dismissing its hypocrisy. Dismissing the memories of sitting through an offensive and, not to mention, incredibly boring Sunday mass. But something shifted. On day 65, Luca opened the Book of Common Prayer. The prayer wasn't magic, but it was the first time in his adult life that he had spoken to a God who didn't seem angry at him.

Day 90 arrived with a stillness that only the passage of time understands. No confetti, no fanfare, no grand announcement of triumph. No perfect, cinematic closure. Just Luca, still himself, yet somehow different, packing his things into a small bag, folding worksheets, tucking away journals, and scribbling therapy notes. He folded them as if they were sacred, something to keep but not to be weighed down. The air in the rehab center was sterile, but Luca didn't feel suffocated by it for the first time in weeks. He didn't feel like he was drowning. He felt lighter in some strange, subtle way, his heart no longer a war zone. It wasn't fixed. It wasn't perfect. But it didn't burn anymore. Not like it used to.

He hugged a few people on his way out. People who had shared their lives, pain, and small victories with him. Strangers, yes. But strangers who had seen him in his darkest moments still chose to stand with him. That meant something. But the door closed behind him, and the finality of it settled in. He was walking out, but the path was still uncertain. And maybe that's how it always is. The path isn't always clear when we begin, but we must walk it anyway.

Mami was there to pick him up. Her car was a silver blur in the parking lot, waiting for him, waiting for the son she had feared she might lose forever. He climbed into the passenger seat, his body heavier than it used to be, weighed down not by the addiction, but by everything that had come before it, the loss, the shame, the years of pretending.

Mama didn't wait for him to speak. She cried when he opened the door and slid into the seat next to her. It wasn't a scream or a wail; it wasn't even messy. It was punched, as if the release had been building in her for months. Her shoulders shook slightly as she turned to face him, her eyes full of something Luca couldn't quite name. "I'm proud of you," she whispered, her voice cracking slightly on the last word. She reached for his hand, squeezing it like she was trying to hold on to something she thought she might lose. Luca didn't know how to answer that. How do you answer something big and complete, born of years of worry, hope, and love? He could've said, "I'm sorry." He could've said, "I'm not proud of myself yet." He could've said nothing at all. But he didn't. Instead, he said, "I'm tired."

They drove in silence after that, the kind of silence that wasn't heavy or loaded. It wasn't the silence of distance or of things left unsaid. A peace had settled between them, a quiet that felt like the calm after a storm, as if they were taking in the moment's gravity. It wasn't a perfect silence. It was tinged with the weight of everything Luca had been through and everything his mother had carried with him. But it was peaceful. It wasn't filled with fear for the first time in a long time.

Luca hadn't left rehab fixed. He hadn't walked out of there whole. He wasn't healed in the way people imagine when they talk about redemption, or recovery, or coming back from the brink. But he was different. And in some ways, that was the most profound thing of all. He had walked in a broken man, but now he was walking out—not fixed, but open. Open to possibility. Open to pain, yes, but also open to healing. Maybe that's what healing is, Luca thought as he looked out of the car window, the landscape passing by like an old memory. It's not about finding the perfect resolution or the smoothest path. It's about choosing to stay open.

And maybe that was the first real step toward living again.

The road stretched ahead, lengthy and uncertain. But for the first time, Luca didn't feel like he was walking it alone.

Nine

QUIET

The day Luca left rehab, he stepped out of those doors a changed man. It's something you could only notice by listening to and observing him. He blinked slower. He breathed deeper. He looked people in the eye for half a second longer. He wasn't healed, but it wasn't obvious; it was subtle, but something inside him had shifted. The wound was no longer gaping. It was beginning to scar.

The silence between them was different now. It didn't hold anger. It held space. Mami tapped her fingers on the steering wheel, a rhythm that reminded him of bedtime stories and making empanadas. Luca watched the world roll by, taking in fences, fields, and people walking their dogs. Ordinary life hadn't paused while he was in limbo.

The hardest part wasn't leaving rehab. It was coming back to a world that hadn't changed while he had. He returned to a suburb where nothing had forgiven him, where people remembered the headlines more than his smile. But he also returned to the few who had always believed he could be more than the worst thing he'd survived.

He didn't dive into life. He waded. Slowly.

He made his bed every morning. That became sacred. A small rebellion against the chaos that once defined him. He texted his sponsor once a day. Went to three meetings a week. Started walking more. Walking without purpose, to feel his feet hit the ground.

He stopped checking Instagram. He stopped reading reviews. He stopped imagining what his exes were doing.

He started lighting candles again.

He picked up a pen.

He returned to journaling. Pages filled with confessions, intentions, and questions that had no answers. He wrote to his future self like he was writing to a child he hadn't met yet:

"I hope we're still choosing softness, saying no to shame, and finding a way to forgive the people who painted us without asking permission."

Luca had been out of rehab for three weeks when he started waking before dawn. The quiet was a cradle now, not a coffin. He made coffee every morning and journaled without expectation. Cheeky, his newly adopted cat from the shelter, purred beside him like punctuation. The sun spilled in just as he finished his third entry. In it, he described an old flame's laugh, how it cracked through his ribs like spring thaw. He wrote about craving, but not for meth; instead, it was for peach jam. For bare feet on cold tile. For being held.

Weeks later, he stepped into a church; he thought, let's see what Annie's on about.

It was strange at first. The pews creaked when he sat, and

the air smelled like old wood and lavender. But it was quiet, not just silent and calm, like a safe room, but also tranquil in the way a person can be when they are finally allowed to exist without apology.

They sang hymns with more love than pitch. The priest, a short woman with buzzed hair and an oversized cross, smiled at him without expectation. No one asked for his story. No one recoiled from his name.

He sat through the service in stunned stillness. And when the priest read a prayer from the Book of Common Prayer that said, "…If I am to sit still, help me to sit quietly. If I am to lie low, help me to do it patiently. And if I am to do nothing, help me to do it gallantly…," Luca felt his eyes fill with tears.

It wasn't a grand spiritual awakening. But a softening.

He kept coming back.

Some days, he cried through the entire service; some days, he just sat; and some days, he helped with coffee hour. They asked him his name, and without a thought, he replied, "Gabriel," his middle name.

He told me later, "It was the first place that didn't try to fix or erase me. They just let me be."

He started cooking again. Nothing fancy, rice, eggs, beans, but he plated it carefully, as if the meal were a ritual.

He began to piece together a routine. It didn't look like a transformation. It looked like a presence. Like living.

And one night, as we sat on the phone, he said:

"I think this is what rebirth is. Not flames. Not trumpets. Just… dishes, and candles, and showing up anyway."

I didn't have words for that. I just whispered, "I'm proud of you."

He said, "I'm also learning to be proud of myself."

Isabella came over that night with groceries and stories to share. She made locro while Luca prepped the chimichurri. They didn't talk about rehab at first. They spoke of tomatoes, rent, and Mami's new obsession with indoor orchids.

"Pride blooms late," Isabella said, holding a pot of cilantro to her nose. "But it blooms."

Later, over bowls of stew, she asked softly, "Are you ready to see people again?"

He nodded. "I think so. Not everyone. Not yet. But... some."

His first trip back to the restaurant was cautious. He arrived before opening hours, keys jingling nervously in his hand. The walls held his fingerprints, and the kitchen held his muscle memory. Isabella had kept things alive, barely. The staff greeted him with warmth and awkwardness, unsure whether to offer a hug or a salute.

"I didn't burn it down," Isabella joked. "Not even once."

Luca smiled. "Then you've exceeded expectations."

He worked that day like a man reacquainting himself with a lover. He touched everything, adjusted knives, refolded towels, tasted sauces, and reawakened every sense. In the corner, a new dishwasher, Luis, maybe 19, watched him with wide eyes.

"You're... him," the boy said.

Luca arched an eyebrow. "I'm who?"

"The one Bjorn painted."

The words hit like stale air. Luca straightened. "Not anymore."

That night, he wrote: Recovery is not erasure. It's a reclamation.

At his next therapy check-in, his counselor encouraged him to consider a peer support group in the city. Luca hesitated. He didn't want to be a poster child. However, he was also beginning to realize the value of presence. He'd read something about narrative therapy helping recovering people with addiction reclaim their identity by reshaping their personal stories. He hadn't realized until then how badly he needed that.

So he went.

The church basement smelled like mildew and burnt coffee. The chairs were misaligned. A woman named Alina led the circle.

"You don't have to tell your whole story today," she said, meeting his eyes. "Just start with a name."

"My name is Luca," he said. "And I'm... tired. But alive."

Heads nodded.

Week by week, he showed up. Sometimes to listen. Sometimes to speak. He met Jesse, who ran marathons to replace his high. Samira, who baked obsessively to quiet her hands. Tyler, who kept relapsing but never stopped trying.

He noticed something: the shame grew quieter when shared. Not gone, but less sharp. And in those silent acknowledgments, he found a kind of belonging he hadn't felt in years.

One day, he stayed afterward to talk to Alina.

"I want to host something," he said. "At the restaurant. Just... food and presence. For us."

She smiled. "That's how healing spreads. Through shared tables."

So he planned it. Called it Noche de Luz. A private night. Long tables. Free empanadas. Soft music. Candles flickering in recycled bottles. People arrived slowly, nervously, dressed in stories they still didn't know how to tell.

He spoke briefly before the meal.

"This isn't about where we've been," he said. "It's about where we're going. Together."

Applause. Silence. Then, clinking glasses.

Yvette came. Ben came. Even Luis from the kitchen showed up in a pressed shirt, eyes darting with nerves. Luca moved from table to table, offering bread and jokes and listening.

Afterward, as they cleaned up, Darius handed him a note scribbled on a napkin. It read: You've made something special here, my dude.

Luca folded it carefully, placed it in his wallet, and thought Darius was corny.

That night, he lay in bed with Meow and Cheeks curled at his feet, full of food, stories, and something resembling peace.

And in the soft dark, he whispered, "I'm still here."

That week, Luca tested a new dessert: a burnt citrus tart with a dulce de leche glaze. It was a bit of metaphor, a bit of therapy. Bitter and sweet, charred and sugar-laced, it was a bit of treatment. He watched customers react to it with delight and curiosity. For once, he felt like he was feeding people without bleeding.

On Friday, Paloma, the lead server at his job, approached him after the family meal. She was in her early fifties, wore bangles that clinked like wind chimes, and was mainly quiet around the back of the house.

"You made that tart?" she asked.

He nodded.

She touched his wrist. "It tasted like something my mom used to make. She would have loved it."

"Haha, oh yeah? Well, tell her to come by and try some next week."

"I would, except she lost a battle to addiction last year."

He wanted to cry, but smiled instead.

They spoke for ten minutes. She asked if he'd ever considered writing about his recovery, not for vanity, but for others. He said he wasn't sure anyone wanted the truth. She said they did.

Later, Luca started scribbling recipes onto order pads and sticking them to the back wall of the walk-in fridge. A gallery of regrets and confessions. His sous chef called it "Luca's fridge diary."

Meanwhile, Isabella pushed him to get a lawyer to send Bjorn a cease-and-desist order.

"You don't owe him silence," she said. "You owe yourself sovereignty."

Luca hesitated. He wasn't afraid of confrontation. He was scared of reopening wounds that were starting to scab over. But he consulted a gay Latinx lawyer who specializes in artists' rights. They drafted a letter, polite, yet firm and protective. And Luca signed it.

He walked home feeling lighter.

He began attending a new support group called "Makers and Shakers." These men were artists, bakers, designers, and barbers who used creation as a form of redemption. They met every Thursday in a warehouse loft in the Mission. Each session began with a quote.

That week, it was from Audre Lorde: "Caring for myself is not self-indulgence, it is self-preservation, and that is an act of political warfare."

Luca shared about the tart, Paloma, and the walk-in fridge. The group clapped.

After the meeting, one of the men, Matteo, offered to collaborate on a zine featuring stories from recovering artists. Luca agreed.

At night, he found himself dreaming in ingredients again.

At the restaurant, he began training Luis more closely. He

saw a bit of his younger self in the kid; wiry, alert, hungry for praise but afraid of his ambition. One night, he caught Luis pacing the alley, muttering to himself.

"You okay?" Luca asked.

Luis nodded. Then shook his head. "Sometimes I still wanna use. Like… real bad."

Luca didn't flinch. He pulled out a cigarette. Handed it to Luis.

"Hold this," he said. "It helps to hold something that burns slower than you."

Luis laughed, eyes glassy.

Back inside, Luca showed him how to make the tart. The boy watched every movement.

"You'll get through it," Luca said. "Just don't try to do it alone."

That night, Luca updated his fridge diary with a new note: Sometimes, healing looks like teaching someone else how to stay.

Ten

LUCA GABRIEL

He started introducing himself as Gabriel everywhere. This wasn't a dramatic self-reinvention Instagram post. It was a casual realization. Like a name worn in secret for years had finally been invited into the daylight.

It happened for a second time at a community cooking class he attended one rainy Tuesday night. The instructor was checking names. "Luca?" she called. He hesitated. Then shook his head. "Gabriel," he said, voice low but firm. "Sorry. It's Gabriel."

The instructor smiled, jotted down the note, and moved on. No questions. No quiz. No cross-examination of his identity. Just an adjustment. A softness. A nod.

That's how the name took root. One class. Then, a church flyer. Then, a new friend's phone number. Then, he had a name badge at the coffee shop where he worked part-time. Slowly, surely, Luca became Gabriel in public spaces.

But at home, in the deepest folds of his memory, he still wrestled. Luca was the name that carried wounds and rituals. Gabriel was the name he used to speak to the person he was becoming.

"I don't hate Luca," he told me once. "Luca survived things. But Gabriel... Gabriel gets to live."

It was the most honest thing I'd heard him say in years.

He kept the name change quiet from most of the family. Not out of shame. Out of protection. Not everyone earned the right to know all the names you carry.

In church, people began to say it like it belonged. "Gabriel, will you read the second passage?" "Gabriel, your stew was divine." "Gabriel, do you want to join the altar guild?"

It made him glow, the way his shoulders eased and his voice warmed. He wore his new name like a well-washed sweatshirt that made room for breath and belonging.

And in the silence of his apartment, candle-lit, coffee-stained, quietly, he wrote in his journal about his day and lists of things he liked: hot soup, cool bed sheets, and kind eye contact.

On quiet nights like these, he would start to feel the weight of the day. He used his skills to stay in the moment: journaling, thinking about food, and sometimes painting. Painting didn't feel like betrayal anymore. Each night, the canvas would feel lighter and freer.

One large, strange, stunning painting hung above his desk. It was a portrait of a person walking into a body of water, shedding garments of old names and stories. Each ripple was a memory. Each step was both surrender and emergence. In the corner of the canvas, he'd scrawled, "Gabriel. Today."

I asked him about it. "It's me," he said. "But it's also not. It's who I'm letting myself be."

Letting. That word sat with me.

Gabriel wasn't a reinvention. He was a reintroduction.

The church community welcomed him as if they had been waiting for someone like him. He was still as strange as ever, still uncertain, walking daily through the wilderness of memory and recovery. But now, he did so with a name that made his tongue feel like home.

He started volunteering more, packing meals, organizing books, and hosting tiny dinners for newcomers in the recovery program. He joked that his calling was to make people feel safe enough to laugh while eating rice.

Mami took longer to adapt. Not because she refused. Because she loved him in all his forms. "Lukisito," she'd say with habit, then catch herself. "Perdón... Gabriel."

He would smile, never correcting her too sharply. "It's okay, Mami. I know what you mean."

But I saw the shift. I saw how her mouth slowly learned to say "Gabriel" like it wasn't new but had always been hiding in the melody of his being.

Some names we're born with. Others we grow into. Gabriel was not an escape. It was an invitation.

And Luca, brave, brilliant, wounded, had made room for Gabriel to arrive.

Eleven

CULINARY

L uca didn't plan on culinary school. Not really. It started as a joke, a comment he made to someone at a potluck, half-laughing as he ladled out lentil soup. "Maybe I should just cook full-time. Be a queer monk-chef hybrid. Open a bodega that also does therapy."

The joke turned into a search tab, an application, and an acceptance letter he didn't expect and almost didn't open.

He taped the letter to the fridge next to a prayer card from church and a photo of Meow sleeping in a box of kale.

"I guess this is happening...," he whispered to no one.

The first few weeks of culinary school were a blur of calloused fingertips, burned tongues, and late nights that smelled of garlic and redemption. Luca arrived with a cheap knife roll and a notebook whose pages were already stained with imagined sauces. He wrote in it like someone afraid memory might betray him; a kind of gospel for the rebirth he hoped to cook his way into.

His uniform didn't fit quite right. The chef coat was stiff and boxy, and the pants ballooned like clown trousers. He cinched them with a shoelace until payday. Everyone looked odd in their boxy uniforms, but no one said anything. They were too focused on mise en place and not chopping their fingers off to judge each other's silhouettes.

The mornings started with knives and ended with blisters. By week two, Luca had learned to hold a carrot like a lover you didn't trust. He diced with reverence, like the cut mattered more than the root. When he julienned, it was personal.

There was a kind of silent prayer in the kitchen's noise; the rhythm of blades against boards, the hiss of onions surrendering to oil, the muttered curses in half a dozen languages. Chef Malek, their instructor, moved like a storm barely contained in a toque. His voice was smoke and steel, and he rarely raised it. He didn't have to. You felt his presence the way you think heat before you touch the pan. "Touch the salt like it's got promise," he told them. "Taste everything. Taste your heart out."

Luca tasted everything.

Family-style Fridays were the only time the students were allowed to cook their dishes; a weekly communion of inherited spice and maternal precision. It was part competition, part confession. On the third Friday, Luca made empanadas de humita. He used yellow corn he'd roasted to coax out a char note. He crumbled queso fresco between his fingers like memory. The dough was too wet. It clung to him like a second skin, sticky and alive, but he didn't mind. It felt like the way his mother used to touch his cheeks when she still recognized him.

Naomi, a wiry girl from New Jersey with a tattoo of a koi fish running up her forearm, brought banana bread. It was her sponsor's recipe. A woman named Miss Liddy, who used to be a pastry chef, until her hands started shaking. Naomi served it warm, each slice laced with something dark and spicy, like cloves and grief. They traded bites with the silent reverence of altar boys.

I, the ghost in his pantry, had sent a jar of chimichurri wrapped in a flannel shirt that still smelled like me. The jar leaked slightly in transit, staining the note: "Para tu alma salada." For your savory soul. The chimichurri was electric; garlic-forward, unapologetically sharp, and green as envy. When he opened it in the school kitchen, the scent alone made him sit down. "It tastes like home-y fire," he told Naomi, his voice caught between laughter and tears.

In week four, Luca learned that stockpots are cauldrons, and bones tell stories if you boil them long enough. He discovered that butter can be angry, and sauces need patience. There were days he left school too tired to cry, so he sat on the subway and let the ache wash over him like he was rinsing water. He loved the discomfort and fatigue and how his body began understanding things his mind couldn't yet process. It felt like penance.

One morning, they were assigned to clean squid. Luca had never held anything so slippery and alien. It pulsed in his hands like a dare. Naomi gagged twice and then found her rhythm, slicing the bodies open like envelopes. "I feel like I'm doing surgery on a wet nightmare," she muttered. He laughed so hard he sliced his glove. Later that night, she sent him a meme of a cartoon squid wearing a chef's hat and the caption: "You ink, therefore you stink."

There were wars in that kitchen. Not all of them had to do with food. Manuel, a tall boy from Miami who talked too much and flirted like he was born in a telenovela, made ceviche so bright it hurt to taste. He called Luca "Argentina" as if it were both a nickname and a challenge. Luca ignored him for the fourth time, then made milanesa, bringing half the class to silence. Manuel grinned and clapped him on the back. "All right, chef. I see you."

Luca didn't know if it was a truce or the beginning of something else.

On Thursdays, they made soups. By the third Thursday, Luca had a working theory that you could tell everything about a person by their soup. He made a sopa paraguaya that wasn't a soup but passed anyway. It was dense, buttery, soaked in history. Chef Malek tasted it and said nothing for a long moment, then nodded once. That nod carried more weight than all the Yelp reviews in the world.

Homework was relentless. Knife drills. Sauce classifications. French terms that refused to stick to his tongue. He studied at night, often cooking pasta when he felt lonely and rice when he was anxious. He burned things intentionally to learn how to repair them. His fingers were nicked and bandaged, and the scabs started to feel like badges.

One evening, after a ruthless day of deconstructing whole chickens and his self-worth, he FaceTimed me. I was on my balcony in Buenos Aires, smoking a cigarette and painting my toenails.

"You look tired," I said.

"I look like beef tartare."

I laughed, sharp and unexpected. "Good. Maybe now you're finally becoming who you're supposed to be."

"I smell like onions."

"You always did."

He told me about the chimichurri and how it made his classmates cry and ask for seconds. I nodded, pleased. "You carry us in your hands, boludo. That's how it works."

By the end of the sixth week, Luca had fallen into something that resembled a rhythm. It wasn't peace exactly, but it was close; the kind of fragile stability that comes from repetition and purpose. He woke up sore and hopeful. He arrived early at the prep stations to slice mushrooms in silence. He learned that potatoes bruise easily and that some onions will make you cry no matter how much you pretend you're immune.

He kept a Polaroid of his father in his locker; a grainy shot from a summer barbecue long ago. He looked at it before service and whispered the same thing daily: "Watch me."

He was watching himself, too.

People arrived shy, arms crossed, hope buried under routine. By dessert, there was laughter. Naomi sang an old Joni Mitchell tune. A man named Hector was obsessed with lentils. He was going to open a lentil food truck. It sounded wild.

Luca didn't lead so much as listen. That was new for him. He used to need to fill space, to be the loudest flavor in the dish.

After everyone left for the day, Raquel helped with the cleaning. She wore one of Luca's aprons, the one with the tomato stains and frayed strings.

"You look nice in that," Luca said.

Raquel kissed his forehead.

"Thank you, Raquel. You're always so sweet at the right times."

That night, Luca lit a candle at his bedside. He tried to give thanks while feeling the silent peace now accessible in his home.

The next morning, Luca met Raquel for coffee. She was preparing for a food justice panel later that day and wore a denim jacket patched with feminist slogans and scorch marks.

They hugged like siblings who missed each other but weren't sure how to say it.

"Been keeping your salt levels up?" she asked.

"Salt, acid, and therapy," he said.

They sat outside, sipping bitter Americanos. Raquel pulled out a flyer from her pocket. "Ever thought about teaching a cooking workshop?"

Luca raised an eyebrow. "To whom?"

"Anyone who eats."

He laughed but didn't say no.

"I have been thinking about leaving Mami's house. I'm in my thirties; I haven't relapsed in a bit. I dunno. Plus, I like you, Raquel, and I feel like maybe we'd make great roommates. Plus, you mentioned that your roommate ran out on you, and I was thinking—"

"Luca," Raquel interrupted.

"Uh, yeah?"

"You had me at I dunno, plus I like you."

"Haha, shut up, dude."

"I'd love it if you moved in, like, asap."

"Hell yeah, let's fucking go."

Later, while walking home, he passed a bakery with a sign: *Now hiring part-time instructor: community baking classes.* He paused. Took a photo. Saved it.

Luca was finding new possible neural pathways everywhere, as Jamal called them. Everything was at his fingertips, which made it overwhelming. He called his sponsor and told him about this feeling: wanting to try everything but worrying about burning out, which led to triggers. His sponsor told him to do one thing. One thing at a time.

He spoke to Mami about leaving and how he finally felt ready.

Mami was so proud but sad she'd be living without him for the first time in his life. She put on a brave mom face and said, "I'm so proud of you, Hijo, ve con Dios."

"Gracias, ma," he said with a tear in his eye.

He moved in that weekend with nothing but a duffle bag to his name. He ordered a mattress online, his first big purchase since rehab.

It started small: the quiet itch for rhythm beyond recipe cards. For a place where he didn't have to succeed, perform, or produce something worth plating. A room that expected nothing except that he show up.

So he walked to church one Sunday after a particularly exhausting double shift and a fight with himself over a forgotten prayer journal.

Not dramatically. No clouds parted, no thunderous internal monologue.

He walked.

The little Episcopal church sat on the corner of Fifth and Laurel, between an old laundromat and a cafe that never seemed open. He had passed it dozens of times before, years ago, even, when his sobriety was new and raw and everything inside him buzzed with the ache of things not yet mended. But now, the banner out front read The Episcopal Church Welcomes You, and just beneath it, a rainbow flag flapped in the wind.

He almost turned around. He nearly decided it was too much, too symbolic, too vulnerable, and too visible. But his feet didn't listen.

He remembered the Book of Common Prayer I sent him and the nights when he called me in silence while I read to him from the same book.

Inside, the sanctuary smelled like lemon wood polish and

lavender oil. The pews creaked the way memory does. The stained-glass windows didn't shout; they glowed. There was no band. No projection screen. Just an organ slightly out of tune and a woman in her sixties handing out bulletins like each one carried a blessing.

He sat in the back.

He thought no one would notice.

They did.

But not in the way he feared. No one asked where he'd been. No one looked surprised that he had come. A man with silver hair and a turquoise cane nodded at him like they were old friends. The priest, Reverend Tina, smiled from the altar as if to say, You're not late. You're right on time.

The service was calming, lyrical, and laced with pauses that didn't feel awkward, just honest. They prayed the Collect for Purity and read from the book of Isaiah. The choir sang off-key and still made the rafters shake.

And then came the sermon.

Reverend Tina stepped to the pulpit in a soft black robe and white stole. She didn't clear her throat. Didn't apologize. She looked around the room like someone scanning the horizon for rain, then spoke:

"Some of us came here today not to find God, but to rest from looking. And that's okay. Sometimes faith begins not in the fire, but in the fatigue."

Luca felt something in his chest crack.

She went on. Not long. Just long enough to say that the gospel wasn't a performance. That Jesus never once handed out a rubric. That grace is most potent when you're too tired to earn it.

Tears slid down Luca's cheeks. He didn't wipe them. He

just bowed his head. After the service, he lingered in the back, pretending to read the bulletin.

On the last page was a photo of the vestry team: ten people smiling awkwardly in front of the altar.

Two of them were in wheelchairs.

One was a woman who signed the gospel weekly in American Sign Language (ASL).

Three were openly queer. Two were openly married to each other.

He stared at the page like it was a postcard from another world.

This wasn't the church of his childhood. This wasn't fire and brimstone and "God made Adam and Eve." This wasn't the closet. This wasn't survival by silence.

This was a table set wide.

In this room, people with tremors handed out the Eucharist with shaking hands, and no one rushed them.

This was a church where a gay couple sat in the front row with their adopted son squirming between them, and nobody whispered.

This was real.

He came back the following week.

And the next.

He didn't speak much and hadn't taken communion yet, but he listened. He stayed for coffee hour. He started recognizing people.

There was Grace, the baker with tattoos of fruits and sourdough recipes up and down her arms.

There was Kyle, a teenager who identified as trans, humming through hymns and scribbling verses in the margins of their bulletin like secret prayers.

There was Ruth, who walked with a limp and called everyone "sweetheart," even the priest.

Gerald and Thomas had been together since the late '80s. They brought different pies to every potluck and argued over which was better.

He called them the Church of Late Bloomers.

Luca found himself sitting beside them more and more. It was a magnetism rooted in recognition he had never really felt.

After a month, he stayed behind to help with the cleaning.

No one asked him to.

He noticed how the chairs wobbled, the cups needed rinsing, the altar cloths were folded with care, and a bit of chaos.

It felt familiar, like a kitchen. But different. Less grease. More grace.

As he folded bulletins into neat stacks one afternoon, Reverend Tina offered him a half-eaten cookie.

"You've got a habit of staying," she said.

"I like the quiet after the singing," he replied.

"Me too," she said. "Sometimes that's where God hides."

They didn't say anything else. They just folded paper together for a while, letting the silence speak. One Sunday, after the service, he stayed behind to help with the cleanup, folding linens and rinsing out cups.

Luca didn't expect to be asked to read. He'd been helping with cleanup for weeks, stacking chairs, refilling the decaf, and folding bulletins with meditative care. He liked its silence and the soft afterglow of service when the sanctuary was emptied, but the spirit lingered.

He talked to Raquel about his church and how it wasn't like other churches; it was chill and welcoming. Raquel insisted it wasn't her thing, so Luca suggested a middle ground.

"Alright, well, the place keeps me busy, which is good for my brain health or whatever, so will you come to the pantry with me. They need help spicing it up and running it, and who is better than us?"

The monthly pantry was called The Memory Pantry, and they were not ready for two chefs in training to hit the ground running the way Luca and Raquel did. Raquel built a website. Luca resisted at first; he wanted it to be intimate. "It can still be small," Raquel said. "But people deserve to find it."

They added a blog. Raquel contributed a piece called *Flavor is Resistance.* Luca wrote about sobriety and strawberry jam. Luca posted a recipe for lentil stew with this preface: *When I couldn't speak, I simmered.*

One thing done, he thought.

His sponsor was right. He would feel a new, buzzing joy when he did one thing at a time. He embraced it all, one step at a time. He started walking more, to notice things and feel the wind ground him. A woman is arguing with her chihuahua. A fence is overgrown with morning glory. An older man is eating soup from a thermos on a park bench. Mindfulness techniques and being in the moment were incredibly lethargic.

When he was home, he would sketch. Not food, but people. Their hands. Their postures. He'd lost so much time to numbness; now everything felt urgent, sacred.

At a Wednesday meeting, Luca shared: "I used to think healing was about arriving. But I think it's about walking. Choosing to stay in motion, even on the bad days."

The group murmured their agreement. Afterward, a teenager named Zion gave him a sticker: *Queer, Sober, Magic.*

He stuck it in his knife case.

And he kept walking.

That night, Luca relapsed.

* * *

Everything seemed to be going great, Luca thought. He was attending meetings and doing everything right. Yet here he was again, engulfed by a wave of self-hate too heavy to bear. He called me, but he hung up the phone. I called back eight times, but he didn't respond.

He hid in his room for four days.

Raquel was worried, yet she covered for him at school. She gave him the space he needed. She was great like that.

It was different than with Mami and me. We, bless our hearts, wouldn't stop harassing him about "healing" whenever he relapsed. Not Raquel. She understood the deal.

When Luca emerged from his room, Raquel asked, "Hey man, you good?"

"Yeah. Thank you for covering."

"Yeah, don't get used to it. Rent's expected on time. I won't do this more than once, especially if it becomes a habit. That's all I have to say about that."

"Heard, Chef."

"Alright, good."

Luca felt like a steaming pile of shit, but he was relieved Raquel didn't make a big deal out of it. She understood the process. Raquel had demons of her own. She had substance issues, too, but had been sober for 12 years. She took her sobriety seriously and respected the process of recovery. Custody battles had been her most tremendous pain in life. Failing her son was something she could never forgive herself for, yet she tried to keep steady for herself and him with all her might. The only thing that mattered was never letting him down again. Luca appreciated that she never tried to mother him. She had one son and her issues to overcome. Luca felt he had found the perfect roommate in Raquel.

Luca didn't dwell on his relapse; he treated it like a recipe. Called his sponsor. He attended his N.A. meeting and shared that night.

"My name is Luca ... and I'm an addict."

"Hi, Luca," they greeted him, no judgment in their voices, the exact greeting he needed.

He cried all night and went to work the next day.

Luca's relationship with food deepened, like the texture of a sauce simmering for hours. He thought about his sponsor's words. He thought he should slow down on all the projects he was taking on. But he simply wouldn't. He was a maniac and wanted to spend all his time with his fingers in dough, paper, blogs, or anything to resist the call of the void. He poured his thoughts into an added page to the Memory Pantry's blog, writing a post called *What We Taste When We're Sober*. Sober, stupid fucking word, he thought. It seemed the weight of that word now surrounded his entire life. But he knew there was agency in it, and though his whole face twitched to the left into a loud noise his mouth would make when he used it for the zine, he used it.

Each issue featured a recipe, a recovery story, and a photo of someone's hands; always hands. Raquel took the images. She captured Joey's knuckles dusted in flour, Naomi's trembling fingers on a coffee mug, and Luca's calloused palms curled around a lemon.

Curtis, skeptical yet loyal, began showing up early to prepare. "I read your blog," he said one morning. "It was… weirdly good." Luca didn't say anything, just smiled with a tinge of disappointment in himself. He talked about it in N.A. that night. How much he hated being praised for being a loser with a disease. His sponsor reminded him to be kind to himself. Luca said he'd try.

Luca visited the church alone the following week. It smelled like wood polish and unanswered prayers. An older gay couple greeted him at the door and handed him a program. The choir was out of tune. The communion bread tasted like cardboard. But the peace, the palpable, awkward, grounded peace, stayed with him.

He sat in the back, breathing.

When the priest said, "Come as you are," he nearly sobbed.

He didn't take communion. But he lit a candle.

When he got home, Raquel waited with leftover polenta fries and aioli. "How was the official Jesus stuff?" she asked.

Luca smiled. "It was peaceful."

They ate in silence.

Raquel preferred the pantry service only. She didn't care for masses or the "officialdom" of it all. Luca liked that they were so different; it allowed him to do things his way.

The next day, Luca added a new section to the Memory Pantry blog called *Small Plates*: short thoughts, recipes, one-liners like *You are not too much. You are just richly seasoned.*

It resonated. People began emailing him stories. A woman recovering from surgery shared a recipe for rice pudding that felt like the return of her appetite. A teen wrote a piece called *Pickles and Pronouns.*

He published them all.

They had to borrow chairs from the bookstore at the next Memory Pantry gathering. Curtis DJ-ed. Raquel taught a biscuit technique over FaceTime. Naomi brought her sister, who had been sober for four days. Raquel read a passage from Baldwin: *"Love takes off masks that we fear we cannot live without and know we cannot live within."*

They served soup and called it Redemption Stew.

And nobody left early.

Culinary school was hot. Physically hot. Emotionally hot. He walked in with a canvas tote and a spiral notebook, and within two weeks, he had burns on both hands and a growing pile of self-doubt.

It was a different kind of discipline than recovery, but just as exacting. Every chop was measured, and every mistake was magnified. Chef instructors spoke in blunt, declarative sentences, leaving no room for existential wonder.

"You cut it wrong."

"You're too slow."

"This stock tastes like apathy."

He started coming home exhausted. He skipped meetings and meals. He convinced himself that one missed call to his sponsor was fine, then two, then a week.

He didn't relapse.

But he thought about it.

He thought about it a lot.

After one fierce day, which included overcooked fish, a failed emulsification, and a classmate who mocked his handwriting on the shared whiteboard, he stood in his kitchen staring at a bottle of cooking wine. It was not good wine, not even real wine, but enough.

His hands shook.

He opened the cap.

And then he did what the version of himself from ninety days ago never would have done. He called his sponsor.

It rang twice.

"Luca?" the voice said. Gentle. Solid. Present.

"I didn't do it," he whispered.

"Okay."

"But I wanted to. I wanted to."

There was a pause. A daunting pause.

"Wanting to isn't failure," his sponsor said. "It's information. It tells us where it still hurts."

Luca sat down on the kitchen floor, back against the fridge. Knees pulled up to his chest.

"I think I'm scared of being good at something," he said. "Because then people expect it. And I'm tired. I don't want to perform. I want to feed people."

"And you will," his sponsor replied. "But first, you have to keep feeding yourself."

They talked for half an hour about grounding, grace, and the difference between pressure and purpose. By the end of the call, the wine was down the drain, the window was open, and the air smelled like basil and the promise of tomorrow.

Culinary school didn't get easier. But he stopped expecting ease.

He packed a protein bar daily, set meeting reminders, and texted his sponsor once a morning, even if it was just a single word: present.

The cuts on his hands healed. His knife skills improved. His joy didn't roar, but it hummed a steady simmer.

Slowly, the kitchen stopped feeling like a battlefield and started to feel like a place where he belonged.

That week, Luca began writing a new menu, which was emotional rather than seasonal. Each dish was themed around a phase of healing. He called it The Restoration Series.

Appetizers: "First Silence," "Tremble Salad." Mains: "Second Wind," "Soft Spine," "Bone of Hunger." Desserts: "After," "Almost Joy."

The names made Isabella laugh and cry in equal measure.

"You're naming meals like poems," she said.

"They are poems," he answered. "Edible ones."

He brought Luis in to help conceptualize the plating. "The food should look like how the body feels when it forgives itself," Luca said.

Luis sighed. "That's... a lot."

"Yeah," Luca said. "But so is recovery."

They sourced ingredients from an LGBTQTIA+-owned urban farm outside the city. Luca spent Saturdays helping to harvest tomatoes, sorrel, and blue kale. Dirt under his nails felt holy. One of the farm managers, Alix, was non-binary and sharp-tongued, and soon became part of Luca's growing circle.

"You're healing out loud," Alix said, loading crates of chard. "That's brave. And messy. But brave."

The culinary school had a deal with neighboring restaurants and cafes. Raquel and Luca applied to Pan y Paz and got in. They prepped for the first night of the new menu. Luca asked Yvette to read a poem before the service. She chose one about roots, returning to the dirt to understand the blossom.

The house was packed. The guests were furling. The plates were left clean.

Word spread quickly. Food critics called it "radical vulnerability disguised as cuisine." Reservations filled weeks in advance. Luca turned down an interview with Bon Appétit. He didn't want to be famous. He wanted to be understood.

One night, an older man approached the counter after his meal. "My son's in rehab," he said. "It's his third time. He hasn't spoken to us in six months. But something about that duck confit reminded me of him. When we used to cook together, maybe he'll find this place, maybe I'll see him here."

Luca didn't have a response. He just reached out and held the man's hand. He was learning the language of comfort, texture, salt, and steam.

Luca returned to his support group, bringing samples from the menu. He let others name what they tasted. "Hope," said one. "Bitterness," said another. "Clean," said a third.

A therapist visiting the group remarked on the powerful therapeutic parallels between culinary creativity and narrative exposure therapy, how each meal allowed Luca and his guests to reframe trauma through flavor.

Later that week, he opened up a space in the back that the owner wanted to revamp. He was doing it again, diving straight into action. Do, and keep moving. Movers and shakers, shake shit up. He would work a full shift at Pan y Paz and then work on the open space. Pan y Paz Cafe, he thought proudly, while he showed the owner, Johnny.

"Dammmmn, looks real good, kid," said Johnny with his infamous half-smirk.

"You got a menu in mind?"

"Yeah."

"Alright, hey, there was something else I wanted to talk to you about. You know I know your story, and you know I'm impressed with how hard you work to stay on track. You know that shit lives in our veins, and we all do our fucking best. But you, you're killing it. And listen, I've got this kid in the family.

Name's Gio calls himself 'G'. This kid thinks he's the last Coca-Cola in the desert, alright?"

Luca laughed and nodded.

"I was wondering if you wouldn't mind, I dunno, taking him under your wing."

"Oh... Johnny, you know I love you, man, but I can't. I don't have...I already have way too much shit on my plate. I mean, I'm a fucking maniac. I do do do. I don't think I got it in me to... I just, fuck, I don't know."

"Alright, look, I need this, alright. This kid is lost, and I think you may be able to help him. I don't know, inspire him or something."

"Is this one of those, he's gay, I'm gay, so we must be a match kind of thing, old man?"

Johnny laughed but immediately dropped his face into an extreme and genuine sadness.

"OK, OK, we need a new cashier for the new cafe. Ignacio was going to do it, but he quit on us last week."

Johnny half-smirked. "Thanks, kid. I'll have Gio come in next week."

Luca half-smirked back.

Pan y Paz, the cafe, started opening one day a month. Word got out that those two sober chefs were involved in the community. People poured in. No pressure. Just access. Community. Trust. Tyler came. Samira brought her teenage daughter. Jesse returned, now sober for six months.

In the quiet afterward, Michela, the fry chef, held Luca's hand and whispered, "You're building something special here."

The pressure was building up in Luca again. Too much. Reality was too much. He didn't know what to call it. He just felt a spider-web as thick as concrete pulsing in the center of his chest. H.A.L.T., he thought, breathe. He called Me.

"Hey, you…"

He hung up.

I am capable of doing this. I'm fine, I'm fine, he repeated to himself.

There were days when he still woke up shaky and unsure. Nights, he thought about using, not out of want, but of habit. He called Harry, his former caseworker, or scribbled in his fridge diary on those nights. He even wrote a letter to Bjorn. Didn't send it. But wrote it and said everything.

"You stole me. But I'm stealing me back."

The letter ended with: This is what I look like when I'm not yours.

He tucked it under a bottle of chimichurri in the fridge.

One month later, the restaurant hosted its first sober pride brunch. Rainbow eggs. Zero-proof cocktails. Drag brunch readings. Laughter spilled into the street.

Luca watched it all from the kitchen window with a small smile.

Twelve

ORDINARY

There are days in a recovering life when nothing dramatic happens, and still, the effort it takes to exist is a quiet revolution. Today was one of those days. Ordinary sunlight spilled across Luca's windowsill. The coffee he brewed was slightly too strong. The cat meowed at nothing in particular. But inside him, something was shifting, a glimmer of peace he didn't yet trust.

He was halfway through his second month of culinary school when he began to notice the texture of his joy. It wasn't loud or fluorescent. It was soft. Textured like sea salt or warm dough. It arrived not with epiphany but through rhythm, knife on board, garlic in oil, a splash of stock. It was in the way he learned to taste as he cooked, trust his senses again, and trust his body not as a battlefield but as an instrument of care.

Each morning, he woke up and greeted the mirror. "Good morning, Luca," he said out loud.

It felt silly. But it was working.

He was still scared, still unsure, still painfully aware of how fragile sobriety could be. But he was also alive in a way that allowed him to feel.

One day, in class, the instructor assigned a solo dish. "Cook something that reminds you of where you come from," she said. Luca nodded, then panicked.

Where did he come from?

Grief? Art? Argentina? New Jersey? Church pews? Hospital rooms? Love?

He closed his eyes and remembered his mother stirring soup at 2 a.m., the first time he cooked rice without burning it, and his past lover licking butter from his thumb. He remembered being Luca, and he honored that memory.

He decided on empanadas.

It wasn't flashy. It wasn't complex. But it was rooted. It was true. He woke up at 5 a.m. to prepare. Grate the cheese slowly. Warmed the pan with care. When it was his turn to present, he said only:

"This dish is from my part that learned to stay."

The instructor didn't smile. She ate. Then she wrote something in her notebook.

Later, he found a note in his locker: You cook like you mean it.

That night, he didn't think about drinking. He didn't know about failure. He lit a candle and prayed in the language he invented as he went.

Not a perfect prayer. But something like grace.

He wrote in his journal:

Today, I felt calm without needing a reason. I think that's new.

And the next morning, when he said, "Good morning, Luca," he almost believed it.

Luca's reintegration into daily life unfolded like a cautious waltz. He resumed small routines: folding laundry, checking the mail, greeting the grocer on the corner. Each task reminded him that he was no longer trapped. He was choosing.

Luca returned to therapy twice a week. His new therapist, Sonia, was a humbling force, with shelves full of orchids and books on trauma-informed resilience. One afternoon, she introduced him to Internal Family Systems therapy.

"There's a whole system of selves in you," she explained. "The person with an addiction, the chef, the lover, the scared boy. They all want a voice. They all want peace."

Luca hesitated. "What if I don't want to hear some of them?"

Sonia smiled. "Then you need to."

Together, they mapped Luca's emotional weather: what triggered the urge to flee, freeze, and fall back. They also celebrated his new victories, hosting sober dinners, mentoring Luis, and even finding the courage to nap.

"You deserve rest without guilt," Sonia reminded him.

Meanwhile, Meow shadowed him like a tiny bodyguard. She slept in his laundry, yowled at his journal, and insisted on midday cuddles. Luca joked she was his emotional support overlord.

He began recording vlogs . In one clip, he stood in the restaurant pantry, holding a jar of cinnamon.

"This spice used to make me crave," he said. "It reminded me of cold nights and bad decisions. Now? It reminds me I can change what things mean."

He shared that one. It gained mild viral popularity in the recovery community.

One Sunday, Raquel brought Mami over for dinner. Luca made roast chicken, potatoes soaked in lemon, and alfajores for dessert.

Mami ate slowly. "You always were the best cook," she said quietly.

He held her hand across the table. "Thanks for waiting for me."

After they left, Luca sat with Meow and played Sade on vinyl. He watched dusk gather in corners and thought, "Maybe this is what healing looks like." Not loud, not perfect, but alive.

He wrote late into the night, often with Meow curled beside him like punctuation.

And one night, just before sleep, he whispered aloud, "I'm proud of you," not sure if he meant Meow, himself, or both.

Luca was elbow-deep in flour when I called.

"I just lit a candle for you," I said. "No pressure, but it was a good one."

He leaned the phone against a jar of chickpeas and wiped his hands. "I'm not sure Gay God takes messages through siblings."

"He does when they're persistent."

Luca smiled. He had become both softer and bolder since we began speaking regularly. We didn't talk about the dark years. We folded that silence into every phone call, like sourdough starter; a past that still fed the present.

He was prepping for Sunday supper, a new menu: mole lentils, citrus slaw, rosemary focaccia, and cardamom panna cotta. Raquel had joked that Luca cooked like someone who'd fallen in love with the earth. Maybe he had.

Curtis came in early and queued up a playlist called *Grace in D Minor*. Mariela sliced fennel with monastic focus. The kitchen moved like poetry now; intentional, lived-in, loving.

Luca spent all his days and nights between the second table at the church and Pan y Paz cafe. They now held sober community dinners bi-weekly at a shared artist co-op with long tables and open windows. I flew in for the first anniversary. I wore a pink jumpsuit and brought hot sauce called "Penitencia."

That night, Luca spoke at the table. "We made it a year without numbing ourselves. A year of showing up hungry and leaving full. Not fixed, not perfect, but fed."

They raised glasses of hibiscus iced tea. Raquel shouted, "To feed our ghosts!"

And everyone cheered.

After dinner, Luca and Raquel stood washing dishes together, shoulders brushing in a rhythm only old friends knew. "Well, well, well, look at what you built," she said, handing him a dripping plate.

"I didn't build it alone," he said. "I just kept showing up."

They discussed the upcoming year, focusing on writing a collaborative cookbook for the Memory Pantry project. Raquel wanted essays. Luca wanted prayers in the margins.

"We'll do both," she said. "Recipe and ritual."

Later, Raquel and Luca walked home slowly, the night warm, alive with city hush. Raquel stopped outside a corner bodega and bought a single sunflower.

"For your recipe notes," she said.

Luca took it carefully. "Raquel, you're giving lavender wife vibes." They looked at each other and laughed uncontrollably.

When they got home, Luca placed the sunflower and a small salt dish in a chipped jar beside his journal. He whispered, "Thank you," and then turned off the light.

He dreamt of his father for the first time in years. Not yelling, not distant; just sitting at the kitchen table, peeling oranges in long spirals. When Luca woke, he could still smell citrus.

He wrote in his journal: *Forgiveness sometimes comes quietly, dressed as simple moments.*

The next morning, he added orange zest to the focaccia. The next afternoon, Luca found himself behind *Pan y Paz* in the back alley, sitting on a milk crate with a cooling tray of lemon shortbread on his knees. Raquel joined him, carrying two cans of yerba mate.

"I never thought I'd be the kind of person who looked forward to Tuesdays," Luca said.

Raquel clinked his can to Luca's. "Tuesdays are simple, but who knew they could be filling?"

The Memory Pantry blog had received a small donation from a local LGBTQIA+ arts fund. Luca used the money to print more copies and host a workshop called *Spice and Story*. People brought family recipes and the grief that came with them. One woman, Ana, read a piece about arroz con leche and her late son. There wasn't a dry eye in the room.

Curtis, unexpectedly moved, offered to edit a video series. "Everyone thinks grief is loud. But it's often a simmer."

That phrase stuck with Luca, who wrote it in his journal beneath a sketch of a garlic bulb.

Later that week, I sent him a care package: lavender soap, a well-worn prayer card, and a picture of us as kids beside a chocolate cake. I scribbled, *You always licked the frosting first.*

He replied with a postcard featuring a matzo ball in flight: *Still licking. Still rising.*

The kitchen had settled into its heartbeat. Mariela started making playlists. Raquel painted a mural on the alley door; a rising sun made of spices. Meow had become a mascot, often sleeping on the pastry shelf during prep.

One evening, a man named Tobias walked in, nervous, clutching a printed copy of the blog. "Is this where the food that tastes like 'love' is made?"

"Yes," Luca said, wiping his hands on his apron. "And also where the cooks learn to love themselves."

Tobias joined that night's Memory Pantry meal. He brought coconut rice and left with three new phone numbers and a volunteer shift.

Later, Luca journaled: *Recovery is a revolving door that leads you home, again and again.*

He reread his earlier entries. So much pain, so much silence. Now, the pages smelled faintly of cinnamon and resolution.

He remembered something Raquel had once said: "Growth isn't always new leaves. Sometimes it's the strength of your roots."

So he kept planting. Feeding. Listening.

He was becoming someone he trusted to stay.

The morning of his thirty-fifth birthday, Luca woke to the sound of rain tapping the window and Meow's soft weight curled beside him. He didn't expect a parade or fanfare; he barely expected anything at all; but Raquel stood in the kitchen wearing an apron that read *Birthday Bitch* and holding a tray of cinnamon buns shaped like hearts.

Luca smirked. "You're ridiculous."

"And you're late for your party," Raquel said, handing him coffee in his favorite chipped mug.

The party was small. It was just a family gathering: Mariela brought Colombian arepas, Naomi brought her homemade hotpot, and Curtis made a playlist called Luca at 35: Slightly Charred, Still Delicious. They played charades and ate three kinds of lasagna.

Mariela gave a toast. "To the chef who taught us that healing comes in spoonfuls."

Luca felt something in his throat then, some unnameable grace, and when he caught my eye on the video call, I said, "You made it, mi nino."

He did make it.

Later that night, when the guests were gone, Luca cleaned alone in the kitchen. Not because he had to, but because it grounded him. He wiped down counters, stacked dishes, and whispered thank you into the quiet.

Thirteen

GIO

Y ou can tell a lot about a person from their first day in a
kitchen. Gio stands there, his eyes wide, his breathing
fast. He hasn't tied his bandana right, and Luca resists
the urge to fix it for him. Instead, Luca watches him. Luca
recalls his early days, with shaky hands, self-doubt, and the
overwhelming scent of onions filling his senses. Gio cuts a
carrot, awkwardly, but he's trying. He wants him to succeed so
badly it hurts.

Gio moves to the stove, turning a knob that only sparks
and clicks, then slamming a pan down as if force will do what
patience cannot. The kitchen noise is a symphony of clattering
pans, sizzling onions, and shouted orders. He's jittery, looking
over his shoulder, waiting for someone to call him out. Luca's
memories echo in the clamor, the chaotic beginning of a shift,
hands shaking, apron already stained. A vegetable roll bounces
across the floor, and Luca sees Gio scrambling to pick it up. It

was like this when Luca started with Raquel, barely keeping up, panic and excitement mixed in every slice. A familiar part of Luca wants to step in, take over, and save Gio. But Luca forced himself to watch instead.

Luca moves beside him, pretending to check the prep list. "How are you doing?" he asks, his voice low amidst the chaos.

"Great!" he says, too loud, the word breaking. He catches himself. "I mean, you know, I'm okay."

Luca smiles, trying not to let his struggle show in his voice. "First days are hard."

Gio looks at Luca, and the defensive bravado is gone for a second. "Yeah."

"You'll get there," Luca says, hoping Gio believes him, hoping he thinks himself.

Gio picks up the knife again, but it wobbles in his hand. Luca glanced at the julienne pile, which consisted of carrots in all shapes and sizes. "Here, let me show you."

They stand side by side at the counter. His uncertainty matches Luca's calm, each breath a counterpoint to the other. Luca takes a carrot, Gio's hands steady, as he shows the movement. Gio's knife presses down, unsteady, uneven, the cuts bruised and jagged. He's trying to keep up, trying to be precise. It's Luca's turn to slice, and Luca sees him watch, curiosity tangled with a fear that looks too familiar. "We start early here," Luca says. "Be on time, and I'll show you the coffee routine."

Gio nods, blinking fast, trying to absorb it all. The prep sheet is marked in Gio's careful handwriting, an attempt to impose order. Luca remembers this so well, overwhelmed by each new technique and each new person, trying to prove himself, not sure if he wanted to stay or run. Luca says nothing; let him find his way. They worked like this for a while; his rough attempts gradually gained shape. Luca's patient, more patient than he should be, Gio's mistakes matter more to him than they should. It's strange how badly he wants Gio to do well, as if fixing him might fix Luca, too.

Gio's relief is palpable when the last order is out and the clatter settles into the dull roar of after-shift cleanup. He's survived, and Luca's not sure if Gio knows he'll have to do it again tomorrow. Luca called him over, his tone as casual as possible. Gio wipes his hands on his apron, more nervous now than he was with a hundred tickets hanging in front of him.

"Come on," Luca says. "Let me show you something."

The kitchen is a ghost of itself once the lunch rush clears, the silence as tangible as the chaos was. Gio follows Luca, hesitating at the door, unsure if he's allowed. Luca led him to the refuge, the space Luca cherishes, where the rituals keep him whole. "This is my morning," Luca says. "Just the kitchen and me. It's where I figure things out."

Gio stands there, not quite seeing it or understanding how quiet can hold so much power.

Gio shifts his weight, torn between interest and doubt. Luca sees the way Gio hesitates, the way he used to when he wasn't sure what to trust. Gio scratches at his bandana, finally looking up, the fear of doing it wrong clashing with the desire to do it. "Keep going," Luca says, but there's a question at the end, like Gio's waiting for him to say it's not enough.

Luca put his hand on Gio's shoulder. "Just show up," Luca says, knowing he can't make Gio do anything, but hoping. They walk back through the now-still dining room, tables empty and chairs stacked. It's supposed to be reassuring, this moment when the restaurant exhales and resets, but Gio's steps are tentative.

Luca stops before he leaves. It's now or never, he thinks to himself. "Hey, Gio. There's a meeting tonight. If you want, I'll take you."

The room holds its breath. Gio's quiet, and Luca feels the weight of each second.

"Think about it," Luca added, pulling back, giving him the space to say no.

"Yeah," he says. "I'll think about it."

Gio's gone, and Luca's left with his voice, the voice that wants to do this right and that simultaneously hopes and fears. He wipes down the counter, each motion a piece of its ritual, each pass of the cloth a small promise to someone else or himself. Tomorrow, Luca thinks, I'll know.

Luca rinses soapy water off the plates and lets it flood his thoughts. "Be careful," Raquel says. Luca knows what she means. Luca's working on the dishes the way he works at everything, with too much force and not enough self-preservation. The kitchen lights glow warmly over him, and the steam is thick enough to breathe. "He reminds me so much of myself," Luca says. "That's why I'm worried," she replies. She's calm, not a drop of anxiety where there should be. "It's why I need to do this," Luca tells her. It's like arguing with a river.

She takes a stack of plates and dries them in perfect order. "I don't parent you, Luca. I respect you as my roommate. We have a good thing going here and at home, and I only caution you to protect that. I'm afraid you'll get lost in this." Her voice is gentle, landing right where it needs to. She always knows.

"That's not fair," Luca says. "I was just trying to help."

"Exactly," she says, loading Luca with more dishes to rinse. "And help turns into something else."

"Not this time." Luca's words are as hard as his scrubbing at the pots.

Her smile is a small, knowing thing. "I've heard that before. I've been here before." The steam carries it over to Luca, heavy and unshakable.

"He reminds me so much of myself," Luca says again, as if repeating it makes it more real. As if it justifies the need that blooms in his chest, the same need Luca can never quite give up. The water is hotter than Luca thought, and Luca likes how it stings.

She sighs, but Luca sees the care behind it. "It's not your job to fix him."

"Someone has to." Luca caught her eye, challenging her to argue and see it differently. Luca wants her to say, 'You're right.'

"He's not your responsibility," she says instead.

The silence holds them. Raquel was starting to sound like me, Luca thought. She had never shown this side of herself to him. She had always played the role of a great friend and respected colleague. The thought of Raquel beginning to act like his sister triggered a response in him. Luca rinsed the last of the plates and started on the silverware. Her words keep repeating in his head, soft and true and unwelcome. The harder Luca tries to push them away, the more they take root.

"Think of everything you're doing right now," she says, waving her hand to take in their apartment and life. "Think of all you've got on your plate. Is this the time to take on more?"

Luca glanced around, seeing it all through her eyes. Cookbooks lined up like soldiers on a mission. A calendar on the wall with the dates carefully marked with milestones, each a piece of survival. Plants everywhere, reaching for the light like they know something Luca doesn't.

"This isn't just more," Luca says, but the argument feels flimsy now, waterlogged and limp.

She dries her hands and sets them on Luca's shoulders. They're strong hands, confident, like she's the one who knows how to save Luca.

"You're doing so well," she says. "Don't get pulled back in."

"It's not like that," Luca insists, even as he sees it is. "I know what I'm doing."

"Do you?" Her eyes are all love and warning.

"He needs this."

"You need this," she counters, right again, the words a gentle catch.

Luca's hands are still wet, suds slipping down his wrists. "I know what it's like to need someone who understands."

"Just remember your boundaries, okay?" she says.

The plates are done, and the silverware is clean. They're standing in a house built on mutual patience, mutual need. Her look is everything, everything. Luca can't say she's wrong. But he won't know she's right, either. The water goes down the drain, and Luca hopes he hasn't gone with it.

Gio's late the next morning, and Raquel's patience is thin. Her shoulders ache from bearing so much of the restaurant's weight. Gio slips in just as the lunch rush begins, avoiding Luca's and Raquel's eyes. Luca catches a whiff of stale alcohol, his stomach twisting with too-familiar recognition. Dark circles shadow Gio's eyes, and Luca wonders if he made it to the meeting or even made it home. Luca, please don't ask, not yet, he tells himself. "Can you keep up today?" he asks, harsher than intended. Gio nods, but Luca can see the anger simmering beneath the surface.

The kitchen erupts into controlled chaos, and Luca shouts orders over the clamor. He wants to pull Gio aside to ask what's going on, but he knows better than to push too soon. Instead, he watches. He sees Gio flinch when a pot crashes to the floor; his hands are slower today, less precise than yesterday. He hacks at a cucumber with more fury than skill, his jaw set, movements rigid. Luca's stomach clenches with every mistake he recognizes.

They collide at the fridge, both reaching for the same container. Luca lets him have it, studying Gio like an ingredient he can't quite identify. "Did you make it to that meeting?" Luca asks.

Gio glares, ice-cold, then softens just enough for Luca to see the truth he doesn't want to admit. "Yeah," Gio mumbles, brushing past Luca, his anger palpable.

"You sure?" Luca asks, half hopeful, half doubting.

"Back off, man." The words are more defensive than angry this time.

Luca should leave it there, but his stubbornness won't let him. He's still thinking of his conversation with Raquel, of the bandana and how it came untied, when he sees the empty bottles in the bathroom trash. The sight knocks the air out of him.

He stares at them, memories flooding back of nights when he thought he could hide, only to realize he couldn't pretend forever. He's holding one of the bottles, unsure how it got there, uncertain how he got here, when a voice from the kitchen calls his name.

"Coming!" Luca shouts back, but his throat is tight, and the word is small. He sets the bottle down carefully, as if it might explode.

Gio's already outside when Luca follows him to the alley, walking through real and mental fog. Steam from the vents mingles with the stench of garbage, clinging to everything. He sees Gio light a cigarette, his hand trembling.

"You think you can hide it?" Luca says, getting straight to the point, straight to the fear.

Gio turns and tries to smirk, but it's thin, like his defenses. "What?"

"You know what," Luca says, and the calm in his voice surprises them both.

"You can't fix me, Luca." Luca's name is a weapon in his mouth.

"Gio, I'm not trying to fix you." He should be gentler, but he isn't.

Gio kicks a crate, frustration and pain wrapped in a single angry motion. "You don't get it," he says, his voice breaking.

"Don't I?" The old hurt surfaces, Luca's past merging with his present.

"I thought I could handle it. Just one drink, you know? To take the edge off." His denial crumbles like dry bread.

"You know it doesn't work like that."

He laughs, a harsh, hollow sound. "What do you care?"

Luca cares more than he should, more than he's allowed. "I'll help you find treatment."

"You can't save me." His eyes are wet, defenses gone. "You can't even save yourself."

The words hit like a dull thud, and Gio runs out of the alley, out of Luca's reach.

Luca stands there, letting Gio's words soak in, letting everything he can't do crush him. The steam from the kitchen feels heavier now, and he turns back inside. The restaurant is loud, oblivious, and moving on. Luca washes his hands, the water scalding, the motion mechanical, each rinse futilely attempting to clean what won't come off.

He grabs his phone, his fingers almost too shaky to dial. Raquel answers on the second ring, her voice an anchor.

"You were right," Luca says, hanging up before she can confirm it.

Fourteen

WINSTON

⊷⊰♥⊱⊶

Luca opened Grindr every night before bed. Some nights, he missed the thrill more than anything, the rush of matching, meeting, and fucking strangers. He struggled to untangle the layers of his addiction. Was he a sex addict or simply a gay man in the 21st century? Straight men have their inner sex lions tempered early in life. Society is built to preserve and protect the male instinct to match with the nearest available partner. Young straight men are encouraged to marry and embrace monogamy. Straight men who cheat are demonized and scolded by every societal pillar. But who tempers gay sex? Society can't agree on whether gay men, or any queer couple, should marry. Monogamy isn't pushed or encouraged; the world of gay, lesbian, trans, and queer sex is...silenced. In circles where it's *accepted*, it's accepted quietly. They don't teach about gay safe sex in mainstream forums; it's absent from sex education, where everyone else learns.

Do Moms and Dads waving gay pride flags pause to ask about safety in bathhouses? At least, Luca hadn't experienced that. Gay sex happens in the dark, he learned early, where predators and wolves linger. It shouldn't have to mirror straight sex in societal expectations; it breathes on its own, allowed to be free, like all sex between consenting adults should.

Where is the middle ground? A friend once told me, "I wish my mother talked to me about boys like she talks to my sister about them. It would be nice to get advice sometimes."

I think of growing gay men and what this means for their desires. How does this shape their interactions with older men and their decisions? If no one teaches our gay youth about safe sex, where do they learn it? More aching still: do they ever learn to be secure in their most vulnerable moments? How much of that learning happens through avoidable situations?

Trying to erase people only harms them; it doesn't cease their existence. Gay men thrive despite opportunities to teach them about anatomical safety being ignored. Luca struggled to open the door to love again. His journey to safe sex was ongoing. He knew only a well, an endless well of desire. One match led to one bathroom fuck, which led to a night at the local bathhouse, which led to a night with Kevin, who always had drugs. Kevin, John, Xavier... they all had drugs. One chat could lead to a pipe, every night. Every night, he opened Grindr, scrolling for hours. He fantasized, he came alone, in his bed. Until he could guarantee one meetup wouldn't lead to the entire wolf's cave of desire, this was the only safe sex he could trust.

The Saturday sun slanted warm and golden through Pan y Paz's windows, catching on a swirl of dust motes and warming Luca's shoulder. The scent of baking bread wrapped around him like an embrace, accompanied by the gentle murmur of conversation and the ring of laughter from the eclectic collection of people scattered around the community room. It was one of those rare afternoons when he felt perfectly at home in his skin, content to observe the ebb and flow of the cafe from his quiet perch.

Across the room, a man stood framed in the doorway, his lean frame shadowed by boxes of fresh herbs from the delivery. He shaded his eyes against the glare, soft curls forming a halo around his face, and offered a shy half-smile to the man beside him. The newcomer leaned against the door jamb with the effortless grace of someone accustomed to charming his way through life. Crisp shirt, sharply cut cheekbones, a thick gold watch flashing at his wrist, he looked expensive and out of place against the scuffed wooden floors.

Raquel caught fragments of their conversation as they maneuvered the boxes through the door. The man introduced himself as Winston, saying he'd been following Luca's zine. Luca's face lit up at that, transforming from guarded to glowing. He tucked an errant curl behind one ear, ducking his head as he invited Winston into his office in the back.

Raquel watched them; she saw their immediate electric energy. The tilt of Winston's head as he stepped closer than strictly necessary to take a box from Luca's hands. The too-broad grin that didn't quite reach his eyes when he coyly asked about past relationships. The way his compliments on the cafe space shifted too quickly into probing questions about Luca's past, skating over boundaries.

Though the late afternoon sun streamed cheerfully through Pan y Paz's windows, Luca sensed an uneasy undercurrent beneath the cafe's drowsy warmth. Luca set down his box on the long oak table that served as a prep station, a shy smile playing at his lips as the man leaned in. "Thanks for inviting me back, I've admired your zine lately, I want to get involved too, it inspires me," the stranger said, his voice smooth as river stones. Luca ducked his head, curls tumbling into his eyes. "You have? I'm glad it resonates."

The man extended a hand, gold watch glinting. "I'm Winston." His grip lingered a beat too long, his thumb brushing Luca's palm.

Raquel shifted as she walked the floor, preparing for service. She caught Winston's eye, and his grin faltered before widening. "Friend of yours?" he asked Luca.

"Raquel. She's part of the Pan y Paz family." Luca's gaze was fond as it drifted her way.

Winston nodded, something calculating in the set of his mouth. "This cafe," he said, glossy oxfords clicking on the wooden floor as he took in the space. "It's very...quaint. Authentic." His appraisal carried an edge that raised the fine hairs on Luca's arms.

Luca straightened, jaw tight. His eyes flicked down to Winston's Italian loafers and the cashmere sweater. He didn't match the usual Pan y Paz crowd, with their paint-splattered jeans and thrift store gems. But he followed Luca's zine, which meant he understood what they stood for...right?

"Thanks," Luca said. "It's not much, but it's ours. The community we've built here is everything."

Winston stepped closer, hand skimming Luca's shoulders, the small of his back. "I'd love to hear more about the man behind the zine." His voice was a conspiratorial murmur, his eyes gleaming obsidian. "Tell me about your journey, how you... came into yourself."

Luca tensed. The shape of that question was too familiar,

curved like a hook, hungry for the soft meat of his past. In his mind, headlines splintered and swirled. Art from anguish. Queer tragedy in the spotlight.

He took a shuddering breath. Met Winston's probing gaze head-on. "I found my peace," he said. "The cafe, the community. They helped me remember who I am, beneath everything else."

Something flickered across Winston's expression, there and gone. His hand on Luca's hip pressed urgently. "Everyone's got a story," he said, gaze dragging over Luca in a way that made him want to shrink and preen in equal measure. "Seems like you've got a real page-turner."

Luca twisted away, busied himself unstacking a crate of basil. "I'm grateful," he said to the bundles of fragrant leaves. "I don't take it for granted."

Silence stretched, thrumming with a sudden energy that crackled in the space between their bodies. Electric, dangerous. An old ache stirred in Luca's blood. Across the room, he felt the weight of Raquel's stare.

Winston took Luca's wrist. His skin was smooth, and his nails were manicured. Luca's head swam with the tang of his cologne, the dizzying nearness of him after so many months of careful solitude. "I gotta say, I came in to see if I could meet THE chef Luca, but I didn't expect you to be so...." Winston said, barely a whisper. His eyes flashed, dark and beseeching. "I want to know you."

The air in the cramped kitchen felt too thick to pull into his lungs. The room tilted, narrowed to the space between their mouths. Winston's fingers grazed the inside of Luca's wrist, skittered up his forearm, raising goosebumps. Those clever hands skimmed over his shoulders, the back of his neck. Dipped beneath the collar of his t-shirt.

It was too much, too fast. Warning bells shrilled distantly, muffled beneath the roar of his quickening pulse. Winston got intimidatingly close.

Luca nearly gave in to an immediate impulse to turn this moment into something else. For a moment, he felt himself being pulled into Winston and sharing a kiss he'd only dreamt about in the last year or so. He felt the kiss sucking the air from his lungs. It was a tangle of tongue and teeth, Winston's fingers shuffling through his hair. Old hunger howled through him, echoing in all the places he'd hollowed out.

Winston's hand slipped beneath the hem of his shirt, calloused fingertips mapping his ribs, his scars. Marking all the secret geographies of Luca's skin. Luca moaned into Winston's mouth, a broken, needful sound. And in a dizzying flash, he was back in Kevin and Xavier's loft, spilled open and panting as appraising eyes dissected his most private agonies—

Except none of that was happening.

Luca blacked out in desire with his eyes open.

"Hey, uh, are you good?". Luca hears Winston say, waking him from his feverish daydream.

Luca wrenched away, stumbling back, creating space between them. His hip barked against the counter, grounding him in the present. He sucked in a ragged breath, reeling.

"Yeah... haha, sorry, I sort of blanked out. Look, I appreciate the love. Was there anything else you wanted to discuss? Dinner service is starting soon."

Winston snarled at him Oh—"

Nausea churned in Luca's gut, hot and acidic. His hands trembled as he touched his chest. He hadn't wanted someone so suddenly and so badly in so long.

His fingers found his sobriety chip, shuffling about the

familiar grooves and edges. It had been well over 256 days since he gave in to this part of his addiction. His pulse pounded, like a panicked bird in the cage of his ribs. He felt shaky, unmoored.

"Hey," Winston said. He reached for Luca again, face etched with concern. "Did I—did I do something wrong?"

Luca jerked back as if scalded. Shame flooded him, chased by a sickening wave of desire. "It was a pleasure meeting you, Winston, but dinner service is starting up and...I think you should go."

Hurt flashed across Winston's features before they smoothed into careful neutrality. "If that's what you want." He straightened his shirt and ran a hand through his artfully rumpled hair. He looked like a god, some feral creature of myth and want. Luca ached.

"I'm sorry," he whispered as Winston turned to leave. What was he apologizing for? Getting too close to him? He didn't know anymore.

Winston paused in the doorway, face in shadow. "I'll see you around, Luca...My number's on your phone." He winked, turned around, and then he was gone, the cafe door chiming brightly in his wake. Luca slumped over the counter, cheek pressed to the cool steel. His reflection warped in the polished surface, dark eyes haunted.

Luca hardly noticed his mind reeling, a gauzy overlay of past and present: random exes' knowing smirks, the sour stink of vodka, skin and sweat, and the coppery bloom of blood under his nails.

He breathed deeply through his nose. Grounded himself in the scents of baking bread, the bright zip of crushed basil. This was what he'd built. His haven, his hope.

He couldn't risk it, not even for the thrill of a Winston's touch igniting nerve endings long gone dormant. He knew too well how quickly passion curdled to poison.

Slowly, carefully, he picked up the shards of shattered ceramic and swept scattered herbs into the trash. His movements were methodical and automatic, wiping away all traces of the past half hour.

But he could still feel the ghost of Winston's mouth, the desperate way their bodies surged together. He pressed a hand to his chest, felt the wild thunder of his heart.

It was like a raw nerve, all the old longing flayed open. The air reeked of spent desire. He swallowed thickly. He'd have to be careful and keep his distance. There were too many landmines in the geography of his past.

Luca straightened and pasted on a smile that felt brittle even to him. He'd have to do better and be stronger than this.

He had a community to protect, a home to guard. He couldn't afford to lose himself again, even for a moment or a few seconds that felt like flying.

Luca touched his lips and took a shuddering breath. He returned to preparing for dinner service.

Luca's skin prickled with remembered heat, the thought of Winston's hands and mouth in the kitchen mere days ago. Now his lover sprawled across Luca's bed like a big cat, radiating lazy satisfaction. This thing between them had moved so fast that Luca felt hurtling down an unknown road, hands grasping for the wheel.

Winston rolled onto his side, tracing idle patterns on Luca's bare chest. "I could get used to this," he purred, nuzzling along the column of Luca's throat. "Waking up with you every morning. Having you all to myself."

Something shifted behind Luca's neck hairs, a nameless

unease. "All to myself". As if Luca were something to be possessed. He brushed it aside. "It's been...intense," Luca murmured, fingers carding through Winston's artfully tousled hair. "A good, intense, mostly," he added at Winston's sharp look.

"Mostly?" Winston propped himself up on an elbow, dark eyes searching.

Luca's eyebrows furrowed. There it was again, that subtle pressure, the implied accusation.

He was spared from answering by a rap at the door. "Yeah?" he called, extricating himself from the sheets. Winston made a low, disgruntled sound.

"It's me," came Gio's voice through the wood. "Sorry to bug you so early, but I wanted to run an idea for a new recipe by you? For the summer menu?"

Luca was already pulling on sweatpants, ignoring Winston's deepening scowl. "Give me one sec."

He slipped into the hall, closing the bedroom door on Winston's sigh.

Gio stood in the narrow hall, a sheaf of notes in his hands and a manic gleam in his eye that Luca knew well. The kid got like this when inspiration struck, a whirling dervish of creative energy, words tripping over themselves in their race to be expressed. Luca loved that about him, that unfettered enthusiasm, the purity of it.

"Okay, wait until you hear this," Gio started, brandishing a pencil-scrawled recipe. "You know how we've been trying to incorporate more of the stuff from the community garden?"

Luca nodded as Gio outlined his vision, a summer salad starring the cafe's homegrown tomatoes and herbs. It was a good idea. As the kid talked, hands sketching shapes in the air, Luca felt some of the morning's tension bleed away. His element was mentoring, collaborating, and giving back to his community.

He was jolted from his reverie by the sound of the bedroom door opening behind him. "Sorry to interrupt this little culinary impromptu," Winston drawled, slinking towards them with a smile that didn't quite reach his eyes. "But I was hoping to steal you back for a bit." His fingers closed around Luca's wrist, a gesture that was both intimate and somehow proprietary.

Gio was startled, taking in Winston's relative undress and the rumpled bed visible through the open doorway. "Oh. Um. Sorry, I can come back later—"

"No, stay," Luca said, a shade too sharply. He softened his tone. "Winston was just...leaving."

He felt the way Winston tensed beside him, and his grip tightened almost imperceptibly. "Right," Winston murmured after a weighted pause. "Wouldn't want to keep you from your essential salad."

The words curled sourly in Luca's gut, even as Gio flushed and stammered. This was the problem, the recurring niggle. By comparison, Winston made everything else feel frivolous, an intrusion on their time together, as if anything that mattered to Luca was only a distraction.

He pasted on a smile, giving Gio's shoulder a reassuring squeeze. "Why don't you head down and get started on a rough draft? I'll be there in a few to go over it with you."

Gio nodded, his eyes still cutting between Luca and Winston like he was trying to solve a particularly challenging recipe. When the kid finally retreated down the hall, recipe notes held to his chest like a shield, Luca sagged against the wall, pinched the bridge of his nose.

"I didn't mean to run the kid off," Winston said, in the carefully modulated tone of one who meant precisely that.

Luca sighed. "He's an important part of what I'm building here. He's...family. I need you to understand that."

"Of course," Winston soothed, crowding into Luca's space. "I just want to be an important part of what you're building, too." His lips skimmed the shell of Luca's ear, hands settling on his hips. "The most important part, maybe."

And just like that, the warmth was back, honeyed and cloying in Luca's veins. He wanted to burrow into it, wrap himself in the addictive heat of Winston's desire. Wanted to stop thinking, stop parsing implications, and feel.

So he did. He let Winston walk him backwards into the bedroom, his mouth latching onto his pulse point. He fell onto rumpled sheets still warm from their bodies, their scent.

Winston was everywhere, the pressure of his fingertips, the wet slide of his tongue. Luca arched into each touch with a desperation that bordered on violence, something ragged clawing beneath his skin. More, more. This gnawing emptiness would finally ease if he took enough and opened himself far enough.

But even as he lost himself in slick heat and urgent friction, some distant part of him remained stubbornly unbothered. Amid feverish grasping, he thought of the cafe and Gio, waiting for guidance. Of the Queer Literature Discussion Group he was meant to lead that evening.

"Stay with me," Winston growled, fingernails biting into the swell of Luca's ass. "Be here."

Luca tried. He shut his eyes, focused on sensation, the sweet sting of teeth against his throat, the stretch and burn as Winston worked him open. But that persistent corner of his brain didn't let go, picking at the loose thread.

Later, after Winston had dozed off and the sweat had cooled on their skin, Luca slipped from the bed. Pulled on pants and a t-shirt, padded into the kitchen to start coffee with unsteady hands.

He was going to be late for the Queer Literature Discussion Group. Guilt and something uncomfortably like shame churned in his stomach.

He stood at the counter, staring out the small window above the sink as the coffee percolated. His reflection was ghostly in the glass, hair askew, love bites blooming along the column of his neck. He looked well-fucked and haunted. As hollow as he felt.

The thought rose unbidden: it's too much. This drowning, consuming thing with Winston…it couldn't be sustained. Not without Luca losing essential parts of himself. All his frantic grasping left him feeling more unbothered than before.

But how did he scale it back without losing it entirely? Without bruising Winston's ego or making him feel like one more side project?

Luca sipped his coffee, hissing as it scalded his tongue. He was going to have to talk to Winston. Talk, not tumble into bed, to avoid the complex parts. Set some boundaries. Make it clear his work here, everything he'd built…it wasn't negotiable.

He hoped he had the strength to see it through. That Winston's greed wouldn't blacken and take root in this tentative thing they'd planted together.

But deep in some wordlessly aching part of himself, Luca already felt the blight setting in. Wondered if he had enough left in him to fight.

* * *

Weeks later, the first thing Luca noticed upon waking was the suitcase. Bold with logos and the shine of expensive leather, it squatted next to the dresser like an uninvited guest. For a disoriented moment, he thought Winston was leaving. Then he registered its haphazard spill of contents, silk shirts puddled on the floor, a watch case gleaming with light. More of Winston's clothes hung in the open closet, crowding out Luca's humble flannels and jeans. He wasn't leaving. He was moving in.

Luca sat up slowly, sheets pooling around his waist. His eyes roamed the small bedroom, taking inventory of the changes—Winston's laptop on the desk, a stack of his marketing briefs there. Beard oil and cola-colored mouthwash lining the bathroom sink. The man himself was conspicuously absent, though the rumpled ghost of him lingered in the sheets.

Something soured in Luca's stomach. It wasn't that he minded sharing space, but…they hadn't discussed this or agreed to cohabitation to twine their lives together in such an irrevocable way.

He was still processing, trying to identify the oily feeling slithering up his spine, when he heard the front door open. A moment later, Winston appeared, a paper bag cradled in one arm and two coffee cups dangling from the opposite hand. His grin was loose and easy.

"Morning, sunshine," he said breezily, setting his offerings on the nightstand. "Scone? They're blackberries, your favorite."

Luca opened his mouth. Closed it. "You moved in," he said. It came out flat.

Winston cocked his head, a bird dog scenting confusion.

116

"Well, yeah. Considering how much time I've been spending here, it just made sense. Figured it would be more convenient for both of us." He was already turning away, shrugging off last night's rumpled shirt. "Now we can have breakfast together every morning. I'll make the coffee, you make the eggs. Very domestic."

Luca watched the light glance off the muscles of Winston's back, gilding them with a deceptive softness. "Don't you think we should have discussed that first?"

Winston paused, hands still on the buttons of a fresh shirt. "What's there to talk about? I want to be with you. You want to be with me. The lease on my place is almost up anyway. I already spoke to Raquel, who said she could always use more rent money. This is the logical next step."

There was a finality in how he said it, as if Luca's reservations had already been considered and dismissed. As if there was some script that Luca hadn't been privy to, choices made that he was expected to accept.

He looked again at the invaded corners of his small sanctuary. His chest felt tight, as if the walls were inching inward.

Winston must have sensed his retreat. He was suddenly back on the bed, nuzzling into the vulnerable crook of Luca's neck. "Hey, it's no big deal. Nothing's changed, not really. We're just cutting out the back and forth, that's all." His palm smoothed down the ladder of Luca's ribs, settling on his hip. "Now, what do you say we christen this new arrangement properly?"

And Luca wanted to push him away and carve out space to think. But Winston's hand was sneaking beneath the elastic of his boxers, and his body had already begun its treacherous purl toward pleasure...

He was nearly late to his standing Tuesday mentoring session with Gio. He arrived at the cafe flushed and flustered, shirt unbuttoned and scarf wound high to hide the evidence of Winston's ardor.

Gio greeted him from behind a fortress of bowls and heaped wet ingredients. "Okay, so, I was thinking lemon meringue today," the boy said without preamble, tapping the spine of a spattered cookbook. "I've got some ideas to amp up the flavor profile. Lavender sugar in the curd, maybe. Or rosemary candied Meyer lemon slices for garnish. But I'm stuck on how to keep the meringue from weeping. Thought you could show me your trick?"

Luca took a breath, willing his racing mind to settle. This, at least, was solid ground. "Absolutely. The key is to make sure not a speck of yolk gets into your whites, and to whip them in a spotlessly clean metal or glass bowl." He shrugged off his coat and rolled up his sleeves. "Plastic bowls can hold onto traces of oil, which prevents the whites from aerating properly."

He stepped up beside Gio and reached for the carton of eggs, grateful for the comforting rhythms of the task. Separating, measuring, and whipping. The luscious lemon curd was bubbling on the stove.

Gio was a quick study, as always. He peppered Luca with questions about the ideal sugar-to-egg-white ratio and the importance of a steady whisking hand. Luca could feel some of the morning's tension bleeding out of him as he explained and demonstrated, buoyed by Gio's eager focus.

They slid the pies into the oven when Luca felt an arm snake around his waist. He startled and nearly dropped the tray.

"Easy there," Winston chuckled, low and intimate against his ear. "Didn't mean to sneak up on you."

Luca extricated himself carefully, acutely aware of Gio's

118

curious gaze. "What are you doing here? I thought you had client meetings all day."

Winston shrugged, leaning a hip against the counter. In his pressed suit jacket and glossy shoes, he looked out of place, an errant sketch from a menswear catalog slipped between Pan y Paz's earthy pages.

" I wrapped up early. Thought I'd swing by and see if you wanted to grab lunch." His gaze slid to Gio, taking in the boy's flour-dusted apron and flushed cheeks. "But I can see you're... occupied."

There was an odd inflection on that last word, a subtle twang of displeasure that raised the fine hairs on Luca's arms. "We're in the middle of a lesson," he said evenly. "You're welcome to hang out in the front until we're finished, if you'd like."

Winston's smile thinned. "No, that's alright. I'd hate to distract you from your very important pie-making." He straightened, adjusting his cuffs. "I'll leave you to it. Gio." He nodded at the boy, a bare chin tilt, before striding out of the kitchen.

Luca watched him go, stomach churning. Beside him, Gio cleared his throat. "Sorry," the boy mumbled, eyes on his shoes. "I didn't mean to monopolize your time or anything."

"No, hey." Luca gripped Gio's shoulder, ducking to meet his gaze. "You have nothing to apologize for. This is our standing appointment. Winston knows that." He gave the boy a gentle squeeze, a bolstering shake. "You're important to me, okay? The work we do together matters. A lot."

Gio's answering smile was fragile but genuine. They returned to their pies, the air between them weighted with things unsaid.

Dinner that night was a strained affair. Winston had insisted on a "family meal" at Luca's place, extending the invitation to

Gio and some of the other core members of the cafe community.

"I just want to get to know the people who are important to you," he'd said, all wide-eyed sincerity.

Now, watching him hold court at the head of Luca's thrift store table, regaling the gathered group with tales of his corporate conquests and nonchalant name-drops, Luca wondered if his motives were at all pure. There was a performative edge to Winston's bonhomie, a glint of calculation behind the megawatt smiles and gregarious toasts.

He seemed to take particular pleasure in needling Gio, peppering the boy with questions about his background and ambitions. "Culinary school, huh?" he mused, swirling Merlot in his glass. "Pricey prospect for someone from your neighborhood. How do you plan to swing that?"

Gio flushed, eyes flicking to Luca. "I'm working on it," he mumbled. "Saving up, looking into scholarships. And Luca's been teaching me a lot."

Winston's brows lifted, a perfect arch of feigned surprise. "Oh, I'm sure. I assumed you'd prefer to pursue a formal education rather than experiment in a community center kitchen. But I'm probably just biased. Some of us put a lot of stock in prestigious degrees and pedigree, as elitist as that may be."

The table went quiet, a thick and muddy silence. Luca could feel the weight of expectant eyes on him, waiting for him to... what? Defend Gio's honor? Put Winston in his place? He remembered similar moments with Xavier, the man's knack for subtle digs and public power plays making others complicit in their intimacy.

"I think," he started, each word an effort, "that there are many paths to success. Just because something is nontraditional doesn't mean it's less than." He met Winston's gaze squarely, his ambitions, hard-fought and still so tenuous, trembling behind his breastbone. "Gio has talent, passion, and the work ethic to match. He'll get where he's going."

Gio looked at him, eyes shining with gratitude. Winston's mouth did something complicated before smoothing into a media-ready smile. "Of course," he demurred. "I didn't mean to imply otherwise. Just playing devil's advocate, you know how I love a healthy debate."

He rose to fetch another bottle of wine, giving Luca's shoulder a proprietary squeeze as he passed. The conversation resumed around them, a chorus of determinedly light chatter.

But for Luca, the evening had calcified into a bitter lump under his tongue. He looked around at the faces of his friends, his chosen family. At the tender roots they'd put down in the fertile soil of Pan y Paz. They'd flourished, not despite their hardships but because of them.

And then he looked at Winston, the man's sharp smile, sharper suit jacket. The hunger in his eyes when he looked at Luca was ravenous and uncomprehending of anything that fell beyond the borders of his want.

I can't do this, Luca thought with sudden, ringing clarity. He pictured a future where this tension was his daily bread, caught between his nurturing instincts and another person's unyielding demands. He chipped away pieces of himself to fit into the gilded birdcage of Winston's affections.

No. He'd fought too complicated for this life, this self. He wouldn't let anyone, not even someone he cared for, undermine that foundation.

The realization settled in his chest, an ember of resolve. He knew what he needed to do. It wouldn't be easy, nor would it be painless. But he'd been through worse fires than this. He knew he could withstand the burning away.

For now, he took a steadying sip of his ginger ale. Reached out to lay a hand over Gio's, giving it a bolstering squeeze. Met Winston's eyes across the table, his gaze level and unflinching.

The future stretched before him, uncertain but shot through with promise. He was ready to take the next step.

Fifteen

FULL HOUSE

"**L**ike this," Luca said, guiding Gio's hands as the boy shaped dough on the floured countertop. "Confident, but gentle. Coaxing, not forcing." It was a tricky balance, too much pressure and you'd overwork the gluten, yielding a tough crust. But timidity would produce an under-baked disappointment, collapsing at first bite.

Gio's brow furrowed in concentration, the tip of his tongue caught between his teeth as he kneaded. Luca was taking in the moment, rejoicing in the peacefulness of mentoring.

The kitchen doors swung open with a bang, startling them both. Winston strode in, all clean lines and cloud-colored cashmere against the room's earthy clutter. "Starting the child labor early today, aren't we?" His voice was light, but Luca knew him well enough by now to hear the serrated edge beneath.

"Gio asked for an extra lesson before his shift," Luca said evenly. "He's hardly a child."

Winston's gaze raked over Gio, a cool nod of appraisal. "No, I suppose not." He stepped closer, fingers trailing across the small of Luca's back, a subtle gesture of possession. "You certainly do dote on him, though. If I didn't know better…" He let the implication twang in the air.

Gio's hands went still at his station. Luca saw the boy's shoulders hunch, bracing. Hot, slick anger pulsed behind his eyes, the first fat drops of a squall.

"Don't." The word was low, adamant. "Don't make this something ugly. Gio is my friend, and I'm his teacher. You don't get to undermine that for childish sport."

Winston scoffed, but there was an eddying pause before he answered. "Come on, baby. You know I'm just teasing, marking my territory a little. No need to be a hard ass about it." He reached out, aiming to be playful.

Luca sidestepped with his hand. "Is there something you needed, or did you just come to lay piss rings around the things you think you own?"

Somewhere beyond the red rush of his anger, he was dimly aware that this was perhaps the most direct he'd ever been with a lover. Blunt force, so unlike his usual tactic of smiles and diplomatic deference. It felt terrifying and freeing.

Winston stared at him for a long, charged moment. "I just wanted to see about lunch plans." Each word was carved from ice. "But I can see you're in the middle of…something." He sneered the last word, face ugly with some unvoiced accusation.

Luca breathed through the boil of his blood. "I'll be finished up here shortly. I'll see you at home later."

Home. The word was ash on his tongue. Winston heard it, though, and some of the coiled tension left him. He nodded once, pleased with this small concession. Assured he had Luca's capitulation, if not his agreement.

When he was gone, Luca sagged against the steel countertop, closed his eyes to will his heartbeat into steadiness. After a long moment, he felt Gio's cautious hand on his shoulder.

"Hey, you okay?" The boy's voice was gentle, threaded through with concern. "I've never seen you two go at it like that before."

Luca mustered a watery smile. "It's nothing you need to worry about, G. Just some stuff he and I need to figure out."

Gio's answering look was skeptical. "He shouldn't talk to you that way. Or make those nasty accusations." His mouth twisted, chin jutting defiantly. "You deserve better."

The words struck Luca square in the chest, a bright, pure ache. He pulled Gio into a swift hug, unmindful of the flour they were both dusted in. "So do you," he murmured fiercely. "Don't ever forget that. Anyone who makes you feel small or ashamed, you cut them loose. No matter how shiny the package."

Gio nodded against his shoulder, a jerky affirmative. They held on for a beat longer, two saplings twined against unseen storms.

The rest of the day passed in a brittle haze. Luca moved through his tasks by rote, his mind churning. He could feel a confrontation brewing on his horizon, dark clouds stacking at the edges of his vision.

When he finally returned to his apartment that evening, he was adamant to find Winston waiting, a glass of amber liquor dangling from his manicured fingers.

"Well, well. He finally deigns to join me." Winston's voice was lacquered with false cheer, an urbane veneer over seething resentment. "You've had quite the busy day tending to your little protege, right?"

Luca set down his bag with deliberate care. He shrugged out of his coat and hung it on the peg by the door, aligning the shoulders just so, these small acts of mindfulness, girding for what was to come.

"We need to talk," he said. No preamble, no softening. A part of him quailed at its baldness, selfish bluntness.

Winston's brows flicked up. "Oh? Are we breaking up with me?" A poor attempt at levity, belied by the white knuckles around his glass.

Luca took a breath. He felt the stretch and ache in his lungs. "I'm not happy, Win. With the way things have been between us lately."

"So I've somehow failed to keep the great Luca Reyes content. What is it this time? Not enough foot rubs and rose petals? Or have I sinned wanting more of your time and attention than you're willing to dole out?"

"It's not about that." Luca fought to keep his voice steady, to collar the whip-snap of his temper. "It's about respect, for me, my work, the commitments I made long before you. You don't get to insert yourself into my life and expect everything to rearrange around you."

"Rearrange—" Winston broke off on a sharp laugh. "God, you egomaniacs are all the same. So focused on your grand purpose, your community service martyr routine. As if folding a little for the person you supposedly love would crumble that house of cards you call an identity." He knocked back the rest of his drink, shuddering from the burn. The glass came down hard on the table, punctuating his next accusation.

* * *

Gio a.k.a. G, was twenty-two, barely sober, and poured drinks with a tremble that made the glasses feel like they were shivering too. Luca's boss was always honest because the kid had eyes that said I know I won't make it, so don't make me try.

He wore his trauma like a second skin. Didn't talk much during training, just nodded, flinched at dropped pans, and disappeared into the walk-in to cry when orders stacked past three.

"Let him fail," Raquel warned. "He'll drown or float."

But Luca knew drowning. He knew what it looked like to beg for air in a world that said, 'Not today.' So he stood near the shallow end. Close enough to catch him if he sank.

The first time G showed up drunk for a shift, he didn't deny it. Didn't try to mask it with gum or Visine. He cried. Apologized. Asked for a second chance, as if it were a cigarette at rock bottom.

Luca didn't fire him. He fed him a bowl of arroz con leche, a cinnamon-heavy and warm treat. Let him sleep between burlap sacks and boxes of dried chisels in the stockroom. Told Winston it was temporary.

"It's not a halfway house," Winston muttered.

"No," Luca said. "It's a restaurant. Built by someone who used to snort coke off prep tables."

Winston didn't laugh.

That night, Luca pulled out the futon mattress he'd stashed behind the service fridge and laid it on the cement. G curled into it like someone who hadn't felt safe since he was twelve. He mumbled something about having a dog once. Named Bean. "She liked to sleep next to my chest. She kept me warm."

"You need a blanket?" Luca asked.

"No. I need to know you won't leave."

Luca paused. "I'll be here in the morning."

It wasn't a promise, just a truth. One morning at a time.

Over the next week, G showed up early, sometimes before Luca. Clean shirt. Teeth brushed. And still, that tremble in his hand like a leftover from war.

He talked more. Not much. But enough to piece together a broken outline: kicked out by conservative parents after a DUI. Slept in a Civic that reeked of old fries and missed chances. Tried rehab once. Lasted nine days. Said he'd rather crawl through gravel naked than go back.

Sobriety, he confessed, felt like being buried alive in your skin.

Luca didn't touch him, not even when G leaned in a little too long after a shared cigarette by the dumpster, where the stars looked like burnt-out lights.

"You want a daddy, not a date," Luca said gently.

G smiled like that hurt more than a slap. He didn't lean in again. But his eyes lingered. Hopeful. Hollow.

Meanwhile, the tension with Winston brewed slowly. Not a fight, not yet, just longer silences. Colder kisses. The absence of skin where there used to be skin.

Winston started staying later at his studio. Said the light was better for editing. Luca didn't ask. He just felt the distance like vinegar on his tongue.

One night, Winston stood in the doorway of Luca's apartment and said, "I don't want to be jealous of a child, Luca."

"Then don't," Luca said. "Be proud of me instead."

Winston looked at him like that was the most unreasonable thing he'd ever heard. "You think it's easy watching you pour the tenderness I waited months for into someone who might not even make it to thirty?"

"He doesn't have anyone."

"Neither did I," Winston said quietly. "But you didn't pull out a mattress for me."

Luca didn't reply. Just returned to the stove where beans simmered, salted to taste but not forgiving.

That night, Winston didn't stay. G didn't speak. And Luca sat on the floor between them, watching the slow ruin of good intentions.

Later, Luca walked into the stockroom to check on G. The boy was half-asleep, a poetry book open on his chest, one of Winston's, left behind months ago. Rilke. The page was dog-eared.

"Didn't know you read," Luca said softly.

"Didn't know you cared," G whispered back.

"I don't."

"Liar."

Luca sat on the edge of the mattress. "You remind me of me. That's not a compliment."

"I know."

"You have a choice," Luca said. "You can burn every bridge you find or learn to build one. Just one."

G rolled onto his side, curled tighter. "I want to build one. I do. I keep setting the wood on fire."

Luca exhaled. "Then we start with concrete. You can't burn that."

In the morning, Winston was gone. But G was still there. Bleary-eyed. Clutching a sticky note on the fridge: Don't lose yourself trying to save him. I love you. But I can't — won't keep doing this.

When he returned, his apron still soaked with saltwater and shame, he held the plates steady. Luca never asked why he had come back out. He understood the weight of silence, knew that sometimes the only reason you kept going was because no one had told you to stop.

G didn't laugh at the staff jokes or join the post-service beers. He lingered near the industrial sink, as if scrubbing long enough might baptize him. Raquel noticed. "Kid scrubs like he's trying to erase the world," she muttered once. Luca just nodded.

On Tuesday, they ran out of cilantro. Carmen, a line cook, barked for a substitute. G froze because someone had yelled, and when people screamed, his body locked like it expected to be hit. He whispered "sorry" twelve times before Luca gently handed him a bunch of parsley. "Here. Different leaf, same love."

On Wednesday, G brought in a box of bruised tomatoes, saying he got them from a vendor who owed him a favor. Luca asked, "What kind of favor?" G shrugged. "The tomato kind." They made salsa roja together, which left their tongues tingling with heat. G smiled, just a little. Luca noted it like a rare bird sighting.

On Thursday, he sliced his hand. Not bad, but the sight of blood made him spiral. He sat on the back step, chain-smoking menthols and rocking like the world had spun too fast. Luca crouched beside him, holding out a gauze pad. "You okay?"

"No."

"Want to talk?"

"No."

"Want to smoke in silence for a while?"

G nodded.

They smoked in silence.

On Friday, a woman entered the restaurant and stared at G for a full minute before turning and leaving. G watched her go, face pale, hands shaking. Later, he told Luca, "That was my mom. She doesn't talk to me since I came out. Said I made her sick. That I smelled like rot."

Luca didn't say, "I'm sorry." He said, "We use rot to make kimchi. And that shit's delicious."

G laughed, a full one, this time. It startled them both.

He started helping with prep at night, volunteering to stay late, chopping onions so fine they looked like snow. Carmen taught him how to fold empanadas with pinched seams. "You got nice hands," she said. "Shaky, but kind."

Luca caught him once in the dry pantry, singing a slow, sad tune. When G saw Luca, he blushed and muttered, "Didn't know I was doing that."

"It was nice."

"I only sing when I'm safe."

"That's rare," Luca said.

"Yeah."

One night, G fell asleep at the counter while shelling peas. Luca threw a blanket over himself. Winston watched from the doorway, arms crossed.

"He's not your kid," Winston said.

"I know."

"Then why does this look like a bedtime story?"

Luca didn't have an answer. He just tightened the blanket around G's shoulders.

The boy was trying and trying, but trying wasn't always enough.

Two weeks later, he relapsed. It started with vodka in a water bottle, followed by a missed shift. Then, showing up at 2 a.m., pounding on the back door, eyes bloodshot, mumbling about being chased by demons made of fire and spit.

Luca let him in, fed him rice and eggs, and sat with him until he stopped shaking. He called in a favor from Matteo to get him a spot in a local support group and told Carmen to give him light duties for a few days.

Winston didn't come home that week.

"Am I the reason he left?" G asked.

"No," Luca lied.

"Do you hate me?"

"No."

"Do you hate yourself?"

"…Sometimes."

"Me too."

The next day, G cleaned the entire kitchen, top to bottom, mopped twice, and organized the spice rack alphabetically. He said it helped him feel in control.

He started writing poems on napkins and left them folded beneath Luca's prep board.

I am not the rot they said I'd be.

I am ginger, salt, and savory love.

I am pickling.

Please don't toss me out before I'm ready.

Luca kept them in a shoe box under the counter. He told no one.

One night, Carmen caught G crying in the walk-in.

"Breakup?" she asked.

"No," he sniffled. "I just…I don't think I deserve this."

"None of us do," she said. "But we take the plate when it's passed to us. You hear me?"

He nodded, wiped his face, and went back to work.

When Winston finally came home, he looked at Luca as if he were a stranger.

"I don't know if you're his chef or savior," Winston said. "But you're not mine anymore."

Luca wanted to argue but didn't. Because maybe it was true.

G wasn't a replacement. He was a reflection. A warped mirror of who Luca used to be. Who he still feared he could become. And yet, he loved the boy. Not romantically. Not even like family. But like someone who understood what it meant to wake up each morning and choose breath over oblivion.

One night, G made dinner: a simple stew. He burned the rice and forgot the salt, but when he served it, his hands didn't shake.

Luca took a bite. "Could use work."

"I'm trying."

"I know."

That evening, Luca went in search of Gio. Raquel stayed behind to run the café. Raquel also grew to care for little Gio; he was now part of the family. When Luca returned, the kitchen felt foreign and familiar: new knives, new stoves, and the same fire.

While Gio was recovering from his latest binge, Luca helped teach at his culinary school. He taught students how to taste intention. "Food without love is just fuel. You want to feed ghosts, you need more than salt."

He cried once, teaching. Midway through a story about the first time he made soup for someone sober. Nobody laughed. They just nodded.

Back home, Raquel had kept things running. The mural now had vines painted along the edges. Someone had left a bouquet of rosemary on the doorstep. "For the chef who feeds us gently."

That evening, at the cafe, Luca found the pantry organized by bold categories she printed freshly from a sticker gun. He smiled at how "Raquel" it all looked.

That night, at home, Raquel asked, "Are you happy?"

Luca thought of the nights he thought he'd never make it. Of the first meeting. The letter to himself. Raquel's lemons. My candles. He thought of soup, laughter, and scars that no longer stung.

"I'm something better," he said. "I'm present."

Raquel kissed his temple. "Aha, who's the lavender wife now?" she said playfully.

Sixteen

SPOONFULS

That week at school, they had a guest chef. He recognized this guy from a cooking show. World-renowned. The chef spent most of his demo criticizing the class.

"You're all too soft," he said. "You want to cook from emotion? Then write a poem. The kitchen isn't a therapy room."

Luca felt his stomach knot.

That night, he stayed late in the school kitchen. Alone. He pulled out ingredients like they were prayer beads. He didn't try to be flashy. He cooked the way he wished someone would speak to him.

He made caldo de pollo, a simple, slow, and traditional dish.

He set a single place at the stainless steel prep table and took a seat.

He ate in silence.

He cried while chewing.

The next day, he submitted a written assignment outlining his culinary philosophy, titled "Cooking as Witness."

I do not cook to impress. I cook to remind. I cook so that memory has a place to sit. I cook so that grief does not starve. I cook to stay.

The instructor wrote: "This is not what I asked for. But it's what I needed to see from you."

A few days later, Kyle from church approached him after the service.

"Hey," they said. "My mom said something awful to me this week. But then I thought about how you and others keep showing up and returning. And it made me feel a little braver."

Luca smiled. Not out of pride. But out of something more profound.

Call it grace. Call it presence. Call it the soup of becoming.

He wrote in his journal that night:

Maybe we're not late bloomers. Perhaps we're just blooming on time, where no one expected flowers to grow.

And he slept profoundly. No nightmares. Just warmth.

Culinary school was chaos. A disciplined chaos that healed parts of Luca he hardly recognized anymore.

He learned the foundations, mise en place, knife cuts, and emulsions. He studied the science of ingredients to understand how the Maillard reaction contributes to the flavor of meat. Salt doesn't just season; it transforms.

Cooking gave Luca something to hold onto. A perfect dish was something he could control in a world where he often couldn't control himself. His recovery journal became a food journal, and his emotions became recipes.

Each month of sobriety became a new dish: a homemade arepa for month three. Sancocho for month six. Month nine?

He served a spicy black bean soup at his church potluck and didn't cry.

At culinary school, he made mistakes. He oversalted a consommé. He burned a duck breast. But he didn't spiral. Instead, he stayed late and tried again.

He met new people, friends who didn't care about his past, instructors who saw potential instead of pathology. One chef, Chef Alina, pulled him aside and said, "You have good instincts. Don't cook like you're proving something. Cook like you're remembering something."

He started doing that, remembering meals with his mom, my favorite toast, and his ex's ridiculous obsession with caramelized onions.

Food became memory. And memory became healing.

By the third month of culinary school, Luca had stopped calling it school and started calling it practice. He had once read that monks practiced prayer, athletes practiced performance, and living also needed to be practiced. Cooking became his new liturgy. Mise en place was meditation. The repetition of dice, chop, stir, and simmer softened him. He let it teach him to breathe again.

It began in silence. Not the oppressive kind that curled around Luca during his darkest nights, but a full-bodied calmness filled him like warm bread. He was standing in the walk-in at Pan y Paz, watching condensation bead across a steel shelf, when he realized he hadn't thought about using it in weeks and hadn't craved. Not planned, and he didn't even flinch in his sleep.

He stepped out into the kitchen and took a deep breath. It smelled of cardamom and roasted beets. Curtis was experimenting with vegetable pâtés and playing an old Bolero tune.

Mariela chopped onions with steady reverence, her silver rings clinking against the cutting board.

Luca felt rooted. He opened his journal and wrote: *The absence of pain is not the same as joy, but it's where joy takes root.*

He began attending step meetings more regularly, but with a new perspective. No longer just for accountability. Now he listened to others like Raquel listened to pots on the verge of boiling; attentively, with both ears and instinct.

One night, a man named Daniel said, "I got clean because I wanted to live. I stayed clean because I learned how to eat again. That's where I met joy."

That night, Luca couldn't sleep. He wrote a recipe called *Joy Stew*:
- 1 hour of silence
- 2 tablespoons of sunlight
- 3 cloves of garlic
- Simmer with chosen family

Raquel found it the next morning taped to the fridge.

"You gonna make this?"

"I already am," Luca said.

* * *

The zine now had a following across state lines. An LGBTQIA+-owned café in Vermont stocked copies, and Raquel was fielding requests for speaking engagements. Luca was invited to a panel on recovery at a culinary conference in Austin. He hesitated. Then said yes.

The flight was early, and the anxiety was even earlier. But Raquel met him at the airport with a sign that read "Chef of

Spoons, Not Daggers."

At the panel, he spoke last. He told a story about his first relapse, the tinny taste of blood after vomiting, and the way lentils brought him back to his body. When he finished, the room was silent.

A chef from New Orleans approached him afterward. "You said something that hit me. About how craving is just hunger with a mask. I think I've been masking for years."

They exchanged contact info. The chef's name was Rue. They started a back-and-forth email chain about recipes, shame, and risotto.

Luca returned from the conference exhausted but expansive. He spent an entire day making tamales with Naomi and Mariela. They laughed more than they spoke.

He went to the church the following Sunday. Dressed in jeans and a cardigan, Raquel was once called "grandpa chic." The pews were hard. The singing was off-key. But when he lit that candle, it flickered steadily.

After, an older woman gave him a crochet square. "In case your hands get cold."

He cried in the parking lot, a joyful, grateful cry.

That night, Luca baked molasses cookies and mailed half to Rue. He tucked in a note: *Chicken Stew pairs well with sweet endings.*

Winter approached, and Luca found himself craving things he didn't use to: slow Sundays, thick socks, clementines peeled in silence. There was a weight to the season that no longer felt threatening but grounding. He moved through the café with new ease, sleeves pushed up, scars exposed like knotted wood. He was not hiding. He was not ashamed.

Pan y Paz thrived on this rhythm. The staff was smaller now, but it was more cohesive. Mariela had become head of pastries. Curtis split his time between the kitchen and an art studio next door. Gio was half-in-charge, half-lost in the moment, and fully content to do inventory.

December brought snow, real and metaphorical. The memory pantry was nominated for a local arts and wellness grant. Luca, ever hesitant with the spotlight, asked Raquel to accept if they won. "It's your legacy too," he insisted. She agreed, but only if he baked her speech into a pie.

The night before Christmas Eve, the kitchen hummed. They were prepping for a "No Family, No Problem" dinner. Raquel invented the name. "For the rest of us," he said, clinking wine glasses with a drag queen named Bailey who volunteered as hostess for the night.

That dinner changed everything. People came in from all over; recently sober, divorced, recently heartbroken. A man named Eli brought gingerbread men iced like his exes. A woman in her sixties shared pickled beets and said, "They're sour, like the holidays." Someone made such delicious mushroom stuffing that Luca is still talking about it.

Luca made turkey mole with cinnamon and dried apricots. "A hug with heat," he told anyone who asked.

Midway through dinner, Raquel tapped a spoon on a glass. "Luca has something to say."

Luca froze. But the room waited, warm and ready.

"I just..." he began, voice cracking. "I'm grateful. Not just for you showing up. But for teaching me that showing up is enough."

Applause. Tears. Laughter.

Later that night, as the last guests filtered out, Luca found a note folded under a dirty plate. It read: *I didn't think I'd make it through today. But I did. Because of this. Thank you.*

Luca kept it in his journal.

January was slower, and he liked it that way. He started sketching portraits of hands and meals again, as well as one of Meow sleeping with his mouth open.

Rue, the chef from New Orleans, came to visit. They co-hosted a pop-up called Feed What's Hungry. The menu was entirely built from reader submissions to the zine. Luca was stunned by the number of people who came. Dozens of faces, once strangers, are now part of his culinary and emotional kin.

One dish, "Grief Rice," from a Chicagoan, became the emotional centerpiece of the evening, a homey dish seasoned with broth, scallions, and the ache of starting over.

When the last plate was cleared, Rue hugged him. "This isn't just recovery. It's revolution."

And maybe it was. Because Luca didn't just feel stable, he felt ignited.

They hosted a perfect pantry dinner that night.

Every guest would receive a copy of the zine's first anthology edition: *The Taste of Staying.*

The night before the dinner, Luca sat alone at Pan y Paz. He lit a candle, not for luck, but for memory. For the Luca who almost didn't make it. For the ones who didn't. For the ones still trying.

He didn't pray. He seasoned the silence with gratitude.

When the wind outside howled, he didn't flinch. He stirred the soup.

And waited for the next beautiful thing to begin.

The night air smelled like burnt sugar and damp pavement. Luca stood in the alley behind Pan y Paz, apron stained, hands smelling garlic and lemon. A quiet had settled into his bones;

the kind that came after feeding people, the sacred hush of satiated hunger.

Isabella wiped down the bar inside while Daniel flirted harmlessly with a pair of tourists. The stereo hummed low, a bolero whispering from the kitchen. The restaurant felt alive, yes, but stable too. That was new.

Luca lit a clove cigarette. He didn't smoke it, just let it burn while staring at the moon. He thought about cravings; not the drug kind, but the soul kind. Connection. Meaning. God, maybe. Or something close.

That week, Luca began writing a new menu. It is not seasonal, but emotional. Each dish is themed around a phase of healing. He called it The Restoration Series.

Appetizers: "First Silence," "Tremble Salad." Mains: "Second Wind," "Soft Spine," "Bone of Hunger." Desserts: "After," "Almost Joy."

The names made Isabella laugh and cry in equal measure.

"You're naming meals like poems," she said.

"They are poems," he answered. "Edible ones."

"You're healing out loud," Alix said, loading crates of chard. "That's brave. And messy. But brave."

They prepped at Pan y Paz for the first night of the new menu. Luca asked Yvette to read a poem before the service. She chose one about roots returning to the dirt to understand the blossom.

The house was packed. Word spread quickly. Food critics called it "radical vulnerability disguised as cuisine." Reservations filled weeks in advance. Luca turned down an interview with Bon Appétit. He didn't want to be famous. He wanted to be understood.

During this time, he returned to his support group, bringing samples from the menu. He let others name what they felt.

"Hope," said one. "Bitterness," said another. "Clean," said a third.

A therapist visiting the group remarked on the powerful therapeutic parallels between culinary creativity and narrative exposure therapy, how each meal allowed Luca and his guests to reframe trauma through flavor.

Later that week, he started a small pilot project called Second Table, inviting people in recovery to prep meals at Pan y Paz one day a month. There was no pressure, just access, community, and trust.

Tyler came. Samira brought her teenage daughter. Jesse returned, now sober for six months.

Darius pulled Luca close after dinner and whispered, "I'm so incredibly proud of you."

But Luca wasn't immune to struggle. There were days when he still woke up shaky and unsure. Nights, he thought about using, not out of want, but of habit. Those nights, he called Nolan, his former caseworker, or scribbled in his fridge diary. He even wrote a letter to Bjorn. Didn't send it. But wrote it. Said everything.

"You stole me. But I'm stealing me back."

The letter ended with, "This is what I look like when I'm not yours."

He tucked it under a bottle of chimichurri in the fridge.

One month later, the restaurant hosted its first sober pride brunch. Rainbow eggs. Zero-proof cocktails. Drag brunch readings. Laughter spilled into the street.

Luca watched it all from the kitchen window with a slight smile.

He slept hard that night. Dreamt of bread rising in time-lapse. Of a strange new face, sharp jaw covered in hair, holding their cat in one arm, stirring soup with the other. Of a future where hunger was met, not just for food, but for gentleness.

The next morning, Luca realized he hungered for something more profound than dinner. He walked to church and sat in the back, as always. When Reverend Tina asked, "Would you consider doing the second reading next Sunday?" he took a step back.

"I, uh, me?" he asked, like someone else had been standing behind him.

She smiled, patient. "You've been here. That's the only qualification."

He nodded, but his stomach turned all week. Every time he picked up the bulletin, his hands remembered the tremble they used to hold back in churches. Not this church. But still. Somewhere in his body, the echo of "You're not welcome here" still pulsed like a low drumbeat.

When Sunday came, he stood at the lectern with his breath shallow and his hands cold. The reading was from Romans. It was about endurance, hope, and suffering producing something holy.

He didn't read it like a preacher. He read it like someone who had felt every word.

And when he sat down, no one clapped. But someone whispered, "Amen."

After that, something shifted.

He began attending vestry meetings. At first, to listen. However, they then asked him to help coordinate logistics for a community dinner.

He brought up composting systems. Someone else suggested sourcing from local farms. Another person said, "Luca, you should lead that effort. You're a chef, right?"

144

He shook his head. "A student. Still learning."

"Well," Reverend Tina said, "we lead from our wounds here. And our kitchens."

Everyone chuckled. But Luca didn't. Not fully. He was still getting used to the idea that leadership didn't require perfection. That authority could come wrapped in softness.

That you could lead without having to wear armor.

The idea for the LGBTQIA+ youth support group came slowly.

First, it was a glance. Luca noticed a teenager sitting alone in the very last pew. Every week, the same hoodie, silence, and quick exit before coffee hour.

Then there was a conversation at the parish picnic. Kyle leaned in while slicing watermelon and whispered, "This church is cool and all, but I wish there were something just for us, the queer kids, I mean."

"Something like what?" Luca asked.

Kyle shrugged. "I dunno. A place to talk. To exist. Not therapy. Not school. Just… not alone."

That night, Luca couldn't sleep.

He remembered being sixteen and sitting in pews like a ghost. Hoping no one would notice. Wishing someone would.

He brought it up at the vestry.

"I was thinking," he said, "what if we hosted a space for LGBTQIA+ youth? Not a conversion seminar. Not a trauma circle. Just a room. With snacks. With adults who've been there."

There was a pause.

Then Miriam, the older blind woman who always hummed through hymns, said, "About damn time."

And it was done. The first meeting was in the parish hall.

Luca made cookies and over-brewed tea. He pushed the tables to the side, laid out blankets, and arranged beanbags. He printed a sign that read, "No one here needs to be fixed."

Five kids came.

Kyle, of course. A bi girl with chipped nail polish and a spiral notebook she never let go of. A gay boy who sat closest to the snacks and didn't talk much. A non-binary teen who cried during introductions but didn't apologize. And the kid from the back pew.

Their name was Sam. They had blue hair and one of those stares that carried every room they'd ever been in.

"I thought I'd just sit in the corner," they said when they arrived.

"You can," Luca said. "But you don't have to."

They didn't smile. But they stayed.

Luca didn't try to be a therapist. He didn't have answers. He didn't quote scripture unless someone asked.

Mostly, he listened.

He told them upfront, "I'm not here to lead. I'm here to hold the room open. For whatever you bring."

They brought poems. And drawings. And questions.

They asked, "Do you believe in God?" and he said, "I don't know yet. Maybe someday, if I'm honest..."

They asked, "Did the church ever make you feel broken?" And he said, "Yes, but not this one."

They asked, "What if we never stop being scared?" he said, "Then we show up scared. And we do it together."

After the third meeting, Sam stayed behind.

They hovered near the snack table, eyes on the leftover Oreos.

"Can I ask something?" they said.

"Always," Luca replied.

"What if I'm too angry to believe in anything?"

Luca paused. Then sat down.

"I think anger is OK," he said.

Sam looked at him, confused. "Why?"

"Because it means you cared," he said. "And it means you still care, even if you don't know how."

They nodded.

Then whispered, "I think I might come back."

"I think I hope you do."

He walked home that night under a sky smeared with stars and streetlight. He didn't feel like a leader. He felt like a candle someone had forgotten they'd lit.

And he thought: maybe this is what church means now.

Not sermons. Not structure.

Just presence. Just a room where people don't have to explain.

Luca sat through coffee hour watching people talk about the weather and casseroles. The air smelled like store-bought cookies and someone's perfume. This gentleness was almost too much. He was used to conversations with sharper teeth.

Tom, the deacon in lavender, introduced him to Miriam, a retired nurse who baked communion bread and told everyone she was "God's carb delivery system." Luca liked her instantly.

He started volunteering, not because he wanted to be holy, but because he didn't want to be alone on Sundays. He set up chairs, arranged flowers, and brewed coffee strong enough to wake grief.

One Sunday, he brought rosemary focaccia instead of cookies. It disappeared in minutes.

"Do that again," Miriam said, mouth full. "This bread is a revelation."

Luca laughed. "Then call me the prophet of olive oil."

They did.

He joined the church's LGBTQIA+ fellowship group, Saints Out Loud. Their meetings were part scripture study, part potluck, part informal therapy. Luca made potato leek soup one week and found himself sobbing between spoonfuls.

He wrote a blog post called "Crying Into Soup: A Liturgical Practice." It went semi-viral.

A gay Episcopalian theologian shared it with the caption: We need more kitchen-based homilies.

Raquel visited during Lent. They attended a foot-washing service together. Luca refused at first, uncomfortable. But when a trans woman in a floral dress knelt and washed his feet with lavender water, he wept. It wasn't just about cleanliness. It was a surrender. Communion. A letting go.

Afterwards, he made lavender shortbread for the entire congregation. Packaged them in wax paper with the label: Blessed Are the Bakers Who Heal Us.

He began dreaming of a side project: Episcopal Eats, a digital cookbook of church suppers and LGBTQIA+ faith cuisine. Raquel agreed to illustrate it. Tom designed the website. The church contributed stories and heirloom recipes.

They hosted a launch dinner in the parish hall. The menu included brisket with quince, lentil shepherd's pie, and communion wafers served with raspberry compote.

Tom gave a toast: "The body of Christ is broken. So are we. But here, we flavor the fragments."

Luca's sobriety anniversary arrived quietly. He spent it kneading dough and writing letters to the versions of himself he didn't become. He burned them in the church courtyard, then made sweet tea for the choir.

During Pentecost, he read a poem from the pulpit. It was

about fire and hunger, about queer rage transmuted into nourishment, and about how the Holy Spirit might speak through a sizzling pan.

A teen in the front row mouthed the words: me too.

Luca knew he would never be a priest. But he was something adjacent. A spiritual sous chef. A reverent roux-maker.

He led a class called "Taste and See," which combined scripture readings with sensory cooking. When they read about manna, they made sourdough. For the loaves and fish, they cooked tilapia and pita. For Holy Saturday, they sat in silence and let the stock simmer.

The bishop visited and wrote in the diocesan newsletter: Pan y Paz is doing the work Jesus talked about: feeding, welcoming, breaking, and rebuilding.

Luca framed that part.

One night, he dreamed of Jesus at Pan y Paz, eating arroz con leche and crying. When he woke up, he added it to the specials board.

"Christ Would've Loved This Pudding," it read.

People ordered it without asking.

Tom died unexpectedly in July of a heart attack. The congregation was gutted. Luca baked for three days straight. At the memorial, he brought a triple-tiered lemon cake. The note said, 'He rose before us.'

The grief turned to ritual. Every Sunday, someone brought something Tom loved. Miriam made tamales. A queer couple brought his favorite tea. Luca brought bread. Always.

He started writing prayers. One was published in a progressive liturgy journal:

God of risings and reductions,
Of burnt edges and salted grace,

149

Thank you for the hunger that brings us here,
And the hands that do not flinch.

On All Saints' Day, the church read the names of the lost. Luca whispered Bjorn's name. Not because he missed him. But because even abusers deserve to be mourned, if only for the damage they caused.

That night, he hosted a vigil in the alley behind Pan y Paz. Candles lined the recycling bins. Raquel read Baldwin and passed out arepas. Luca stood with a spoon over his heart.

They sang. Not hymns. But a melody Raquel made up on the spot. The refrain was: Even ruin remembers love.

Luca remembered it every time he stirred soup.

The rhythm of ritual became another kind of recipe. Luca found himself craving Sunday mornings, not for salvation, but for the quiet procession of intention. The way the priest blessed the bread reminded him of plating; I sang off-key beside him, which reminded him of the dinners they used to cook in their mother's too-small kitchen. Everything worth remembering had a scent, and this one was a blend of cinnamon, lavender, and wax.

He began dreaming in liturgies and leftovers. One night, he dreamed of baptizing a loaf of challah, whispering, "This is my body, raised not broken."

Inspired by the church's community outreach, Luca pitched the idea of a weekly pop-up food clinic that combines nutrition education with low-cost meals for the unhoused LGBTQIA+ population in their neighborhood. Tom loved it. Raquel offered to teach fermentation. Tom offered to be the DJ.

The first pop-up was held in the church basement. The same room where Alcoholics Anonymous and grief groups met, now transformed with tealights and card tables. They called it *The

Loaf and Lantern.*

They served chickpea stew with preserved lemon, beet hummus, and date bars that night. Luca opened the meal with a small blessing: "May what you eat remind you that your story matters."

People cried. People danced. Someone proposed to their partner over a bowl of soup.

From then on, the basement became a sanctuary of spoons and second chances every Tuesday. A rotating crew of volunteers showed up; some from the church, some from rehab, some who just wandered in once and never left.

He met a retired Episcopal bishop, Peter, who crocheted rainbow coasters and told stories about sneaking his boyfriend into seminaries in the '70s. Peter said, "The church finally caught up with me. Took it long enough."

Back at Pan y Paz, Luca incorporated some of the Tuesday recipes into the regular menu. "Hearth Hash" became a bestseller, as did "Liturgical Lentils" and "Grace Gnocchi."

He added a shelf in the café lined with zines on gender-queer studies, consent guides, and spiral-bound cookbooks from mutual aid groups. Above it hung a sign: *Food is Faith. Feed Both.*

One evening, while closing up, Luca found a handwritten note tucked inside a copy of *Radical Hospitality.* It read: *This place saved my life. I'm not ready to say thank you in person yet. But know that I'm clean. And I'm full.*

He framed it.

Luca started taking long walks again, the kind he used to dread. Now, they felt as though they were a part of his wellness routines. He listened to LGBTQIA+-led podcasts about faith and healing. He wrote down recipes dictated by memory: his father's roasted chicken, his mother's flan, and his version of arroz negro with sobbed-in squid ink.

He tried to reconnect with his extended family, sending letters scented with vanilla and humility. Some responded. Some didn't. That was okay.

Raquel's mural expanded to the side of the building, now featuring a table with infinite seats. Luca added a painted banner across the top: *There Is No Last Supper. We Always Eat Again.*

That Easter, the church invited Luca to bake the communion bread. He wept while kneading, whispering every name he'd once prayed for. He added lemon zest and rosemary. Tom called it "the Body of Christ with a twist of joy."

After the service, Luca handed out mini-loaves wrapped in linen. A teenager came out to her parents at the altar. I read a passage from a poem I'd written. Raquel held Luca's hand the entire time.

That night, they made strawberry shortcake for dinner and watched old cooking shows until they fell asleep in a pile of blankets and a purring cat.

When Luca opened his eyes the next morning, the world felt baked, not broken. He got up, tied on his apron, and smiled at the rising dough.

Seventeen

WHAT'S IN A NAME

G abriel had begun to understand that names could carry temperature. "Gabriel," his middle name, felt like warmth, like black beans simmering with garlic and cumin. It curled on his tongue like the first sip of something deeply familiar that remembered him, even on the days he forgot himself.

But names could also be heavy.

One Friday morning, the church bulletin misprinted his name. "Luca will be hosting Sunday's hospitality table." It was a mistake. A small one. The kind that wouldn't register to most. But for Gabriel, it felt like a hand reaching from the past to tap his shoulder and say: You're still him. You can't just paint over that.

He sat with the bulletin in his lap, staring. Part of him wanted to laugh. Part of him wanted to cry. And a quieter, deeper part of him wanted to disappear, just long enough to remember who he was trying to be.

Instead, he walked into the church kitchen. He tied on his apron. He sliced bread. He cut fruit. He brewed the strongest pot of coffee that fellowship hour had ever known. He greeted everyone who walked in the door as if he were greeting a guest in his own home.

Because he was. Because the church, like a well-worn cutting board, was where grace met repetition.

That afternoon, he texted me:

They got my name wrong in the bulletin. But I stayed anyway. That feels like something.

I replied: You've come so far, and I'm over the moon proud of you.

He cherished those words.

By then, culinary school had become more than instruction. It had become a crucible, testing something different every week: technique, timing, and teamwork. But it also tested whether he could stay present in a room that demanded both perfection and humility.

He burned things, wept, remade sauces, apologized, felt, corrected, and kept going.

He began developing recipes instinctively, without measurements, relying solely on memory. Sazón y intuición. Like his mother taught him. Like his tía did before she got too tired to stand for long hours at the stove. He began to teach a few classmates how to fold dough for empanadas. He told stories while they worked. One girl, an introverted baker from upstate New York, said, "You should teach this for real. Like, teach people how to cook their memories."

He smiled. He wrote it down in his journal.

Cooking memories. Teaching tenderness.

That week, Kyle from church asked him to speak at their youth group for just a few minutes, about cooking and why he kept showing up.

He panicked. He practiced in front of his cat. He stuttered in front of the mirror. But on the day of, he walked in with a small pot of soup and an even smaller index card. He said:

"Hi. My name's Gabriel. I cook to remember. I cook because healing isn't linear, but flavor is. I cook because sometimes the world forgets we're here, and food reminds us we're still hungry. That's all."

They clapped.

One kid cried.

Gabriel didn't run.

He stayed.

That night, he wrote this in his journal:

I'm not a prophet. I'm not a saint. But I might be a soft place to land.

And maybe that's enough.

The Episcopal church helped him imagine a version of faith rooted in love rather than shame. It helped him forgive himself for who he became in the wolves' cave.

He learned that Episcopalians don't see doubt as a flaw, but as part of the journey. He read about Bishop Gene Robinson, the first openly gay bishop in the Episcopal Church, and felt a strange pride he didn't know he was capable of. He discovered that the Episcopal Church uses the Revised Common Lectionary, which means every parish reads the same scriptures at the same time across the world. He wasn't just sitting in a pew. He was part of something vast and connected.

He called his sponsor that night.

"Hey."

"Hey," he responded firmly.

"I'm good, I've been terrific actually. Too good?" He says shakily.

"Oh yeah? How are all the plates?"

"Haha, good one, well, I have been saying yes again. I'm scared because I gave in to reality too often the last time. It's like, well, living in the present. At first, it's so hard. It's strange to show up to each moment. Excruciating even. But now, it keeps me centered. Saying yes keeps me here. Yet somehow, I still, sometimes in the deep of the night I feel like a steaming pile of shit. Do you know what I mean?"

"That's the disease, kid," Walt said. "Addiction doesn't leave easily. It just changes costumes. Sometimes it appears to be a fear of missing out. Sometimes, like not feeling good enough. Most days, it sounds like your voice, trying to talk you out of being present."

Gabriel exhaled slowly. "I keep thinking if I just get the restaurant right, or Gio right, or—hell—if I could just fix every broken thing, then maybe I could feel whole again."

Walt chuckled, but it was soft, not cruel. "You remember Step Eleven?"

"You mean the prayer one?"

"Yeah. 'Sought through prayer and meditation to improve our conscious contact with God... praying only for knowledge of His will for us and the power to carry that out.' You know what that means?" Walt leaned into the phone. "It means we stop trying to play God. We stop needing all the answers. We learn to say yes."

"To what?" Gabriel asked.

"To this day. To the mess. To the kid with too much hurt in his hands who shows up anyway. To burning a fucking tomato

156

and starting over. To be afraid and still choose to love."

Gabriel rubbed his eyes. "I'm scared all the time, Walt."

"I know. But you're sober. And you're showing up. Step Ten: daily inventory, making it right, staying aware. That's presence, Gabriel. That's all God asks."

Gabriel stared out the window, where a pigeon pecked at something invisible on the sidewalk. The city didn't stop. But for a second, he felt still. Present.

"What if I mess it all up?"

"You will," Walt said, smiling now. "But you'll also get some of it right. You'll say yes when it counts. And that's enough."

Gabriel nodded, the lump in his throat too big for words. He didn't have to be perfect. He just had to be here.

Maybe Walt was right. Perhaps he is precisely where he's meant to be.

That Sunday, he met Jo for the second time, before he became Jo in his heart.

Later, he met Jo at a park near the waterfront. They lay on a worn quilt and watched kites snag the late summer wind. Jo fed him slices of mango with lime and cayenne.

"You're smiling a lot lately," Jo said.

"How do you know that? You've been watching me, huh?"

Luca bit into a piece and let the juice run down his chin. "I think I finally believe I deserve to."

They kissed without hurry. It was a softness Luca hadn't known before recovery. It felt like the beginning of something edible, something whole.

Eighteen

YES, CHEF

~∞∞~

Gabriel always kept three bags packed: knives, notebooks, and pens.

Every morning began in the dark, the kind of dark you only recognize when your eyes are too tired to adjust. Before sunrise, he walked to the kitchen with keys in one hand and bruised fingertips in the other. The city was still asleep, or pretending to be. The world was damp with the breath of everything unspoken.

He didn't speak either. Just slipped on his apron and began.

Mise en place.

Order in place.

Peace.

He lined up the carrots, peeled the potatoes, and started the daily brine. Each cut was an act of faith: that precision could hold chaos, that repetition could keep him here, present. The quiet hum of the walk-in cooler was a hymn in another language, one his body understood without translation.

At noon, he sat in a folding chair in a church basement that smelled like old vinyl and powdered creamer. Someone read from a booklet. Someone else passed around the basket. The chair creaked beneath him. Everything felt right in its place.

They talked about powerlessness that day. He watched the floor, the patterns of dirt and old coffee stains that told a story older than scripture.

Sometimes the silence between shares was the most honest part.

He folded his hands.

He closed his eyes.

He tried to believe that stillness could save. Evenings were spent at church again, not in pews this time, but in the back rooms. Bulletins to fold. Coffee urns to scrub. A vase to fill with flowers that didn't match, but he tried.

Someone had to make the church look like a beacon of hope.

Someone had to sweep the crumbs of communion.

He never asked why it was always him.

He just stayed. And then it all started to blur. He was still showing up. That wasn't the issue.

It was the weight.

The timing.

The way his name was said twice before he realized someone was speaking to him.

He called it tiredness.

But it wasn't tiredness.

It was deception dressed as devotion.

The lines between spaces faded. One morning, he caught himself slicing zucchini and whispering a Psalm. That afternoon, he wrote grace on a sticky note and stuck it to a tray of demi-glace.

He laughed at himself, then didn't. He missed a meeting and didn't tell anyone.

Slept through a vestry email and deleted it unread.

Burned a sauce and blamed the pan.

When Reverend Tina asked him if he was okay, he said, "Just tired."

She nodded, but didn't smile. "Take a breath," she said. "You don't have to do everything."

But he did.

Didn't he?

Who else would stir the soup, pass the peace, rinse the wine cups, carry the chairs, read the passage, close the meeting, whisper the prayer, say I'm fine when he wasn't?

Who else could?

By Thursday, he was walking differently.

Not limping, not quite, but as if each step required more permission than he had to give.

He dropped a spoon in class and didn't pick it up for six seconds.

Someone joked that he was slowing down.

He laughed, but it caught in his throat.

He forgot the name of the new vestry member.

Forgot to call his sponsor.

Forgot to drink water.

That night, after folding bulletins, he stared at the sink for longer than was reasonable.

It was full of someone else's dishes.

He washed them anyway. And then Sunday came.

The sanctuary was soft with morning light; the pews were half-filled with coats, coughs, and longing.

Gabriel stood at the lectern with the reading in front of him, the bookmark tucked just so, his hands flat like paperweights.

It was Isaiah, something about water in the wilderness.

He knew it. I had read it before and cried once in a bathroom at a restaurant.

But the words blurred.

Not all at once, slowly. As if the page were melting.

His brow furrowed.

Cleared his throat.

Found his place again.

Finished the reading. Sat down. Took deep breaths. Waited for his heart to return to his chest.

No one said anything, which was worse than if they had. After the service, he stayed behind.

He wiped down the fellowship table, stacked chairs, and folded linens with hands that trembled just enough to be embarrassing.

Someone said, "Thanks again for staying."

He nodded.

He picked up a dish towel, damp, soft, still warm from another hand.

And he stood there.

Just stood there.

The towel in his hand.

The buzz of the old refrigerator in the corner.

The sanctuary is empty now.

Only crumbs and bulletins left.

And he whispered, not loud, not dramatic, not for anyone but the tiles beneath him:

"I can't do this much longer."

Not even a cry.

161

Just an exhale.

And the room, kind as ever, said nothing.

The day began like many others at Pan y Paz: quiet, rhythmic, present. Gabriel stood at the prep table slicing heirloom tomatoes, their skins still sun-warm from the queer co-op farm outside the city. Meow, his one-eyed tabby, lounged on the counter beside a basket of sourdough rolls, licking her paw with ecclesiastical grace.

Raquel called just after the first tray of biscuits came out of the oven. "I think I found your next project," she said.

"I already have too many."

"You'll want this one."

She forwarded him a grant for culinary community healing initiatives through a national LGBTQIA+ wellness fund. It was aimed at programs that integrated recovery, queer identity, and food sovereignty. "It's got your name baked into it," Raquel said.

Gabriel read the proposal twice before calling me. "Would the church co-sponsor a queer recovery culinary school? It could just be an addition to the Memory Pantry."

There was silence on the other end. Then: "If it's anything like your focaccia, they will." We both laughed.

Gabriel thought about everything. He thought about how there had to be a balance, yes, until he broke between saying and saying no, until the same happened. He called Raquel.

"I'm going to say no to this one, Raquel, but I just met this guy, Jo. He's dreamy and is super involved in community projects, too."

"Right on, pass me his number, also good for you dude".

"Ha, thanks."

Jo and Raquel drafted a vision: Memory Pantry's: The Table School Thursdays within weeks. A rotating curriculum with guest chefs from the community, trauma-informed cooking therapy, and meals that mirrored the twelve steps. Each module paired a culinary technique with a step. Knife skills aligned with Step One: cutting through denial. Bread baking accompanied Step Two: rising with hope.

Jo wasn't a chef, but he was in the restaurant industry. He had been in the Front of the House most of his career, and he loved it.

They pitched it to St. Thomas's vestry. Tom wept openly. "I'm so proud of what this has become".

The grant came through.

Renovations started on a defunct kitchen hall behind the church. Gabriel supervised every tile. Tom painted the walls with vines and scriptures adapted from local poets. Raquel recruited her herbalist friend to plant a rooftop garden. Jo created playlists titled "Be Ye Tender" and "Marinate."

Classes began with twelve students, each referred through sober networks, shelters, or faith circles. There was Hugo, a former seminary dropout; Jaz, a non-binary drag performer; and Reed, a chef who lost their restaurant to addiction and divorce.

Jo taught the first session. "You will not be graded. You will be fed. And yes, you will probably cry over onions."

The Table School quickly became more than a curriculum. It was a confessional line, a kitchen brigade, a sanctuary. Students shared their griefs like they shared garlic: raw, fragrant, healing when warmed.

They hosted monthly community feasts. The menu? Whatever students created. Dishes were plated with edible flowers and blessings.

A guest speaker from an addiction recovery center visited

for one week. She discussed the neurochemical role of food in regulating dopamine and facilitating recovery from trauma. Gabriel followed her talk with a lemon-thyme tart. "Science and sugar," he winked.

The students built a zine called Hotplate Theology. Raquel managed submissions. Gabriel edited with pride and disbelief at the simple beauties he was experiencing.

They gained local press. Gabriel was invited to speak at a conference on LGBTQIA+ mental health, but he declined. "The food speaks louder than I ever could."

In therapy, Gabriel explored his fear of leadership. "You're afraid of being admired," his therapist said. "Because you know how dangerous charisma can be."

He nodded. "And how quickly love turns to smoke."

Still, he showed up.

One day, a new student arrived late, reeking of vodka and shame. His name was Miles. He refused to wear an apron. "I'm just here to peel," he said.

Gabriel let him. They gave him a mountain of carrots.

Two weeks later, Miles taught the group how to make birria tacos and shared that he was seven days sober.

"I was gonna … you know, I was fantasizing death that night when I read your story in Queer Spoon magazine. Figured I'd try cooking instead."

Gabriel didn't say anything. Just hugged him. Miles cried into his shoulder like an altar boy who'd finally been seen.

That night, Gabriel wrote in his journal: The knife can carve harm or grace. Same tool. Same hands. Just a different choice.

The Table School became a spiritual fermentation vessel. Ideas bubbled and burst. A new group formed within it; Kitchen Apostles Anonymous, an NA-style support circle built around food, vulnerability, and queer kinship. Meetings began with a bite, not a bell. Gabriel always ensured there was something warm on the stove: mushroom barley soup, cornbread, and miso rice.

Each person who shared introduced themselves not only by name, but by a dish that brought them back from the brink. "I'm Devon. And arroz con leche kept me from relapsing last winter."

They met in the church's vestry kitchen. There were folding chairs, string lights, and a sign over the sink: We Do Not Bake Alone.

Gabriel noticed how food softened the stories, how the trauma cracked open more gently when stirred through something sweet or savory. He incorporated more research, drawing from articles on culinary therapy's efficacy in trauma healing and substance abuse treatment. According to a PubMed study, culinary engagement activates reward pathways similar to meditation.

He began to see it clearly: kitchens as temples, cutting boards as confessionals, broth as balm.

Meanwhile, his Sundays at St. Thomas's grew more intimate. He watched older churchgoers tentatively chop onions beside queer youth in crop tops. There was silence. Then stories. Then laughter.

Tom played the piano while Jo read excerpts from poems he was workshopping. Gio embroidered apron pockets with lines from affirming scriptures.

Gabriel crafted menus that mirrored the liturgical calendar. For Lent: a fasting soup made of dandelion greens and regret. For Easter: Sour Cherry Galette with Lemon Basil Chantilly. "Resurrection," he told the guests. "Tastes tart before it's sweet."

One afternoon, Gabriel entered the chapel to find Gio lighting a votive. "I'm not here to pray," Gio said. "Just… remembering."

"For whom?"

"For me."

That night, Gio stayed late to help clean pans. "You think God forgives us?" he asked.

"I think God's been waiting for us at the table this whole time," Gabriel replied.

Recovery no longer felt like an isolated island. It was an archipelago, with each meal, prayer, relapse, and re-commitment a bridge back to himself. Having Gio, Jo, and Raquel fold into his world like butter in a pastry so effortlessly was his north star.

In his journal, Gabriel wrote: Gay God walks in flour footprints and cries at night. Gay God is you and me.

Carmen was already soaked in oil, Raquel was arguing with a supplier on the phone, and Gabriel stood in the doorway, feeling the strange steadiness of a routine.

The café had become an altar. Not a temple of redemption, but of repetition. Whisk. Wipe. Fold. Plate. The sacred rituals of the simply mundane. Gabriel had stopped searching for language to define himself. He preferred verbs such as "cook," "hold," and "notice."

After rehab, the idea of being better felt violent. He didn't want to be better. He wanted to be rooted.

And so, each day, he cooked. Not to fix himself, but to feed himself and others. Not just with food, but with presence.

Gio now worked weekends, showing up early with his one good spatula and a list of songs he swore made bread rise faster. Raquel began inviting elders from the community to "story lunches," where they'd cook ancestral meals and share stories while the yeast rose.

One week, an older trans woman named Miss Gigi made collard greens with smoked tempeh and talked about the Stonewall riots like a recipe. "First, you get fed up. Then, you get your sisters. Then you throw whatever you got."

Jo had a growing interest in the cafe and Gabriel's world. He would come in and order a different dish every day. He would never impose himself on Gabriel. He would go on some days, and Gabriel wouldn't even know. He just wanted to taste the menu. He tried to get to know Gabriel, and so far, it seemed the best way to do that was to learn how he moves in his favorite place. Jo understood the love for the restaurant after all. There was no art like it. The rush, the connection with all things life, the smells, the sensations, the yelling, the pots and pans, the farms, the heat, the salt, the fermentation. The chaos contained all for one purpose: to make life ... tasteful... one table at a time.

Jo loved the restaurant, possibly more than Gabriel. So he had to see it for himself, try the menu, and see his team. That is how we would see if this beautiful man was worth giving his heart to.

Every day, Jo was greeted by a new server: Marsha, Audre, Pedro, and Divine. All dedicated, knowledgeable, and lovely. Gabriel sent a special treat when he noticed Jo was there. He had never been more intrigued or afraid of a man. Jo seemed to understand. He was so different from Win. He didn't demand his time. The opposite, instead, floated near him. Blended in. He wasn't an obstruction but a bouquet in his restaurant's painting.

In the evenings, Gabriel attended his group meetings. He hadn't been sharing lately, but he brought focaccia and sat beside a lesbian poet named Babs who smelled like cardamom and always had at least three theories about lunar capitalism.

"What's the gayest thing you've done this week?" she asked one night.

"Besides this focaccia?"

They laughed. And it was nice.

Gabriel started walking more. On Tuesdays, he would walk to the old local bookstore two miles away. There he'd buy old cookbooks and zines and once, a used copy of Episcopalian Liturgies for the Radical Queer Soul written by a local author.

The inside cover read: For the misfits who stayed. You are not the wound. You are the faith.

That night, he cried for an hour, then baked clove-studded orange bread.

The Table School on Thursdays continued to grow. No rules. Just community, carbs, and a question each week. One day, it was: What did your ancestors eat that you still crave?

The answers were messy, beautiful, and full of tears. They made molasses bread, pozole, rice with pigeon peas, Turkish coffee, and cake from memory.

Gabriel spoke last. "I miss Mami's arroz con huevo frito. It wasn't fancy. But it was the only meal where she sat with us and didn't rush. It felt like quality time together."

The following week, they served arroz con huevos to everyone for free. The sign read, "Comfort feels better when shared."

He stopped going to NA, not out of defiance, but because his recovery now lived in other spaces: in the way he folded napkins, in how he said "no" without explanation, in how he kissed Luis on the forehead after burning the empanadas and didn't apologize.

He still reads recovery articles, mostly about neurodivergence, trauma recovery, and how community kitchens reduce relapse in high-risk populations. He adds annotations to his cookbooks. He keeps showing up for the day. That was his promise, that was his recovery vow. That and always talking to Walt. He told himself, no matter what happened, he would keep Walt around.

That night's journal entry: Add turmeric to the stew. Boosts serotonin and memory. It's also pretty.

One quiet Sunday, a woman came in with her son. He looked like Gabriel with the same curious gaze and messy curls. The mother said, "We're new here. He just got out of treatment."

Gabriel knelt beside the boy, looked him in the eye, and said, "Try the stew. It's got your name in it."

They both smiled earnestly.

Nineteen

JO

⚜

J o returned to church the same way you return to a song you haven't heard in years, slowly, afraid it might not sound the same anymore.

That first morning, he sat two pews behind Gabriel. He wore a slate blue sweater and jeans, his nice jeans that weren't too tight. His silence was reverent but not hesitant. He moved like someone familiar with sacred spaces, someone who knew how to make room for God.

People noticed him, of course, the Moroccan man with honey-warm skin and a posture that held both elegance and grief.

Gabriel watched him in small glances. Jo didn't sing, but he listened to hymns like personal letters. He kept his hands open on his lap during prayers. And when it was time to pass the peace, his "Peace be with you" was always soft. Like he meant it, like peace costs something. Jo's mother died when he was very young, so young that he had to be told she had existed in the first place. Her name was preserved in photographs and family recipes. The women of the neighborhood said she had been sharp-eyed and brilliant. Jo only knew she was gone.

But his father, his father, was the kind of man who made each moment as full as he could for his boy. He was quiet, yes, but joy shone through his voice when he spoke to Jo, as if love was something you conveyed through tone. He was a mechanic. Sang when he worked. Wore a St. Christopher pendant that hung low over grease-stained shirts. I made tea every night without asking if Jo wanted any because, of course, Jo wanted tea.

He had been raised Catholic, attending strict Latin Masses with incense that stung the lungs. But when Jo was born, something shifted. By the time Jo was walking and talking, and by the time Jo started asking questions about dresses, dolls, Jesus, and why the priest always seemed afraid of children, Jo's father understood.

He understood that acceptance wasn't enough.

Children like Jo didn't just need to be tolerated; they needed to be celebrated, protected, and seen.

So he left the Church. Not out of anger, but love.

And when Jo was four, they discovered the small Episcopal congregation on the city's edge, with hand-knit pew cushions and a priest who referred to God as "she."

That church raised them. In his soft shoes and loud opinions. Jo, who asked a thousand questions during Children's Chapel. Jo, who cried during baptisms, even if they didn't know why.

And Jo's father, always a step behind, always smiling, always asking, "Do you feel loved here?"

Years passed. Jo left. Life happened. Cities. Lovers. Languages. Shame, too, for a while. Not because of who he was, but because of who the world refused to become.

But when he came back, when Jo returned, as all wanderers do, it was because of the silence. Because of the memory of soft hands on the shoulder. Because of the taste of bread and wine in a place that had never asked him to pretend.

Gabriel didn't date casually. Not anymore. If he was going to open the door again to romance, it had to come with parameters, with boundaries drawn in permanent marker and reviewed in the mirror every morning. He scribbled them on a notepad that lay by his bed:

No drugs.

No clubs.

No men without careers or direction.

No lying to my sister.

No weird possessive men.

He even texted me when he reinstalled Grindr.

"If I spiral, come tackle me."

I replied, "Only if you promise to live-blog it."

We joked, but we both knew what was at stake. Grindr wasn't just an app. It was a portal, sometimes a connection, sometimes a craving. Sometimes to care, but often to chaos. And Gabriel had finally stitched his skin back together. He couldn't afford another tear.

Still, he was lonely. There was no shame in that. Loneliness is not a failure. It's just a truth. And he wanted, deeply, to be seen, to be held. He was emotionally drained from tasting the same dry cocktail: being passed around, the flickering bar lights topped off later beneath sheets with a stranger. He wanted real eye contact. Real laughter. Real safety.

He set the app's settings to strict filters, no profiles without a bio. No one is without a job. No ass only pics. No torsos only.

You didn't get access to him if you didn't show your face.

He matched with a few people. Polite chats. Two coffees. One dinner. Three nameless hookups. Each time he tried, he found himself scanning for red flags, listening for addiction in the silences, and watching for manipulation in the compliments.

And worse, whenever someone flirted, his skin buzzed in the same place where past cravings lived. Not for a drink. Not for drugs. But for oblivion. For that quick, all-consuming validation that didn't ask you to stay afterward.

He wanted closeness, but it scared him. Real closeness is something that needs to be seen, not just desired.

And that's where the spiral began.

A string of sleepless nights. A week without journaling. Two meetings skipped. Three days in a row, he woke up and didn't open the blinds.

His meals became cereal and toast. His prayers became silent. His breath became shallow.

He didn't use. He didn't drink. But he hovered so close to the edge that even his dreams started whispering again.

Just a sip.

Just one night.

To remember what it feels like to feel nothing.

Then, one Saturday, he found himself staring at a message. A guy, handsome, sweet, even, had a career, respected his rules, and said all the right things.

But something about the way he said, "Let's keep this light," made something old and angry crack open inside Gabriel.

He stood in his kitchen and said out loud: "No."

Then he cried for ten minutes.

Then he got dressed.

Then he walked to a meeting.

He didn't speak at first. He just listened. The listening that happens when you need the words of others more than your breath.

A woman named Carla shared about how she relapsed because she believed loneliness was worse than shame. Gabriel's throat tightened.

A man in his seventies discussed deleting the apps again. Someone else cried about how hard it was to feel lovable and broken.

When Gabriel finally spoke, his voice cracked:

"I thought I could date and stay detached. I thought I had rules. But I forgot that loneliness doesn't follow rules. And desire doesn't come with disclaimers. And I don't want to be perfect. I want to stay."

After the meeting, someone gave him a hug that lasted too long. But it didn't scare him. It felt like scaffolding.

The next morning, he went to church.

The sermon was on Jacob wrestling the angel.

Reverend Tina said, "Sometimes the fight is the blessing. Sometimes the limp proves that you stayed long enough to be changed."

Gabriel took communion with wet eyes.

He stood near the coffee table afterward, holding a Styrofoam cup like it was the last warm thing in the world. That's when someone tapped his shoulder.

He had close-cropped hair. Dark eyes like wet stone. A calmness that radiated like early light.

"Hey," he said. "I liked your reading last week."

Gabriel smiled nervously. "Oh. Thank you."

"I'm Jo," he said. His voice was warm and measured, with an accent that carried the gentle rhythm of Casablanca.

174

He nodded. "Gabriel."

They smiled. And for once, Gabriel didn't scan him for danger. He noticed Jo's presence was steadying, like a candle that didn't flicker.

That night, he wrote:

I almost didn't make it. But I did. Today, I met someone whose name feels like a chapter I haven't read yet.

Their first real date wasn't planned. Not really. After church, Jo lingered near the stairs where people shuffled out with coats and quiet chatter. Still high on the comfort of hymns and sugar from the lemon bars, Gabriel found himself drifting that way without thinking.

"Do you want to walk?" Jo asked.

Gabriel hesitated for a second, then nodded.

They walked. That was it. They didn't even say where. They just wandered through the old streets near the church, past brick buildings with chipped paint, under bare trees whose shadows made poetry on the pavement.

Jo talked about how he liked the cold. "It sharpens you," he said. "Like winter edits the world down to its bones."

Gabriel liked that. He liked the sound of Jo's voice. Low, patient. He liked how Jo didn't fill every silence, how he didn't rush to impress.

They stopped at a bench across from a closed bakery.

"I almost didn't come to church today," Gabriel confessed.

Jo smiled. "Me neither. Which is why I did."

They didn't talk about the past. Not yet. Just books. Food. How music changes when you're sober. How neither of them knew how to whistle.

When they hugged goodbye, Jo's coat smelled like bergamot and cloves. Gabriel stood still after he left, holding the air like it might explain something.

Their second date was less of a date and more of a dinner that happened because Gabriel couldn't stop thinking about the way Jo said turmeric with a slight trill.

"I'm making lentil stew," Gabriel texted. "Come over if you're hungry."

Jo showed up with fresh bread and a small container of za'atar. "For the top," he said. "Always finish what you begin."

The stew simmered while they talked. Jo told him about growing up in a Moroccan household where food and faith were braided together, where his Auntie taught him to marinate olives with lemon and garlic while reciting ayat from the Qur'an.

"I wasn't always sure how to be all of me," Jo said. "Queer. Arab. Devout. It didn't always line up."

"And now?"

"Now I just follow the thread of what feels like home. And sometimes that's bread."

Gabriel liked that answer.

When Jo left that night, he kissed Gabriel on the cheek. Soft. No pressure. Just presence.

Gabriel closed the door and stood with his back against it, breath caught between fear and reverence.

That night, his journal entry was one line:

I want to devour him, but I will gladly enjoy his tapas of affection.

Gabriel didn't tell anyone about Jo right away.

Not because he was hiding anything. Not this time. But because the thing between them felt delicate, like layering the mascarpone in the tiramisu. You don't poke it. You wait. You watch. You let it become.

Still, the weight of the new stirred old fears.

He found himself dreaming again, not of using but of losing. Dreams where Jo disappeared mid-sentence, where intimacy became a trapdoor, where he suddenly and completely reverted to a version of himself that no longer fit.

He brought it up at therapy.

"My body's remembering things," he said.

The therapist nodded, slow as always. "That's what bodies do. Especially when they're starting to feel safe again."

"It's exhausting," he admitted. "To be this close to something good and not know how to hold it."

"You're not failing," she said. "You're waking up."

He told his sponsor, too. Over coffee, after a long walk.

"I'm scared that if he touches me, I'll disintegrate. Or worse, I won't flinch and instead become consumed by him."

His sponsor stirred his drink. "You don't owe anyone your body. But you do owe yourself your honesty."

That night, Jo came over again. They didn't cook. They ordered pizza and watched a documentary about desert rain frogs. Jo rested his hand near Gabriel's on the couch, not touching, just close enough that if Gabriel wanted to bridge the gap, he could.

He didn't. Not yet. But he didn't move away either.

Later, when Jo went to the bathroom, Gabriel walked into the kitchen and whispered to himself:

"It's okay, everything's okay."

When Jo returned, he sat down and picked up where he left off in their conversation. No pressure. No questions. Just presence.

Gabriel exhaled.

Jo invited him to an interfaith dinner hosted at a Unitarian church nearby the following week. There were candles on every table, lentil soup, warm bread, and readings from different traditions. Jo read an Arabic poem about patience. Gabriel didn't understand every word, but the cadence made something in him weep.

When they walked home afterward, Jo offered his hand.

Gabriel took it.

It was a simple gesture. But it felt perfect.

That night, they didn't kiss. They just sat. On the floor. Eating leftover cookies and talking about the idea of mercy.

"I used to think God was only watching when I messed up," Gabriel said.

Jo smiled. "Maybe that's when God watches closest. Like a parent in a pool, standing right there, waiting to catch you."

The room got quiet.

Gabriel rested his head on Jo's shoulder.

He felt the beat of Jo's breath and thought, This is what being here makes possible.

In his journal, he wrote:

I didn't flinch. I didn't run. I stayed.

Their third real date was more intentional. Gabriel invited Jo over with a plan, music, candles, and one of the few dishes he felt brave enough to serve with pride: arroz con pollo, which he made the way his grandmother taught him, minus the shortcuts and microwave cheats.

Jo brought figs and a small, hand-written poem folded into a square. He tucked it into Gabriel's notebook and said, "For later."

Dinner was good. Good. Not because it was perfect, but because they ate slowly, laughed deeply, and didn't try to be anything but what they were.

Afterward, they sat on the floor again, legs stretched in opposite directions, surrounded by crumbs, empty bowls, and the peace of being present together.

Gabriel exhaled.

"I've never dated someone like you," he said.

Jo tilted his head. "Why?"

"Because you don't make me feel I need to perform."

"That's good, right?"

"It's terrifying."

Jo nodded. He didn't press. He didn't soothe. He just let the words hang in the air like incense.

Eventually, Jo kissed him.

It wasn't a fire. It wasn't hunger. It was gentler, like light spilling through blinds, like a memory being rewritten in real time. And when Gabriel pulled back, he didn't feel the usual tremor of panic.

He felt the warm flush of having made it through a gate he once thought was locked.

Later, when Jo had left, Gabriel opened his notebook.

The poem was short. A single stanza:

To walk beside someone and not behind or in front,

This is love without a map.

He placed the paper under his pillow. The next few weeks unfolded like a slow season. There were no major climaxes or dramatic reversals. There were just morning texts, shared meals, and long walks that blurred the line between prayer and partnership.

Gabriel told his mother. She smiled and touched his hand. "Is he kind?"

"Yes."

"Then I'm happy."

He told me too. I listened without question, letting his voice run like water. I heard the slight fear in his pauses, the way he checked himself before saying "relationship". But I also listened to the wonder.

Jo cooked a lamb tagine one night, fragrant with apricots and saffron. It was beautiful, and it made Gabriel cry.

Jo reached across the table. "Tell me what's happening."

Gabriel wiped his face and laughed. "This is the first time someone's made something this good for me and expected nothing in return."

Jo said, "That's how I was raised. If I feed you, it means I see you."

They didn't sleep together that night either. They held each other. They listened to a playlist Jo had made called "Maybe You and Me." It was mostly instrumental music, including one Nina Simone track that Gabriel played thrice.

The next morning, he woke up alone but not empty. He stood by the window, coffee in hand, and whispered to himself:

"This doesn't have to end in fire."

In his journal that day, he wrote:

My body is starting to believe what my spirit already knows. I can be held without being hurt. I can be loved without losing myself.

He had never written anything like that before.

Spring leaned into summer, and with it came softness. Not easy, life was still jagged around the edges, but softness, like a favorite song heard again in an unexpected place.

Jo and Gabriel developed a rhythm: texts at 8 a.m., walks after class, and dinner at either of their apartments weekly. It wasn't official. They hadn't labeled anything, but the air around them started to feel cleaner, filtered, pure.

One afternoon, Jo invited Gabriel to meet his cousin Amal, who was visiting from D.C. They met at a bookstore café and spent two hours discussing gender-queer studies, fermented foods, and Nina Simone. Amal was sharp, playful, and intensely protective.

The last clatter of dishes fades, swallowed by the kitchen's settling hush. Gabriel leans against the counter, shoulders curled inward, one hand absently twirling a wooden spoon in an empty metal mixing bowl. The hollow scrape and whisk are loud in the quiet, but he barely hears them over the static of his thoughts. Late afternoon sun slants through the high windows, painting everything in bold light and stretched shadow, a chiaroscuro reflecting his tangled emotions. He releases a slow breath, glancing up at Jo through his lashes. The words sit heavy on his tongue, fragile as spun sugar.

Jo meets his gaze, and his dark eyes are warm and patient. He knows that look on Gabriel's face has traced its lines in the blue light of sleepless nights, has kissed its furrows smooth in gentle morning light. He waits and lets the silence stretch like resting dough.

Gabriel sets the bowl down with a soft clink. "I want to tell you about Winston." His voice is low, tentative, the name bitter-sharp in his mouth.

Jo nods, shifting his weight to settle more fully against the counter. His arm brushes Gabriel's, grounding and steady. "I'm listening, love."

Gabriel swallows hard. His fingers twitch, aching for something to hold onto. He thinks of Winston's hands, how they could grip so tightly that they bruised. "I just got out of that, and it was way too much and all wrong." The words spill out, a rushing confession. "And worst of all, he didn't understand how Gio showed up like a sudden burst of light, pulling me out of places I thought I'd never escape."

The memory rises, vivid and visceral. Winston's snarl, the wall hard against Gabriel's back. Breath hot and sour with liquor. "You're nothing without me, you know that? Just a fucked up little junkie playing at chef." Gabriel blinks and shakes his head like he can physically dislodge the images.

"I thought… I thought I deserved it, for a long time. That I wasn't worth more than how he made me feel." Gabriel's throat is tight, the words scraped thin. "Like everything I touched was tainted."

Jo makes a soft sound, an empathetic sigh. His hand finds Gabriel's, lacing their fingers together in wordless support.

Gabriel squeezes back, takes a shuddering breath. "But then Gio came along and he… he saw me. Saw me." A wavering smile flickers across his face, there and gone. "From that first day in the kitchen, it was like he looked at me and saw something worth believing in."

The memory shifts and warms. Gio's eyes are bright with determination over a sputtering stovetop. Their first genuine smile was tentative and real, something easing in Gabriel's chest, like a knot slowly loosening.

"He never gave up on me, even when I gave him every reason to." Gabriel's eyes are distant, lost in remembering. "He pushed me, challenged me. Made me want to be better. For him, for myself." He laughs a little, wet and wondering. "He was a pain in my ass, and the best thing that ever happened to me."

Jo smiles, soft and knowing. He lifts their joined hands and presses a kiss to Gabriel's knuckles. "That's amazing, love. I'm so glad Gio is part of your story, and I can't wait to get to know him more."

Gabriel blinks hard, overcome. He tugs Jo closer and rests their foreheads together. He breathes him in, the scent of lemon and rosemary, and home. "Thank you," he whispers. "For listening. For being here."

"Always," Jo murmurs back. His free hand comes up, brushing a strand of hair behind Gabriel's ear with infinite gentleness. "I'm so proud of you, Gabriel. Of how far you've come."

Gabriel shudders, lets the words wash over him. Feels them start to take root, delicate but determined. He thinks of Gio, of Jo. Of Pan y Paz, a dream made real. Of how much he has to lose now, and how much more this moment means because of it.

The kitchen in Gabriel's home sighs around them, holding the quieting pulse of their hearts, the mixing bowl gleams, empty and waiting. Gabriel straightens and meets Jo's gaze. Feels the pieces of himself slowly knitting back together, stronger in the broken places.

"Come on," he says, a smile playing at the corners of his mouth. "Let's finish cleaning up. It's going to be a big day tomorrow."

Jo grins, squeezing his hand. "Lead the way, chef."

Together, they turn to the work ahead. The sun catches on the tile, tinting it gold. In the space between shadow and light, Gabriel lets himself believe that this kitchen, this love, this life, might be his to keep.

Twenty

JOY

Joy, it turns out, is not a final destination. It's a fragile room with windows that rattle when the wind kicks up. And Gabriel, new to joy, still learning its contours, found himself tiptoeing across the floorboards of this room like someone afraid they might accidentally break it.

It wasn't sadness that came next. There was doubt.

He'd be brushing his teeth, stirring lentils, or walking home from Jo's and suddenly thinking, Do I deserve this? Not in a melodramatic, self-pitying way. But in that bone-deep, post-trauma sort of whisper: Is this safe? Am I allowed to be happy for this long without consequence?

He began rereading his old journals.

The earlier ones were jagged, full of longing and apology. Pages soaked in ink and confessions, check-boxes and relapse markers. He read entries from the first week of rehab. He winced at his handwriting. He didn't recognize the voice. Or maybe he did, and that's what made him ache.

But then, in a faded Moleskine journal from year two of sobriety, he found a note scribbled next to a half-eaten list of grocery items:

Someday, I will feed people not because I owe them, but because I overflow.

He read it ten times. That one line cracked something open again. And in the quiet of his kitchen, surrounded by candle stubs and soft music, he said aloud:

"I am allowed to overflow."

He talked to his sponsor. They met at their usual spot: a dusty diner with good hash-browns and terrible coffee.

"I feel like joy is asking too much of me," Gabriel said.

His sponsor stirred sugar into the coffee without looking up. "Or maybe joy is asking you to stay."

Gabriel nodded. "I don't trust it."

"You don't have to trust it yet," his sponsor said. "Just don't run from it."

He told his mother over the phone one night.

"I'm scared I'll mess it all up," he whispered.

Her voice, steady and worn with love, came through the line like prayer.

"Gabriel, you have always been worthy, even when you forgot. Even when you were breaking, your worth never went away."

He called me too. I, of course, didn't tell him what he wanted to hear, but told him what was true.

"You don't have to be ready," I said. "You just have to be honest. And you are. That's why you're still here."

Gabriel sat with that.

He journaled:

Joy scares me. But I'm still showing up to it. Showing up is my superpower.

Gabriel's days felt braided now, a rhythm of work, calm, Jo, and moments that shimmered like flares in a darkened field. He wasn't searching anymore. He was staying. Anchoring. Even the word "healing" felt foreign, like a sweater someone else had left on his chair. What he had now was different. It was living.

Raquel had started organizing "Midnight Breakfasts" at the cafe once a month. No advertising, no RSVP, just a chalkboard sign at the front: Come hungry. Leave fed.

People showed up in pajamas, in tuxedos, in drag, in silence. Jo lit candles. Curtis played vinyls from his "Queer Slow Jams" collection. Orlando recited poetry between bites of warm peach cobbler.

They served herbal teas instead of coffee and oat porridge featuring rose petals. They also served pancakes made with buckwheat and topped with date molasses. Everything was soft, not just in texture but in intention.

Jo explained it once: "It's not about food. It's about softness. The kind the world doesn't give us often."

Gabriel watched them, his community, his people, eating, laughing, and sometimes crying. One night, a couple proposed in front of the kitchen counter. Next, someone read an anonymous letter about surviving conversion therapy. Nobody clapped. They just nodded, passed a napkin, and shared more cobbler.

He realized that night: community and family are all about this.

They hosted a series called "Queer Roots." Each event celebrated food from a different diaspora. Jo's masterpiece was the Caribbean night. He served tamarind-glazed eggplant, coconut rice with scotch bonnet relish, and mango lime pudding. They paired each dish with a memory.

"My dad once told me salt is a time traveler," Jo shared. "I didn't understand until I cooked this rice."

Gabriel started attending yoga with Raquel. He laughed at first, "Me? Yoga?" but found moving his body without judgment comforting. The teacher, a gentle Black gay elder named Marcus, said at the first class: "Let's be honest. Most of us learned to contort for survival. This is about something else."

At home, Gabriel took longer showers, not out of necessity. But he liked the feel of water on his back. The pulse. The reminder. He started writing postcards to people he had never sent them to. "Thank you for teaching me about sorrow." "I found a way through." "You were wrong. I'm still here."

Jo bought them new sheets of linen and navy. Gabriel gasped when he touched them. "What is this?"

"Peace," Jo said. "Imported."

They hosted dinner with Calla's cousins from New York. Raquel taught them how to make her version of matzo ball soup infused with lemongrass. Curtis played dominoes with someone's grandma and lost. Jo served flan. Orlando did a dramatic reading of a Yelp review.

Between the soup and the laughter, Gabriel caught his reflection in the oven door and smiled confidently.

* * *

The joy spilling into Pan y Paz wasn't planned. It began with people, tired people, bruised from the world, hungry for a feeling. It started in Gabriel's apartment, over jam-streaked toast and Jo's third-hand wine glasses. Gio was chopping parsley as if it were penance. Raquel is dropping off donated books and staying for dessert.

The four of them didn't sit down and plan a movement. They didn't stop saying yes.

Yes to one more folding chair. Yes to skipping the booze and serving crispy chickpeas with za'atar instead. Yes to replacing the dim, anonymous fog of bathhouses with something warm-blooded and bright: open seating, games played in the back, well-kept novels traded over tapas. Pan y Paz didn't declare itself a cultural center; it just became one.

Raquel curated the shelves as if she were an art collector. Fiction with queer brown joy. Cookbooks that read like memoirs. Zines tucked into bathroom nooks beside safe-sex kits and tiny plants someone kept remembering to water. Gabriel cooked as if every meal was a statement; he was eloquent with each dish. Jo brought the charm, the playlists, and the volunteers. Gio swept up, learned fast, and grew under their eyes like something miraculous.

On Thursday nights, people gathered not to escape the world but to be rebuilt by it. They ate slowly, spoke loudly, and took up a lot of space. Elders sat with teens. Artists taught knife skills. Bears and drag queens debated the spiciness of their food. No one was right. Everyone was home.

The idea was simple: eat, love, make money, and be exactly who you are. Johnny loved every minute of it. His little cafe was now his cash cow, and his cafe becoming the "most inclusive cafe in town" was a bonus he was proud of. "He gave Gabriel the keys to the place, you're running this place better than I could have imagined, keep doing you," He told him one night.

They weren't reinventing the wheel. They were seasoning it.

People left thank-you notes in the folds of napkins. They donated their time, tomatoes, and heirloom recipes passed down like family traditions. They fed each other, read to each other, and lived in bright colors between bites.

And each time someone walked through the door, uncertain and hopeful, they were reminded: this wasn't about business.

It was about belonging.

Jo bought a second cat. Named them Paprika.

Meow hated her. Raquel said it was "feminist inter-species tension."

One night, Gabriel and Jo created a simple menu to clean out the walk-in. They served roasted fennel with blood orange glaze, lavender polenta, cardamom panna cotta, and a main course called Salt on Toast, which turned out to be black garlic focaccia with pickled peaches and goat cheese.

They discussed their favorite snacks from childhood, haircuts, unusual smells, and why some people like cilantro while others don't.

When everyone left, Gabriel looked around the mess of plates, crumbs, and empty wine bottles and whispered, "This is it, huh?"

Jo leaned into him. "Yeah. It is."

That week, the café received an anonymous donation. A note was attached: For whatever you feed next.

Gabriel didn't ask where it came from. He knew.

He folded the note into the other, still tucked into his apron.

Twenty-One

TRES

The restaurant was loud. It was always audible. Knives on boards, burners roaring, the constant hiss of steam and spit of oil. And beneath all of that, voices. Orders. Instructions. The music of a kitchen trying not to fall apart.

Gabriel had been a chef for nearly three years now. Quiet, dependable, deliberate. He didn't show off. He didn't cut corners. He prayed with reverence. When he was on the grill, the flames bowed to him. When he was on salad, the vinaigrette sang. But he stayed low-key. Humble. He didn't seek praise.

Until he saw the flyer taped above the prep sink.

"Now Hiring: Front of the House Managers (Internal applicants encouraged)."

His heart jumped.

He tore it down.

He brought it home. Smoothed it out on the counter. Stared at it for a week.

Then, one night after dinner, he talked to Jo.

"Are you still looking to get back into management?"

"Yes…"

"We are hiring a Front-of-the-house manager."

"You're kidding…"

"I'm not?" Gabriel chuckled nervously.

"It sounds perfect, love… You wouldn't hate seeing me even more than you do now?"

"Do I see you a lot? Hmm, hadn't noticed," Gabriel smirked.

"Stop!!, When do I start?" Jo exclaimed in between laughs.

They both kissed in a mix of hope and fulfillment.

In the late-morning lull before the prep list starts breathing fire, Gio stands by the dry goods shelf, a kitchen towel twisted between his hands like he's worried it might betray him. The stainless steel counters at Pan y Paz gleam with the menace only a well-run line can offer.

Gabriel nods toward him from the walk-in, already three tasks deep and humming the opening bars of a song no one else knows. He's not the kind of chef who yells. That's the myth. He's the kind who notices when someone's wearing the same shirt three days in a row and leaves a clean one on their hook without a word.

Jo sweeps past carrying an empty bread crate and a half smile. He's running front today but still checks on the flour bin, hand soap, and music volume. The man has the eyes of a hawk and the timing of a stage manager on opening night. He shoots a look at Gio. Not a command, just an invitation to keep up.

Lunch service begins as a trickle. Gio starts plating garnishes, chopping citrus, and chasing chives around the cutting board. Jo brings menus to the two-top near the window and refills a water pitcher, as if it were a performance with an intermission and an encore. Gabriel tastes a chickpea stew, nods to himself, adjusts the salt, and doesn't speak. His approval is in the way his brow unfurls.

By noon, the kitchen starts to breathe heavier. Orders come in short bursts: three sandwiches, two bowls, six drinks, a modification that makes Gabriel mutter under his breath and reach for the smoked paprika. Jo glides through the dining room like he's rearranging air. Gio, sleeves rolled and hair damp with effort, begins to move with rhythm, if not grace.

Gabriel barks out a "behind" just as Gio turns, and their shoulders almost collide. Jo watches this from the pass and smirks. Later, he'll tease them both about their tragic pas de deux.

By two, the lunch rush has crested and collapsed. Gabriel pulls a loaf of focaccia from the oven like it owes him money. Gio leans against the counter, a smear of aioli across one forearm. Jo slides him a soda with a lime wedge balanced on the rim, a silent reward. They don't say much. That's the rhythm, too.

Cleanup is automatic: dish racks, bleach spray, someone wrestling the mop bucket as if it were alive. Jo handles a refund for a guest who wanted less flavor and more Instagram appeal. Gabriel snorts. Gio mouths "Philistines" and scrubs harder.

The afternoon brings deliveries, inventory, and an espresso each. Jo folds linen napkins with methodical flair. Gio trims herbs, and Gabriel checks invoices. A box of lemons goes missing and turns up by the broom closet. Someone blames the ghost. Jo blames Gio. Gabriel blames himself. Then they all shrug.

They eat together in bursts. Shared bites, bread ends dipped in leftover sauces, stolen radishes. Gio watches Jo laugh at something Gabriel says and looks away too fast. Gabriel hands him a pickle without explanation. Jo pours more water. It's not a moment. But it's not a moment.

Dinner creeps in slower, like it knows it's the main act. Staff arrive. The music changes. The air thickens with garlic and intent.

Gio works sauté tonight, which means real fire and real consequences. Gabriel checks his prep twice and says nothing. Jo gives him a wink from the host stand. The orders begin. Gio misses one cue but recovers fast. The rhythm catches him. The pans hiss. His hands remember. Jo calls back a compliment from the floor. Gabriel hums again.

By the time they plate the last dessert, Gio is wrecked in the best way. He leans on the counter, grinning like an idiot. Gabriel hands him a piece of burnt caramel. Jo clinks his glass to Gio's soda. No speeches. Just small things done well. Over and over.

Later, the three of them stand in the alley, backs to the door, steam rising from their shirts. Jo lights a cigarette and doesn't offer. Gabriel stretches his back—Gio's arms dangle, loose and tired.

"I didn't burn anything," Gio says.

"You nearly flambéed your eyebrows," Jo corrects.

Gabriel nods. That's praise.

Jo glances sideways. "You'll get faster. But don't lose the focus."

Gio shrugs. "Trying."

Gabriel elbows him. "You're doing."

The streetlight hums. Trash bags line the curb. None of it matters.

Inside, the kitchen will cool, and the prep will begin again.

But now, Gio is part of something he doesn't have to name. Not safe. Not sacred. Just real. Just theirs.

He's found his place. He earned it, minute by minute, onion by onion.

Gabriel will keep teaching. Jo will keep watching. Gio will keep showing up.

That's the thing about restaurants. You don't build them once. You build them every day.

Together.

On Jo's second day, Gio stifles a yawn against the back of his wrist, blinking gritty eyes as he reaches for another sprig of rosemary. Jo sits facing him, methodically plucking leaves from a thyme stem and laying them in one of the waiting ramekins. The earthy scent of the herbs rises between them, cut through with the bright zing of lemon peel.

They work in comfortable silence, the rasp of finger pads against stems and the occasional clink of glass the only accompaniment. It's become a ritual, this early morning communion, a moment of quiet stolen for themselves before the day's demands descend.

From the doorway to the kitchen, Gabriel watches them, shoulder propped against the jamb. Two mugs of coffee steam gently in his hands, the rich aroma mingling with the perfume of the herbs. He savors the tableau before him, the effortless synchronicity of Jo and Gio's movements, the way the lamplight gilds the planes and angles of their sleep-soft faces.

Gio pauses, a tremor running through the fingers cradling his current sprig. It's woody and pliable, the leaves a blue-tinged green. Gio stares at it, something painful and distant settling behind his eyes. The scent fills his head, conjuring sense-memory…

Astringent, medicinal. Grayish tile, a hard bench, a tree in a cement planter outside the window. Rosemary, stubbornly thriving in its metal cage. The rasp of a wool blanket, the sear of smoke and shame in the back of his throat.

Gio swallows thickly, a muscle jumping in his jaw. Jo looks up, gaze sharpening as he takes in the sudden tension in Gio's shoulders, the way his fingers have gone white-knuckled around the stem. Silently, Jo reaches out, resting his hand over Gio's.

"Tell me what you remember," he says, so gently it aches.

Gio shakes his head, lips pressing into a bloodless line. But he doesn't pull away from Jo's touch.

Jo shifts closer, his knee bumping Gio's. "Breathe with me," he murmurs. "In through your nose, out through your mouth. Nice and slow."

He demonstrates, exaggerating the rise and fall of his chest. Gio drags in an unsteady breath, trying to match him. Holds it until his lungs burn, then lets it shudder out. Again, and again, until the roaring in his ears begins to fade, replaced by the soft, rhythmic whisper of their synchronized breathing.

Gabriel takes this as his cue, padding on silent feet to lower himself to the floor beside them. He sets a mug down at Jo's elbow, then extends the other to Gio, waiting patiently until he uncurls a hand to accept it.

"It's good to remember," he says, holding Gio's gaze. "Even the hard things. Maybe especially those."

Gio's throat works as he swallows, fingers tightening around the warm ceramic. Slowly, haltingly, he begins to speak.

"It was my first morning waking up sober," he says, eyes fixed on the steam curling from his mug. "Sober, not just… not drunk yet. In this clinic. There was this bush outside my window…"

He goes on, painting the scene in jagged bits and pieces. Jo and Gabriel listen, sipping their coffee, offering only their silent support. When Gio's words finally trickle to a stop, Gabriel lets the quiet breathe for a long moment before humming softly.

"My first day at culinary school," he offers, "I woke up so nervous I couldn't even drink my coffee. My Mom sat with me, made me breathe with her like this. She used to grow herbs in old coffee cans on the balcony…"

As he speaks, Jo reaches out, finding Gio's hand again and tangling their fingers together. Gio lets him, clinging to the connection like an anchor line.

"I still say my morning prayers at sunrise," Jo says. "Facing east, greeting the new day. It reminds me that each morning is a blessing, a chance to begin again."

They trade stories like this, stitching together a patchwork of memory and ritual. The hazy light outside the windows gradually turns to gold as they speak, filling the dining room with dawn's pale, expectant glow.

When their mugs are empty and the ramekins filled, Jo sits back on his heels, surveying their work satisfactorily. He lifts his mug on impulse, clinking it gently against Gio's.

"To new beginnings," he says.

Gio looks up, meeting his eyes. A slow, hesitant smile tugs at the corners of his mouth, softening the sharp edges of his face into something young and unguarded.

Gabriel leans in, adding his mug to the toast with a muted clink. "To new beginnings," he echoes, "and to mornings spent together."

Gio's smile widens and brightens. He raises his mug, tapping it against the others'. Their arms form a triangle, a circle of connection. In their faces, Gabriel sees past, present, and future entwined, their disparate paths converging in this single, crystalline moment.

Gio's startled, rusty laugh rings through the hush like a bell. Jo and Gabriel can't help but join him, the sound rising in a bright crescendo.

It floats up through the ceiling vents, past the rafters and roof tiles, dissipating into the pale morning. In its wake, the restaurant feels subtly transformed, not just a place of work, but a shared space, a home.

Wreathed in the steam of coffee and rosemary's green, growing scent, Gabriel, Jo, and Gio sit together and greet the new day.

* * *

"You've never glowed like this before," Jo said the next day, watching Gabriel prep vegetables at the kitchen island.

"What do you mean?" Gabriel asked, feigning surprise. "I'm a moth baby!"

Jo laughed and kissed the top of his head. "Whatever it is, keep going."

And so he did.

Gabriel started designing a tasting menu rooted in memories. A "story menu," he called it. Five courses:

The House I Grew Up In: Sopa de plátano, smoky and warm, with a swirl of crema de ajo.

The Closet I Escaped From: Charred eggplant with pomegranate glaze and coriander.

The Night I Didn't Die: Beet tartare with citrus zest, served cold.

The Lover Who Stayed: Lamb in spiced honey with rose and cardamom.

The God I Finally Trusted: A single fig poached in wine, soft cheese, and a whisper of mint.

He tested every dish three times and tasted each with Jo. He would send Mom and me recipe index cards, stained with soy sauce and spices. He'd call us in the morning to ensure we understood the recipes, and then at night for our feedback.

"Alright, girl, tell me what's up … what is missing?"

I always kept my cool, trying not to scare him away with my excitement and pride in his love and purpose with food.

When he finally served the owner, he was calm.

They didn't speak for a while after eating.

Then the owner leaned forward and said, "This should be on the menu. No edits."

Gabriel nodded. "Thank you."

He didn't cry this time. He just closed his notebook and walked back into the kitchen, apron on, heart steady.

Later, in his journal:

Love is a palette.

As summer peaked, the restaurant was busier than ever. Lines out the door. Press interest. A feature in a local magazine titled "The Sous Chef Who Cooks in Metaphor."

But Gabriel stayed grounded. His rituals held him.

Morning journal. Prayer candles. Three deep breaths before every service. Meetings on Thursdays. Holding Jo's hand at dinners and checking in on Gio.

He didn't try to be invincible. He didn't chase perfection. He just kept choosing the current feeling. His feelings were clearer these days, and his understanding of them grew stronger daily.

One day, his mother came to visit in person. The first time she'd stepped into one of his kitchens.

She wore a simple blue dress and held a rosary in her hand like armor. When he walked out to greet her, she pulled him into a long hug and whispered, "M'hijo… look what you built."

He gave her a tour. Showed her the spices. Introduced her to the team. Let her taste everything.

When she tried the lamb, she started to cry.

"This tastes like… like your happiness, Hijo," she said.

"I think it is," he replied.

They sat on the back steps and drank coffee in silence. And in that silence, everything unspoken was heard.

Later that night, he wrote:

I feel a blooming inside of me. Blooming into the version of myself I had always been too scared to believe in.

The story menu stayed on the board for two months, and every night it was ordered, Gabriel stood at the pass and watched the plates return empty. Something about that visual: a dish returned clean, scraped down to memory, and felt like a full circle.

Jo came in on Wednesdays, never in uniform, always with a pen or pencil tucked behind his ear. He didn't hover. He didn't check tickets or count silverware. He liked the air when it smelled like sautéed shallots and rising dough, like Gabriel's brow furrowed while composing a plate like a short story with a surprise ending.

Gabriel had just tasted a new marinade, eyes narrowed at the balance of heat and smoke. "It's a collaboration," he replied, "whether we admit it or not."

The truth was, they operated like a couple of artisans building something from the inside out. Jo understood the room's tempo and how to adjust the lights by ten percent depending on the weather outside. Gabriel understood that anchovy butter would bring the kale to life, but only if it was chilled. Neither one chased perfection. They chased the thing just behind it, the moment a guest closed their eyes after the first bite.

Their affection lived in logistics. In the way Jo would refill Gabriel's water glass before he asked. In the way Gabriel would tweak the set list for Jo's favorite shift songs. They never over-explained. They rarely argued. When they did, it was about practical things like table placement, dish rotation, and whether the flour should be stored above or below the sugar.

Gio was their shared delight. He came in daily, nervous and fast-talking, all elbows and ambition. Gabriel watched his knife work like a coach tracking a rookie. Jo made him memorize the seating chart and threw him into a lunch shift to test recall under pressure. When Gio forgot a table number, Jo made him draw the whole room from memory. When Gio burned the shallots, Gabriel made him eat them. "Know the error," he said. "Then you won't repeat it."

They didn't coddle. But they didn't withhold either. Every genuine success Gio earned was met with one of Gabriel's nods, that small, dense gesture packed with meaning, or a clap from Jo, usually accompanied by a running joke about unionizing the garnish station.

By month two, Gio started showing up early to polish the silverware, not because he had to, but because Jo mentioned once that it helped the light bounce.

Dinners turned into small masterclasses. Gabriel would test a sauce and slide a spoon toward Gio without instruction. Jo would whisper critiques like secrets, like gossip—"That vinaigrette's got commitment issues." They let Gio help rework the pickled daikon recipe. They made him run the expo. They made him taste the olives with closed eyes and name every flavor he could.

"He's going to be better than both of us," Jo said one night.

Without looking up from his prep, Gabriel replied, "I truly hope so."

Gabriel loved the spreadsheets more than he admitted. The ordering systems, the seasonality grids. He kept the menu chalkboard tidy and his inbox color-coded. The restaurant owner adored Gabriel. He wore linen year-round and used the word "conceptual" too often, which suited him just fine. Praise was useful when it came with more autonomy. Johnny was barely around lately. The cafe was in perfect hands, as far as he was concerned.

Jo loved the rush. He loved Table Eleven's questions and the woman at Table Four, who always asked for her fork to be warmed. He loved the logistics of bodies in motion, the elegance of timing a reservation to land between two regulars without causing overlap. He handled complaints like a therapist with a wine key.

At home, Jo kept sticky notes of compliments from guests. At the restaurant, Gabriel kept a notebook of tasting notes and failures that tasted like progress.

They rarely talked about the relationship. But you could see it in the easy choreography between them. The way Jo would catch Gabriel's eye during a rough service and tilt his head toward the back, and Gabriel would take a minute to breathe. Gabriel always ensured there was a staff meal Jo would like, even if Jo claimed he was skipping carbs.

Gio noticed everything. He wasn't nosy. He just paid attention. The way Jo's shoulders relaxed when Gabriel made him laugh. The way Gabriel looked toward the host stand every time the front door jingled. It wasn't sappy. It wasn't even overt. But it was built, service by service.

When Gabriel got a call from the owner praising the new menu layout, he didn't tell Jo for three days. Jo already knew. He saw it in how Gabriel stood that night, prouder, straighter, like he'd finally caught up to himself.

Gio spilled coffee and swore in three languages. Jo called him a poet of profanity. Gabriel said nothing but handed him a clean towel.

Later, as service slowed and the playlist softened, the three sat on milk crates behind the kitchen. Gabriel offered them a spoonful of mole, which was so rich it made Gio tear up.

"You okay?" Jo asked, nudging him with his knee.

Gio nodded, then said, "Yeah, it's the spice."

They all busted out in laughter.

The rhythm continued. Tuesdays were inventory. Thursdays were testing sauces. Saturdays were when Jo let Gio practice table turns under pressure. Sundays were brunch, which none liked, but they endured with strong coffee and synchronized eye rolls.

They built something stable and consistent. Guests came back. Staff didn't quit. The food got better. The front ran smoother.

Jo never said he loved Gabriel at work. He didn't need to. It was how he walked in early when he wasn't scheduled in, folded Gabriel's apron, and left it by the locker room when it slipped off the hook.

Gio loved them both. Differently. Fiercely. He loved how Jo made him feel seen, how Gabriel made him want to be better.

One night, Gabriel forgot to bring up a staff meal. Jo noticed.

Gio cooked it instead. Fried rice with too much garlic, the way Jo liked it. Gabriel took a bite and nodded.

Jo looked at Gio like he'd just watched him land a triple axle. "Not bad, kid."

Gio just shrugged, flushed with pride.

The restaurant continued, with more guests, prep, new menus, hard days, and easy laughs. There were no days off, just different kinds of work.

They weren't perfect. They weren't trying to be. They were running a place where things tasted like effort and affection, where the lines between work and care blurred just enough to make it feel worth it.

They didn't chase magic.

They built something better.

They kept showing up.

The Saturday morning sun brushes buttery light over the Mission's facades, highlighting details in the tile and the chipped enamel of street signs. On the corner of 24th, a sidewalk vendor unfurls her wares, glinting rows of CDs, the spines of secondhand books, pyramids of glossy loquats, and blood oranges. The air is a mélange of diesel, sizzling carnitas, sharp-sweet citrus, and the distant brine of the bay.

A silver hatchback idles at the curb, windows cracked to catch the breeze. Behind the wheel, Jo drums his fingers against the worn ridge of the steering wheel, an errant curl escaping his knit cap to tickle his brow. Gio slouches in the passenger seat, fiddling with the radio dial. From the back, Gabriel leans forward, one arm slung over the headrest, the other brandishing a sheaf of printouts.

"If we take Folsom, we can hit that place on Shotwell first," he muses, tracing a fingertip over the penciled stars marching down the paper's margins.

"Folsom's a parking nightmare this time of day," Jo says, glancing at Gabriel in the rear-view mirror.

Gabriel waves this off. "So we'll park a couple of blocks away and walk. The exercise will do you good."

He punctuates this with a poke to Jo's shoulder, grinning when Jo swats at him without heat.

Gio snorts, propping an elbow against the windowsill. "Yeah, Jo, maybe it'll put some hair on your chest."

Jo gasps in mock affront, pushing his pom-pom into Gio's face until he sputters and bats it away. Gabriel laughs, leaning back again and kicking the back of Gio's seat in solidarity.

They set off amid good-natured ribbing, the car merging into traffic with an obliging honk. Through the windshield, the city scrolls by in a sun-soaked panorama of bodegas and murals, early dog walkers, and teenagers on skateboards. Brick, stucco, and Victorians draped in bougainvillea, a palimpsest of old and new.

The first apartment building hunches on a corner lot, shouldering against its neighbors as if bracing for a fight. Three stories of pitted stucco and ironwork balconies, with a FOR RENT sign drooping in one grime-streaked window.

"That's it?" Gio asks, dubious.

Gabriel shuffles his papers, squinting at the address. "It looked…better in the photos."

Jo hums, already angling the car toward the curb. "Don't judge a book, Gio. That's rule number one of apartment hunting."

They pile out onto the sidewalk, Gabriel fishing a set of keys from the padded envelope in his hand. Gio hangs back as Gabriel fits a key into the tarnished lock, exchanging a dubious glance with Jo. The door swings inward with a groan of hinges, revealing a dim foyer with a checkerboard tile floor, an elderly elevator cage huddled in the rear.

Bypassing the elevator, Gio takes the stairs two at a time, the thump of his sneakers echoing in the close stairwell. He's the first to reach the apartment door, labeled 3B in peeling gilt numbers. Ducking beneath the skeptical jut of Gio's chin, Gabriel wrestles the second key into the lock, shouldering the door open.

Inside, the apartment is a narrow railroad of rooms, all scuffed hardwood and high ceilings webbed with crown molding. Gio paces the length of the front room, sneakers rasping against the bare floor. He tests the window sash, frowning at the street noise filtering in.

Gabriel pulls open cabinets in the adjacent kitchen, noting counter space and outlets. The appliances are dingy white, with missing dials and burners crusted with unidentifiable substances.

Jo drifts in from the bedroom, measuring tape clenched between his teeth. He extracts it to announce, "The closet is approximately the size of a coffin. A small, narrow coffin."

"But the ceilings, Jo!" Gabriel enthuses, tipping his head back to encompass the lofty planes. "Think of the light we could get in here."

"Think of how much it'll cost to heat," Gio counters, poking his head in from the living room. He frowns at the ancient radiator hunched in the corner like a gargoyle.

Jo hums, propping a shoulder against the wall. "A little paint, some throw rugs...plants in the windows..."

He paints the picture, his hands sketching vague shapes in the air. Gio chews his lip, trying to see it. But all he can focus on is the patch of ceiling where the plaster is crumbling and the faint scurrying behind the walls that might be mice or worse.

"I don't know," he says, rubbing the back of his neck. "It feels…cold."

Gabriel glances up from his notes, taking in Gio's hunched shoulders, the tight pinch of his face. He catches Jo's eye, something unspoken passing between them.

"You're right," Gabriel agrees easily, flipping his pad closed. "Let's see the next one, yeah?"

The next apartment is marginally better, a boxy two-bedroom with thin carpet and a galley kitchen. Gio itches to throw open a window, to draw a proper breath without the stale undertone of old cigarette smoke. Jo makes a disapproving noise in the single bathroom, eyeing the chipped porcelain on the sink.

"It's too far from the restaurant," he points out, pacing to the window to squint at the unfamiliar street signs. "We'd spend half our lives stuck in traffic."

Gio huffs, toeing at a suspicious stain on the carpet. "And there's no room for Gabriel's books."

His eyebrows raised, Gabriel looks up from where he's measuring the narrow linen closet. "I can pare down my collection."

"You shouldn't have to," Gio says staunchly. "A man needs his books."

Gabriel's face softens, a slow smile spreading across his face. He tucks his measuring tape away, coming to clap Gio on the shoulder.

"I appreciate that, Gio. Truly. But we may need to compromise to stay in the city."

Gio opens his mouth to argue, but Jo cuts in smoothly. "Why don't we look at the last place before discussing concessions? It's still early."

They troop back down to the car, Gabriel trailing behind to snap a few last photos of the building's exterior. Gio kicks at a pebble, sending it skittering into the gutter. His earlier excitement is ebbing, frustration rising to take its place. What's the point if they can't find somewhere that feels right? Somewhere that feels like…

"Home," Jo says, like he's reading Gio's mind. He leans his elbows on the car's roof, fixing Gio with a steady look over the gleaming silver. "That's the goal here. Not just a place to sleep, but a home. For all of us."

Gio ducks his head, stuffing his hands into his pockets. "Yeah, well. Doesn't seem like the city is overflowing with those."

Jo's hand lands on his shoulder, warm and solid through the thin fabric of Gio's hoodie. "Have a little faith," he says, eyes crinkling at the corners. "The right place is out there. We'll find it."

Gio allows himself to be folded back into the car, Gabriel sliding in beside him with a rustle of paperwork and a sympathetic elbow nudge against ribs. Jo steers them deftly through the thickening traffic, humming to the radio under his breath.

They almost miss the last building, tucked away on a drowsy side street lined with ginkgo trees and three-flats with window boxes spilling over with geraniums. Gabriel has to circle the block twice before Jo spots the FOR RENT sign, nearly obscured by the fanning leaves of a banana plant in a large ceramic pot.

Gio is out of the car before it's fully stopped, drawn by some impulse he doesn't fully understand. The building looks like something out of a storybook, all climbing ivy and beveled glass. He leaps up the steps to the front door, running reverent fingers over the carved mahogany panel before stepping back. Jo joins him on the stoop, key ring jangling in his hand.

The foyer is tiled in honey-colored hexagons, with the walls lined by wainscoting rubbed smooth with age. Gio hops from foot to foot as Jo fits the key to a door marked 2A, breath catching in his throat.

The door swings open, and Gio steps over the threshold into a sun-washed living room with polished pine floors and three tall windows overlooking a small green yard. To the left, an arched doorway leads to a kitchen with checkerboard tile and a farmhouse sink, a pot rack already installed over the vintage stove. Gio runs his hand along the bull-nose counter, trying to picture it scattered with mixing bowls and chopping boards, bunches of herbs in glass jars by the sink.

He barely registers Gabriel moving through the space behind him, an indistinct murmur of conversation with Jo. He's too caught up in how the light slants across the floorboards, the faint smell of lemon wood polish, and something green and growing.

He steps to the window, hip propped against the sill, taking in the slightly overgrown yard. A small brick patio, dappled with shade from a drooping oak, is just big enough for a café table and chairs. He imagines sitting out there with his morning coffee, bare toes buried in the soft grass, Gabriel on one side and Jo on the other, shoulders brushing, laughing, and conversation tangling together in the golden morning air.

He's startled out of his reverie by a sudden impact between his shoulder blades. He turns to see a small rubber ball bouncing across the floor, Jo standing in the doorway with a sheepish grin.

"Sorry," he says, holding up his hands. "I found it in the hall closet, couldn't resist."

Gio stoops to snag the ball, eyebrow cocked. "Oh, it's on, old man."

He slings the ball back, catching Jo square in the chest. Jo clutches at his shirt in exaggerated shock, staggering back a step. "Who are you calling old?"

And then they're off, the ball flying between them as they dart and dodge around the empty room. Gabriel appears in the kitchen doorway, lips pressed against a smile as he watches them ricochet off the walls, narrowly missing light fixtures and window panes.

Gio scoops the ball off the floor, whipping it at Jo's knees. Jo intercepts it neatly, spinning to lob it back. Their laughter mingles and multiplies, echoing off the high ceilings.

As quickly as it began, the game winds down, the ball rolling to a stop at Gabriel's feet. He bends to retrieve it, turning it thoughtfully in his long fingers. Gio and Jo stand panting and grinning at each other from opposite sides of the room, faces flushed and hair askew.

"So," Gabriel says, amusement threading through his voice. "I take it you like this one, Gio?"

Gio's grin softens and morphs into something calmer but no less bright. He looks from Jo to Gabriel, taking in the twin looks of hope and expectation on their faces.

"Yeah," he says, rocking back on his heels. "Yeah, I do."

The ride back to the restaurant is filled with excited chatter, the three of them talking over each other in their eagerness to dissect each property. Gabriel passes around his phone, showing off the photos he snapped when the others were distracted. Jo has a yellow legal pad balanced on his knees, columns of pros and cons marching down the page in his slanting scrawl.

They pause at a taqueria to pick up a late lunch, the car filled with the savory scent of pork and cilantro as they idle at a red light. Gio reaches into the greasy paper sack, extracting a foil-wrapped tamale and passing it to Gabriel before fishing out two more.

"I think we can make the Shotwell place work," Gabriel says around a mouthful of masa and mole. "It's got good bones, and the location is ideal."

Jo makes a considering noise, licking a spot of salsa verde off his thumb. "The bathroom needs work, though. And I don't love being on the ground floor in that neighborhood."

"I still think the last place is the winner," Gio puts in, crumpling his wrapper and tossing it back into the bag. "It felt right, you know? Like somewhere we could make our own."

Gabriel and Jo exchanged glances, something warm and proud passing between them. Jo squeezes Gio's knee, leaving a smear of guacamole on the denim.

"You're not wrong," he says, a smile spreading slowly and sweetly. "It did feel pretty special."

"We've got a lot to think about," Gabriel says, swallowing his last bite. "Deposit, utilities, renter's insurance. Not to mention furnishing the place."

He says it gently, but Gio's heart still stutters nervously behind his ribs. This is real, he realizes with a start. They're doing this, building a life together, a family. It's exhilarating and terrifying in equal measure.

As if sensing his sudden tangle of emotions, Jo twists awkwardly in his seat, fixing Gio with a steady look. "Hey. We've got this, remember? One step at a time."

Gio draws a shaky breath and nods jerkily. In the rear-view mirror, he sees Gabriel smiling at him, eyes crinkled and fond.

"Together," Gabriel agrees, reaching to clasp Gio's shoulder. "No matter what."

And as they sit parked on the sun-warmed asphalt, an empty lot where an apartment building recently burned, Gio finds he believes them wholly and completely, down to the marrow of his bones.

This is their beginning, messy and uncertain as it might be. But with Gabriel and Jo by his side, he knows they'll find their way.

The future is as bright and limitless as the cloudless blue sky. Gio leans back in his seat, letting the moment wash over him. The fear is still there, an itch beneath his skin. But it's tempered now by a blooming sense of hope, of possibility.

Of home, waiting just over the horizon.

Twenty-Two

MAPS

❧

Gabriel shared more of his past with Jo, including the time he spent in the rehab center during the winter. About the overdose, he hadn't meant to survive. About the drawings he used to make in Gabriel's room, and the ones he burned. About the prayer book he'd kept all these years, even when he didn't believe a word inside it.

Jo listened. Asked only one question: "What helped you come back?"

Gabriel thought for a while. Then answered, "The promise that I hadn't ruined the chance to be loved."

Jo held his hand across the counter.

One Saturday morning, Gabriel stayed in bed past sunrise. Jo was gone, teaching a morning seminar to the new servers, and Gabriel had the whole apartment to himself.

He got up, brewed coffee, lit a candle, and opened his journal.

I am no longer trying to outrun the past. I am building

something alongside it. Brick by brick. Plate by plate. Breath by breath.

Then he sat and stared at the flame in deep meditation.

Later that evening, Jo made a stew from his grandmother's recipe. It was thick with spice, layered with cumin, cinnamon, and history.

Gabriel took a spoonful and closed his eyes.

"It tastes like you do when you're glowing," he said.

Jo laughed. "That's the nicest thing anyone's ever said to me."

They ate in silence for a few minutes. Then Gabriel said:

"Today was perfect."

The summer ended, but Gabriel didn't shrink. He didn't revert. He kept waking up. Kept choosing himself. He kept standing in the kitchen and believed the food would tell the story better than he ever could.

At church one Sunday, he stood beside Jo and me and lit a candle for the version of himself who almost didn't make it. He whispered a thank you. And then, a promise:

"I'm not going anywhere. I'm staying. I'm staying. I'm staying."

They were brushing their teeth when the question dropped.

Jo looked at Gabriel in the mirror and said, "Would you ever want to get married?"

The toothbrush paused in Gabriel's mouth. He spit, rinsed, and stared at his reflection like he was trying to recognize the version of himself who could answer that without flinching.

"I don't know," he said honestly.

Jo didn't push. "Okay."

But it lingered.

It wasn't the question that scared him; it was the answer he hadn't made peace with. Because to marry meant to believe in permanence. To think in permanence meant to think he was worthy of staying. And despite everything, despite healing, despite love, there were nights he still woke up afraid that his presence was a burden.

They fought for the first time that week. A small thing. A missed text. Jo felt ignored. Gabriel shut down instead of explaining. It escalated, not into shouting, but into silence that burned.

Later, Jo sat at the edge of the bed and said, "Sometimes I don't know if you're here. Like you're with me, but you're somewhere else too."

Gabriel looked down.

"I am somewhere else sometimes," he said. "I go back. To the pain. To the shame. To those fucking paintings."

Jo was quiet.

"The ones Bjorn made?"

Gabriel nodded.

"They made me famous and invisible simultaneously," he said. "They turned my worst years into everyone's favorite tragedy. They made me into an idea. Not a person."

Jo reached for his hand. "You can talk about them if you want. You don't have to carry them alone."

So he did.

For the first time, Gabriel sat down and told the whole story, about Bjorn, about the intimacy that had felt like freedom until it wasn't, about how the exhibit had felt like a betrayal with good lighting, and about the way people praised the work while he was still detoxing in a rehab bed.

"It changed my life," he said.

He found out on a Tuesday.

Jo had gone to the gym. Gabriel was scrolling through his phone in bed, lazy and half-asleep, when the headline appeared like a punch:

"BJORN VLATKIS RETURNS WITH 'LUKAS UNFIN-ISHED': A RETROSPECTIVE OF RAGE AND REBIRTH."

He clicked.

There it was. His face. Again. Splashed across a full-color press release. One of the old portraits, blurred and bleeding, hyper-exposed, paired with a new one: sharper, almost digital, his body sliced into triptychs. An image he had never consented to. A moment he didn't even remember. Captured. Printed. Priced.

"A meditation on addiction and distance," the article read. "Vlatkis' LUKAS series returns with previously unreleased works and new 'reflections on intimacy through authenticity.'"

His hands began to shake.

The article listed opening dates. It was touring. Again.

He dropped the phone as if it were hot.

Jo walked in minutes later and immediately saw the color drained from Gabriel's face.

"What happened?"

Gabriel couldn't speak. Just pointed.

Jo read. Then sat on the edge of the bed, jaw locked.

"Did he even?"

"No," Gabriel said. "He didn't call. Didn't email. He just… made me into a gallery again."

"I don't understand how he can keep doing this. Even after the lawsuit."

"Yeah, he changes two fucking letters in my name and suddenly he's an AUTHENTIC fucking Renaissance. "

Jo reached for him, but Gabriel pulled away. "I need to be

215

alone."

"Okay," Jo said softly. "But don't disappear."

Gabriel didn't sleep that night.

He sat on the floor, back against the kitchen cabinets, staring at the dark. He thought about everything he'd worked for: sobriety, self-worth, food, love, and how fragile it all suddenly felt.

He wanted to drink. Just once. To feel nothing. To calm the rising tide inside him.

He opened the cupboard where they kept wine for guests and touched the bottle. Then slammed the door shut.

"No," he whispered.

Then louder. "NO."

He grabbed his keys.

He didn't text Jo. Didn't call anyone. He drove. Out of the city. Onto the highway. The silence in the car was deafening. The road was wet. Every mile marker felt like a heartbeat.

He drove through the night, all the way to New Jersey.

To me.

When I opened the door at 3:12 a.m., I didn't say anything, just pulled him inside and held him.

"I couldn't be alone," he said into my shoulder.

"You're not, papi," I whispered.

He slept on the couch, wrapped in a blanket he once picked out for me at a thrift store. He didn't cry. Didn't speak. Just breathed.

And that, in itself, was a triumph.

We didn't talk right away.

I made him coffee the next morning, set it down near his hand on the couch, and sat beside him. We didn't need filler. The silence wasn't heavy. It was a container, wide enough to hold what he was still learning to name.

When he finally looked up, his eyes were bloodshot but clear.

"It's not just about the painting," he said.

I nodded.

"It's about being frozen in time by someone else. Being captured in the worst version of yourself and then being watched. Reviewed. Sold."

He swallowed. I took a moment.

"He painted my body. But what he did was steal my recovery. He made a myth out of something I hadn't survived yet."

I stayed quiet. Let him keep going.

"I was still bleeding. Still overdosing. And he was oiling up the canvas."

He rubbed his hands together like he was scrubbing something off. Then he looked at me and said the line that gutted me:

"People saw those paintings before I saw myself again."

I didn't cry. Not yet. But I reached for his hand.

"I thought I was over it," he whispered. "But seeing them again, seeing people celebrate them again… it makes me feel like I was never a person. Just a beautiful tragedy to put on a wall."

I squeezed his hand. "You're not a painting."

He shook his head. "I'm not Gabriel anymore. But those pieces keep bringing him back."

That afternoon, we walked. No destination. Just movement. He asked if I still kept my old notebooks. I did. We sat on my porch with two of them spread open between us.

"Do you think healing ever stops?" he asked.

"No," I said. "But I think it changes shape."

He nodded.

217

Then, after a long pause, "I think I want to write."

"Good."

"Not a memoir. Not a tell-all. Just… something that's mine. Something no one else gets to narrate."

"Yes," I said. "Tell your own story. Paint your portrait."

He looked at the skyline.

"Maybe it's not about undoing the painting. Maybe it's about painting over it. In bold, ugly, honest colors."

We sat for another hour.

By the time Jo called, he was ready to pick up.

"I'm safe," he told him. "I needed distance. But I'm coming home."

And he did. Two days later. But not before writing twenty-seven pages in my guestroom. Raw. Unedited. Fierce. Beautiful.

And all his.

That's how he began again.

He returned to the city differently.

Not hardened. Not hollow. But sure. The kind of sure that only comes after a storm, when you're still dripping but alive. He pulled up in front of the apartment, left the engine running, and stared at the front steps for a while. Then, with a warm smile, he turned off the ignition.

The first thing he did when he walked through the door? He blocked Bjorn on every platform. No announcement. No ceremony. Just a single gesture of closure.

Then he sat on the floor. Opened his phone. Scrolled through photos, his dishes, Jo's hands, candles from church, laughter at dinner, the fig dessert that once made someone cry, and whispered, "You're doing great."

He meant it.

He showered. Changed into a clean shirt. Lit a small incense stick that Jo had left on the bookshelf. And when Jo walked through the door an hour later, Gabriel didn't hesitate.

He crossed the room and kissed him.

Not just a kiss. A movie kiss. A kiss with love, and yearning, and surrender. A kiss that said: I choose you, again and again, through the memory and the myth and the miracle of surviving myself.

Jo stepped back only to breathe.

"What was that for?"

"For being here, in this moment, with me," Gabriel said.

Then quieter, with tears brimming:

"For loving me before I knew I was still lovable."

Jo cupped his face. "I'd do it again. Every day. Every version of you."

"I love you," Gabriel said. "And I'm ready now. For the next part. For growing. For being seen. For staying in this."

Jo nodded. Eyes glassy. "Then let's grow. Let's make joy boring."

They laughed. Cried. Kissed again.

That night, they lay on the couch together, their legs tangled, and a movie playing low in the background. Gabriel looked at the ceiling and whispered:

I'm not the painting. I'm the brush.

And for the first time, he believed it.

That month, they took a break from everything that usually occupied them. A pause, a reset, whatever you wanted to call it. A stay-cation, they called it, laughing as they canceled calendar reminders and turned down invitations. They decided to be away without being gone, close without being overwhelmed, together without distraction. They unhooked from work, friends, and routines that sometimes felt like routines even when they weren't. They made a pact: to tell each other stories, to write new ones in the spaces they forgot to fill. They took the car and drove north into the mountains, where the air was crisp and the sky was an unpainted blue, which Gabriel said reminded him of Jo's eyes in the morning.

"Before coffee?" Jo asked.

"Especially before coffee," Gabriel replied, his voice a soft smile.

They stayed in a small cabin. Rustic and perfect. No Wi-Fi. No cell service. Just the two of them and the wild, quiet breathing of the woods. They read books the owner left behind for all vacationers to share. They hiked trails without maps. They got lost and found each other simultaneously. They drank cocoa like children, letting marshmallows melt down their chins, laughing at the sticky collapse of sugar. He wrote me a postcard, Gabriel did, and said: It's beautiful here. I think we'll stay forever.

He didn't mean the cabin, not really. He suggested the feeling. The stability. The hopefulness. He told Jo everything he hadn't told him before, the parts that still wore old scars, the chapters he thought were too unfinished to be shared. This was their rebirth. This was their retreat into permanence, letting go of letting go, their refuge from uncertainty. It wasn't the question Jo had asked when he looked at Gabriel in the mirror and asked, Would you ever want to get married? It wasn't the question but something bigger and more beautiful. It was their new answer, the beginning of the next piece of their imperfect, precious, written-together, painted-over life. It was everything Gabriel had been too afraid to say out loud, everything he had been too scared to hold, and now, here, it was his. It was theirs. And he truly, deeply, madly, believed it.

The night had turned everything to honey and amber, the granite beneath them still warm from the day's sun despite the cooling air that carried the sharp sweetness of pine resin and mountain wildflowers. Gabriel shifted his weight against the stone, feeling the rough texture through his thin cotton shirt, and watched Jo's profile as he gazed out over the valley below. They had climbed here without planning, following a deer trail that wound between boulders and twisted manzanita bushes, their conversation trailing off into comfortable silence as the path grew steeper and their breathing became more labored.

Now, perched on this natural viewing platform with the world spread beneath them like a rumpled green quilt, Gabriel felt something loosening in his chest. The kind of loosening that happened when you realized you were exactly where you were supposed to be. Jo sat cross-legged beside him, his dark curls catching the slanted light and moving gently in the breeze that swept up from the valley floor. His camera rested forgotten beside his hip, its black body starkly contrasted against the pale granite, while his hands worked methodically at the thermos he'd carried up the mountain.

"I brought chamomile," Jo said, his voice carrying that careful precision Gabriel had learned meant he was thinking about more than just tea. The metal cap came off with a soft pop, releasing a cloud of herbal steam that smelled like summer afternoons and his grandmother's kitchen. "Thought we might need something warm once the sun started falling."

Gabriel accepted the cup Jo offered him, their fingers brushing in the transfer, and felt the familiar spark of connection that seemed to happen every time they touched. The tea was perfect; it was not too hot and sweetened with honey that dissolved on

221

his tongue like liquid gold. He wrapped his hands around the ceramic mug and let the warmth seep through his palms while Jo poured his cup and settled back against the granite.

The valley stretched endlessly before them, a wilderness of evergreens and rocky outcroppings that caught the light like scattered jewels. Gabriel could see a hawk circling far below, riding the thermals with barely moving wings, and the faint glitter of a stream winding between the trees somewhere in the distance. The silence up here felt different from city silence, not empty, but full of small sounds that required listening: the whisper of wind through pine needles, the distant call of a jay, the soft rustle of some small creature moving through the brush below them.

Jo sipped his tea and carefully set the cup down on the stone beside him. His movements had a deliberate quality that Gabriel recognized, the careful choreography Jo performed when he was gathering courage for something challenging. Gabriel had seen it before in the way Jo arranged his camera equipment when he was nervous about a shoot, or how he organized his lesson plans when he was preparing to discuss a particularly challenging piece of literature with his students.

"This place reminds me of home," Jo said quietly, his gaze fixed on the darkening mountains in the distance. "Not the Caribbean, that was all ocean and humidity and flowers that bloomed so bright they hurt your eyes. But Morocco. The Atlas Mountains. My grandmother used to take me hiking when I was small, before we moved to the islands. She said mountains taught you how to be patient with yourself."

Gabriel waited, recognizing the cadence of someone working up to something larger. Jo's accent grew slightly more pronounced when he talked about his childhood, the careful

English he'd cultivated as a teacher giving way to something more musical, more rooted in the multiple languages that lived in his throat.

"I stopped taking pictures for almost two years," Jo continued, his voice catching slightly on the confession. "After the hurricane. After we lost everything." He picked up his camera and turned it over in his hands, fingers tracing the familiar contours like a prayer. "People kept telling me I should document the aftermath, that it was important, that my perspective mattered. But every time I tried to raise the viewfinder, all I could see was the water rushing in. The way everything we'd built just... disappeared."

Gabriel set down his tea and shifted closer, close enough that their shoulders touched when Jo breathed. The contact seemed to steady him, and he continued talking, his voice gaining strength as it remained soft.

"I used to wake up screaming," Jo said. "Still do, sometimes. These dreams were of the ground opening up and swallowing everything whole. My students, camera, you, everything I love fall into this endless dark." He shuddered slightly, and Gabriel felt the tremor pass through the granite beneath them. "I know it sounds dramatic, but when you've seen the earth move like that, seen water turn into something that destroys instead of nurtures, it changes how you understand the world. Makes you realize how fragile everything is."

The confession hung between them like morning mist, delicate and requiring careful handling. Gabriel had learned, through his journey with trauma, that sometimes the most important thing you could do was simply witness someone else's pain without trying to fix it or minimize it or wrap it in false comfort. So he stayed quiet and let Jo continue, offering only the steady pressure of his shoulder and the warmth of his presence.

Jo set the camera down again and turned to face Gabriel fully, his dark eyes bright with unshed tears. "That's not even the worst part," he said, and Gabriel felt his heart clench at the raw vulnerability in Jo's voice. "The worst part is what happened when I finally tried to love someone again."

Gabriel's throat tightened, but he forced himself to remain still, to create space for whatever Jo needed to share. He could sense the magnitude of what was coming, could feel it in the way Jo's breathing had become shallow and careful, and his hands had begun to shake slightly as they rested on his knees.

"His name was Marcus," Jo said, the words coming out in a rush as if he needed to expel them before he lost his nerve. "I was nineteen, attending a small college in Saint John's, still trying to rebuild my life after the storm. He was also a freelance photographer, working for several tourism boards. Beautiful and confident and everything I thought I wanted to be."

Jo paused to take a shaky sip of his tea, and Gabriel found himself holding his breath, afraid that any movement might break the spell of honesty that had settled over them like a protective cocoon.

"He pursued me," Jo continued, his voice growing smaller with each word. "Made me feel special, chosen. He said he'd never met anyone who saw the world like I did. We spent three months together, and I thought... I could trust someone with all of myself. With my body, with my heart, with my dreams of becoming a real artist instead of just someone who taught other people about art."

Gabriel felt a cold knot of dread form in his stomach, but he kept his expression neut his body language open and receptive.

Jo needed to tell this story, needed to give voice to whatever had been living in the shadows of his carefully constructed life.

"The night we slept together for the first time," Jo said, his voice barely above a whisper now, "I told him I loved him. I was a virgin, scared, and overwhelmed by how much I felt for him. And he said he loved me too." Jo's hands had begun to shake more visibly now, and Gabriel had to resist the urge to reach for them. "But the next Monday at school, everything changed. He started telling people about us. About me. But not in a proud way. In a… mocking way."

Gabriel's jaw clenched involuntarily, anger flaring hot in his chest, but he forced himself to remain calm. This wasn't about his rage. This was about Jo's pain and courage in sharing it.

"He told them I was pathetic," Jo continued, tears spilling over and tracking down his cheeks. "That I cried during sex, that I was clingy and desperate and that I practically begged him to fuck me, which just wasn't true. He made jokes about my accent and how I talked about photography. He turned our most intimate moments into entertainment for his friends."

The words hit Gabriel like physical blows, and he felt his own hands curl into fists against his thighs. The idea of someone taking Jo's vulnerability, his first experience of love, and weaponizing it filled Gabriel with a rage so pure and protective it took his breath away.

"I had to see him every day," Jo said, his voice breaking. "The island was small, the immigrant community smaller. I couldn't escape him, the stories he told, or how people looked at me afterward. Like I was this tragic, broken thing that wasn't quite brave enough to deserve love without humiliation."

Gabriel couldn't stay still any longer. He reached out slowly, telegraphing his movement so Jo could pull away if he wanted to, and placed his hand gently on Jo's thigh. The denim was warm from the sun and soft from wear, and Gabriel could feel the tremor in Jo's muscles even through the fabric.

"Jo," Gabriel said quietly, his voice thick with emotion. "I'm so sorry. What he did to you wasn't love. That was cruelty disguised as intimacy."

Jo looked down at Gabriel's hand on his leg, and his expression shifted. He became less guarded and more open. "I know that now," he said. "Intellectually, I know it. However, it had been living in my body for years. This fear is that if I let someone see all of me, they'd find something worth mocking. Something worth discarding."

Gabriel's thumb traced a small circle against Jo's face, a gesture of comfort and connection. "Is that why you've been so careful with us? With me?"

Jo nodded, fresh tears starting to flow. "I kept waiting for you to see whatever it was Marcus saw. Whatever made me so easy to humiliate? I waited until you realized I was too much, not enough, or just… wrong somehow."

The admission broke something open in Gabriel, and his eyes burned with tears. The idea that Jo had been carrying this fear, this expectation of abandonment, throughout their entire relationship made Gabriel want to wrap Jo in enough love and safety that the old wounds could finally begin to heal.

"Jo," Gabriel said, his voice steady despite the emotion threatening to overwhelm him. "Look at me."

Jo raised his eyes to meet Gabriel's gaze, and Gabriel saw everything there- the fear, the hope, the desperate desire to be known and loved without condition. Gabriel moved his hand from Jo's thigh to cup his face, thumb brushing away the tears that continued to fall.

"Nothing about you is worth mocking," Gabriel said, each word deliberate and weighted with truth. "Nothing about you that is too much or not enough. You are not broken, and you are not a tragedy. You are the most beautiful man I have ever known, inside and out, and anyone who can't see that is blind and stupid and doesn't deserve even a moment of your attention."

Jo closed his eyes and leaned into Gabriel's touch, his breath coming in shaky exhales that seemed to release years of held tension. Gabriel waited, letting his words sink in, letting Jo feel the truth of them in his bones.

When Jo opened his eyes again, there was something different in them, a lightness that hadn't been there before, as if sharing his deepest wounds had somehow made them less powerful, less capable of defining him.

"There's something else," Jo said, his voice soft but no longer trembling. "Something I've never told anyone."

Gabriel's heart clenched with a mixture of honor and terror. To be trusted with Jo's secrets felt like being handed something precious and fragile, something that required the most careful handling.

"You can tell me anything," Gabriel said, and meant it entirely.

Jo took a deep breath, gathering courage for this final confession. "I've never told anyone I love them the way I love you," he said, the words coming out in a rush. "Not just the words, I said those to Marcus because I thought I was supposed to, because it felt like what you did when someone made you feel special. But this... this feeling I have for you, it's like nothing I've ever experienced. It's like you've become part of my cellular structure, like I can't imagine existing in a world where you don't exist, too."

227

Gabriel felt his breath catch in his throat, overwhelmed by the magnitude of what Jo was sharing. "Jo..."

"I'm terrified of it," Jo continued, tears flowing freely now but somehow cleaner, less bitter than before. "I'm terrified of needing someone this much, of building my happiness around another person who could disappear or change or decide I'm not worth staying for. But I'm more terrified of the alternative. Of holding back, of protecting myself so carefully that I miss out on the most beautiful thing ever happening to me."

Gabriel felt his tears start to fall as Jo's words washed over him like a benediction. He had spent so many years believing he was unworthy of this kind of love, this complete and generous devotion, that hearing it spoken aloud felt like a miracle he was still learning to accept.

"I love you," Jo whispered, his voice raw with emotion. "I love you so much that it might scare me sometimes. I love your hands when you cook, how you hum under your breath when you're concentrating, and how you cry at movies even when they're not that sad. I love your scars, stories, and how you've turned your pain into something that feeds people. I love your courage and gentleness; you make me feel worth protecting."

Gabriel pressed his palm over Jo's heart, feeling the rapid flutter of his pulse beneath the thin cotton of his shirt. "I'm here," he said, the words carrying the weight of a promise. "I'm not going anywhere. I'm not Marcus and won't hurt you like he did. I will love you how you deserve to be loved, completely, honestly, without condition."

Jo opened his eyes and looked at Gabriel with an expression of such trust and vulnerability that Gabriel felt his own heart might break from its beauty. The golden light was fading now, painting the sky in shades of lavender and rose, and a night bird began to call somewhere below them.

Jo leaned forward and rested his forehead against Gabriel's, their breath mingling in the cooling air. "I want to believe that," he whispered. "I want to believe we can build something that lasts."

"We can," Gabriel said, his voice certain despite the tears streaming down his face. "We are. Every day we choose each other, every conversation like this one, every moment we decide to stay instead of run, we're building something that can weather any storm."

The wind picked up slightly, rustling through the pine trees below them with a sound like whispered prayers, and Gabriel felt something settle in his chest, something that had been anxious and uncertain, finally finding its proper place. This was what love looked like when it was real, when it was built on truth instead of pretense, on vulnerability instead of performance.

Jo lifted his head and smiled through his tears, and Gabriel saw his wonder reflected in him. They had climbed this mountain to escape, to find peace in the wilderness, but what they had found instead was something more valuable: the courage to be wholly known and the faith to believe they were worth knowing.

The valley below them had fallen into a purple shadow, and the first stars began to appear in the darkening sky. Gabriel pulled Jo closer, wrapping his arms around him as they sat together on their granite throne, witnesses to their transformation. The night air was growing cold, but Gabriel felt warm through his bones, heated by the fire of honest love and the promise of all the tomorrows they would write together.

In the silence that followed, broken only by the soft sounds of the mountain settling into evening, Gabriel felt the truth of what they had just shared settling into his bones like a new kind of gravity. They were no longer two separate people trying to find their way toward each other. They were something new, something neither of them had been capable of becoming alone.

The stars grew brighter as they sat together, and Gabriel knew that whatever challenges waited for them back in the world below, they would face them as they faced this moment, together, honestly, with hearts wide open to the terrible and beautiful possibility of being completely loved.

Twenty-Three

ROAD TRIP

When they got home, they had an easier time discussing complex topics. Nothing was off-limits. One night, lying on their backs in bed, a breeze curling through the window, Gabriel asked, "What was it like? Coming out where you came from?"

Jo exhaled, his breath catching slightly.

"I was fifteen when my Auntie found my journal," he said. "She read everything. All my poems. Letters I'd written to boys I never gave."

Gabriel turned to face him.

"She told me I was breaking her heart," Jo continued. "That I'd brought shame into the house. She stopped touching my face when she kissed me goodnight. Started praying louder after dinner."

Gabriel reached for his hand.

"She wasn't cruel. But she was afraid. And I became afraid of myself."

Jo paused.

"My father, though… he stayed. He didn't say, 'I accept you,' but he never let me forget I was still his son and never stopped trying to understand."

"My father made me feel comfortable in my skin. My Auntie, who had stepped in to help, made me miss my mother so much. I wondered if they were alike, and prayed at night that they weren't."

Gabriel pressed his lips to Jo's temple. "She failed you. But you didn't fail her."

Jo nodded, tears gathering. "I've learned to grieve the mother I wished I had. And honor the one I did."

They talked more over the days. They had open, halting conversations about pain but also about desire and possibility.

They talked about open relationships. Boundaries. Trust after betrayal. The fear of becoming the thing you once swore you'd never be.

"What do you think about monogamy?" Gabriel asked one night.

"I believe in honesty more than rules," Jo said. "But with you? I want the kind of love that looks no further."

Gabriel smiled. "Me too."

They talked about cheating.

"Have you ever?" Gabriel asked.

Jo looked him in the eye. "No. I've been cheated on. That was enough."

"I have," Gabriel admitted. "Before sobriety. It was about emptiness, not cruelty. But still."

Jo nodded. "Thank you for telling me. You're not that person anymore."

They talked about substances.

"If I ever relapse," Gabriel said, "promise me you'll leave. But not without hugging me first."

Jo pulled him close. "If you relapse, I'll hold you. Then I'll call your sponsor. Then I'll make soup."

Gabriel laughed. "That's dangerously romantic."

"It's just love," Jo whispered. "The kind that holds all your chapters."

Joy wasn't loud anymore. It had softened into something simpler, something steadier. It sat with them on weekday mornings and wrapped around them on tired Thursday nights when they fell asleep with books half-open and tea cooling on the counter.

Gabriel had once thought healing would feel like a trumpet, like banners, like being reborn in front of a cheering crowd. However, it felt more like doing laundry together, like the click of Jo's pen as he prepared schedules, groceries, and like sharing silence and knowing it didn't mean something was wrong.

They were building something.

And building required repetition.

Gabriel now woke up most mornings before his alarm. He'd make coffee for both of them, kiss Jo's shoulder while he packed his work bag, and jot down three things he was grateful for in a notebook that lived by the toaster.

Some days he wrote:

Jo's hands. No nightmares. Cilantro that survived the window garden.

Other days:

I didn't feel like apologizing for existing today. Jo made him laugh so hard that I dropped a plate. I was still there.

One Sunday after church, Jo suggested they cook for the

neighborhood mutual aid group, which was struggling to find volunteers.

Gabriel didn't hesitate.

They made lentils. Gallons of them. They filled trays with roasted vegetables, rice, and homemade flatbread, then cleaned up late. A little boy with grass-stained knees hugged Gabriel's leg before leaving.

Jo saw Gabriel watching the door long after the last family left.

"You're doing it again," he said.

"Doing what?"

"Making me feel like we can do anything together."

Gabriel smiled and shouted, "Cheesy alert!! Someone come get this cheese-ball!!" They couldn't stop laughing.

The next day, Jo surprised him with a small print: a sketch of hands passing a bowl titled Still Feeding.

Gabriel hung it by the stove.

"I think I want to open my place one day," he said.

Jo's eyes lit up. "What would it be?"

"A restaurant," Gabriel said. "But also not. More like a home. A kitchen that feeds not just hunger, but grief. Recovery. Questions."

"So… a temple."

Gabriel grinned. "With soup."

The idea didn't go away. It lived on sticky notes. Scribbled in margins and whispered between bites of dinner and after the last dish was washed.

Gabriel started dreaming it into shape.

The name came to him in a dream. "La Mesa," The Table.

He woke up with it in his mouth and ran to his journal.

La Mesa: a space for the exiled, the mourning, the rebuilding.

A kitchen for the in-between.

He told Jo over breakfast, cheeks glowing.

Jo smiled. "Then let's get to work."

And they did.

Jo sketched layout ideas on printer paper with ballpoint pens, and Gabriel drafted menus on the backs of receipts. They walked past vacant buildings, peered in windows, visited community centers, asked questions, and made lists.

But they didn't rush. They let it take the shape it needed, like proofing dough.

They cooked for friends every Sunday, small dinners that doubled as test kitchens. Word got out. People asked to be invited. Writers, activists, lonely students, estranged sons, and healers.

Each meal ended the same way: with silence.

Gabriel began collecting stories.

He asked each guest to write a memory connected to food on a note card.

One said, "Rice with cumin always makes me cry."

Another, "My grandmother made tea so sweet it healed arguments."

A third, "I learned I was gay over a bowl of pho. My friend passed the chili oil and told me, 'It's okay, I see you.'"

Gabriel posted the cards on a corkboard in their kitchen. It began to look like a shrine.

Jo called it The Archive of Tenderness. One night, after a particularly joyful gathering, Gabriel sat on the floor while Jo strummed an old guitar.

Gabriel stared at the flicker of candlelight across the windowpane and whispered, "I think I finally believe I deserve this."

Jo strummed softer. "Good. Because you do."

Gabriel closed his eyes.

And the room didn't feel borrowed anymore. It felt built.

They weren't rushing to build La Mesa but living inside its promise. Every recipe they tested, every guest they welcomed, and every story they collected was a brick in its foundation.

And with each passing day, Gabriel found his voice expanding.

One night, Jo handed him a manila envelope.

"What's this?" Gabriel asked.

"Open it."

Inside: a grant application packet. A small fund for emerging culinary artists doing community-centered work.

"I thought we could apply together," Jo said. "I'll help with the writing. You tell the story."

Gabriel bit his lip.

"What if they say no?"

"Then we try again. But what if they say yes?"

They stayed up past midnight drafting. The application became a love letter to soup, community, and the long healing arc that moved through kitchens and time.

They submitted it in early spring. While they waited, they lived.

They took a weekend trip to a cabin without service: just books, soup, and each other.

And through it all, Gabriel kept repeating a phrase under his breath:

This is what the after looks like.

Presence.

Peace.

A kitchen filled with light.

The email arrived on a Wednesday afternoon, sandwiched

between a discount code from a spice vendor and a reminder from the electric company. Jo saw it first.

"They wrote back," he called from the couch.

Gabriel dropped the whisk he was using, wiped his hands on his apron, and crossed the room.

Jo turned the screen toward him.

Subject: Grant Approval – La Mesa

Gabriel scratched his head nervously. Could you read it twice? Then a third time.

He sat down slowly. "We got it."

Jo laughed and kissed his cheek. "You got it."

They held each other for a long time.

The next morning, Jo jumped on their bed with a chirping happiness that Gabriel was unprepared for.

"Good Morning!!" he sang, the sound of wind and movement behind his voice. "You ready?"

Gabriel smiled, his voice catching. "Ready for what?"

Jo's laughter came like honey poured too fast. "Surprise. I packed our bags. Pride month. You and me. A road trip. We're reaching as many states as possible. Rainbow flags, good music, odd diners, maybe a roadside tarot reading. And we'll be home just in time for the big reveal."

Gabriel sank onto the back stoop, stunned. "You're serious."

"As serious as cumin in lentils," Jo replied, which, for them, meant gospel.

And that was that.

They left the next morning. Jo had scribbled a loose itinerary on a diner napkin, now smudged and folded into quarters. In the glove-box: a GPS they barely used, a playlist titled "Love, Loudly," and an unspoken agreement to let joy steer.

First stop: Delaware. Then Pennsylvania. Then, Ohio,

where they danced barefoot in a pasture at a farm-hosted Pride celebration while a local choir covered Fleetwood Mac under string lights.

They kissed under rainbow streamers in Kentucky, sunlight catching the glitter still stuck to their necks from the night before.

Held hands on a ferry bound for Michigan, where Jo fed Gabriel cherry pie and said, "Every version of you is worth traveling with."

In Illinois, Jo wore a sunflower crown, and Gabriel bought an oversized thrifted leather jacket simply because Jo said, "It makes you look like a poet who's survived something."

They journaled at gas stations. Sang at rest stops, shared peach cobbler from paper plates with a T4T couple celebrating ten years together. "We got married the same week you opened that kitchen," one said.

Gabriel whispered between flags, homemade signs, and impromptu parades in town after town: "We made it."

Texas greeted them with humidity and hymns. At the Austin Pride march, the energy was a pulse of purpose: signs for trans justice, reproductive freedom, and chosen kinship. Gabriel wept during a spoken word set performed by a non-binary poet who closed with: "We are not survivors. We are the architects of dawn."

That night, Jo held Gabriel tighter than he ever had.

In New Mexico, they found a cozier kind of Pride; more of a circle than a spectacle. In the desert, barefoot and surrounded by strangers who felt like mirrors, they passed sage and told stories.

Gabriel stood, voice steady. "I've been many things. A painting. A son. A ghost. A cook. A partner. And now I'm something else too. I'm someone who believes he deserves to be here."

A soft applause. A shared silence. A woman pressed an amethyst into his palm. "For clarity," she said.

He kept it in his pocket the rest of the trip.

When they reached California, the car smelled like sunscreen and lavender. Gabriel's face hurt from grinning. In San Francisco, they stayed three nights. Castro Street. The trolley. Sunset over Ocean Beach. Jo gave him a matching enamel pin that said "Still Blooming."

Gabriel wore it on his apron the next morning.

In Oregon, they hiked a mossy trail and swam in a glacial lake, naked and laughing like boys who hadn't yet known the sharp end of the world.

Washington brought drizzle and bookstores. They bought their favorite novels secondhand and read them aloud by candlelight in a rented cabin near the coast.

In Idaho, no festival. Just an LGBTQIA+-owned diner with the best pancakes either of them had ever tasted. They left a note on the check: "Thank you for making space in a place where they told us there'd be none." The owner cried.

They looped back through the mountains, slowing down. They sang louder. Slept in. Lost track of the map.

Found each other again and again, between roadside pie and midnight conversation, in the open air of becoming.

And still, they drove.

It was somewhere along a narrow Montana highway, mountains on either side, when Gabriel reached over and placed his hand over Jo's. No words, just a simple touch that said I'm here, and I see you. The sound of tires and Jo's joy filled the air.

They began a new ritual. At every border crossing, they

shared one secret; nothing dramatic, just unspoken. In Utah, Jo admitted he'd once wanted to become a florist. Gabriel confessed he still dreamed about old kitchens and sometimes missed the chaos. In Wyoming, Jo revealed he used to write anonymous love letters and leave them in library books. Gabriel told him he once skipped school three times to watch Call Me By Your Name alone.

They laughed. Cried a little. Kissed under motel parking lot lights.

Outside Denver, they stopped at a tiny coffee shack run by an LGBTQIA+.. Jo ordered two lattes and tipped with a drawing of Gabriel's face on a napkin. The barista pinned it on the wall next to a rainbow sticker that read: Queers Fuel Here.

One night in Nebraska, they stayed in a roadside B&B run by an old lesbian couple, Nora and Martha. Martha said over cornbread and vegetable stew, "We've been together 48 years, and the secret is sleeping in sometimes and apologizing with dessert."

Gabriel and Jo looked at each other, eyes soft with the weight of their shared road.

In South Dakota, they lay under the stars, wrapped in a blanket in the bed of their car. Jo whispered, "I didn't know peace could sound like your breath." Gabriel replied, "I didn't know love could smell like dry grass and your shampoo."

They made a playlist of every sound they'd grown to love on the trip: distant coyotes, Jo's laugh when he dreamed, the beep of gas pumps, diner music through cracked windows. It was their LGBTQIA+ symphony.

They attended a backyard Pride potluck in Minnesota and brought their now-famous road trip lemon-thyme cake. The host asked, "What are you two?" Jo said, "We're still figuring that out, but it's edible."

That night, Gabriel wrote in his journal: This journey isn't about arrival. It's about the cuisine of our connection, slow-cooked and seasoned with memory.

They stopped calling it a road trip. They started calling it the roam.

Every new city was a kitchen. Every meal is a new prayer.

In Wisconsin, they stayed above a radical LGBTQIA+ bookstore. Gabriel gave an impromptu reading from his new manuscript to a group of strangers who brought him cherry soda and hugs. Jo danced with a 70-year-old leather daddy in a mesh tank top.

Their laughter fed whole blocks.

Back in the car, Jo said, "I don't want to go back to how things were."

Gabriel whispered, "We don't have to. We are something new."

In Missouri, they got matching tattoos; tiny forks inked on their wrists, a reminder that they always had a seat at each other's table.

At night, they curled into each other like puzzle pieces, finally remembering how to fit.

One morning in Arkansas, Jo made roadside coffee using an old camp stove and whispered, "This is how I want to start every day; with you, outdoors, over something warm."

Gabriel nodded, silent but full.

By the time they reached Louisiana, the journey had become a map of everything they'd built. Not a destination, but a direction. Not a finish line, but a feast.

And when they turned toward home, Jo reached over and pressed play on their final playlist.

Gabriel leaned back, the wind curling through the open windows.

They drove, two hearts salted and slow-roasted by the long miles, returning not to where they began, but to each other; again and again. And when the home skyline finally came into view, Gabriel reached for Jo's hand across the console and whispered, "I've never been more ready."

Because home wasn't a place.

It was a person. It was a table. It was a journey.

And it was waiting.

The sun was setting as they pulled into the driveway.

The house looked the same, with white shutters, chipped paint, and flower pots on the porch, but everything felt different. Lighter. Like something had been waiting for them to come home and see it with new eyes.

Mami was already outside. She waved, apron on, arms open, like a lighthouse in a storm.

Gabriel jumped out of the car before Jo even parked.

He wrapped her up in a hug so tight she laughed.

"You made it," she whispered.

"Of course we did," he said. "Wouldn't miss this."

Jo stepped out and hugged her, too. She kissed both their cheeks and wiped a tear from her chin like it was just wind.

The sun was setting as they pulled into the driveway.

The house looked the same: white shutters, chipped paint, and flower pots on the porch, but everything felt different. Lighter. Like something had been waiting for them to come home and see it with new eyes.

Gabriel felt the weight of time in his chest not heavy but full. Like his lungs had learned a new way to breathe somewhere between the Montana skies and the Louisiana heat, he touched the doorknob as if asking permission from every memory that once lived inside.

Jo reached out and squeezed his hand. "You ready?"

Gabriel nodded. "Let's do it."

Mami was already outside. Apron on. Arms open. Like a lighthouse in a storm. She stood at the edge of the porch with that unwavering steadiness that only mothers and gods seemed to possess.

Gabriel jumped out of the car before Jo even parked. He ran, feet clumsy and heart open, and wrapped her up in a hug so tight she laughed like something holy.

"You made it," she whispered, brushing his hair back with one hand.

"Of course we did," he said, voice cracking. "Wouldn't miss this."

Jo stepped out next, slower, reverent. He walked up and hugged her with depth. "You boys hungry?" she asked, voice thick with emotion and mischief.

"Always," Jo grinned.

Inside, the house was warm with a sense of nostalgia. The table was already set; candles flickering like they knew what was coming. Empanadas stacked high. Mango slices glistening. A pitcher of cold tea beaded with condensation. And in the middle, a cake that smelled like almond and orange blossom.

They sat down together, the three of them. The plates clinked. Forks hovered. The air was saturated with the kind of love that never needed explaining.

And then I came in.

Hands behind my back. Grinning like the sun had told me a secret. I paused in the doorway, breath caught somewhere between anticipation and awe.

Gabriel stood. "You okay?"

I nodded, feeling every cell in my body buzz. "Better than okay. I've got news."

Mami raised her eyebrows, already reading something on my face.

Jo leaned forward, eyes wide.

I breathed, pulled my hands around, and held up a tiny pair of baby shoes.

"We're pregnant," I said. "Twins."

For a moment, the house stood still. A beat suspended in time.

Then Mami gasped; her hand over her mouth, her eyes spilling over. Jo jumped to his feet like he'd been lit from within. Gabriel covered his mouth with both hands, his eyes shining like sunrise after too many nights.

"You're;"

"Yes," I laughed, barely holding it in. "Twins!! Can you believe it?"

Gabriel crossed the room in two strides and pulled me into a hug so fierce and full, it felt like a promise.

"We're gonna be uncles," he whispered, voice thick with wonder.

Mami wiped her eyes and pulled us both into her arms. "The three musketeers… and two more coming."

Just behind me, Darius yelled, "And me and Jo!!" from the doorway.

We all turned and laughed, tangled in hugs and joy. Arms over shoulders, hands clutching backs, faces pressed together like a prayer.

Mami. Me. Gabriel. Jo. Darius. And the loves that made our worlds feel livable and luminous.

The windows glowed gold. Outside, the wind carried the scent of jasmine and memory.

Inside, the table waited.

We sat down again, this time five of us. Plates full, hearts fuller.

This was what it meant to arrive.

And we knew; this wasn't the end.

It was the table we'd been building all along.

And now, it had room for more.

Later that night, while the others cleared dishes and laughter echoed down the hallway, Gabriel slipped upstairs. The room he used to sleep in still smelled faintly like cedar and dust, like the afterglow of every dream he never told anyone.

He closed the door gently, sat on the edge of the bed, and took a deep breath.

Uncle. Twins. Tiny feet. Stories not yet written.

His hands trembled.

He lay back against the quilt, one he hadn't seen since he was eighteen and scared of everything. He stared at the ceiling, watching the light shift in small patterns.

Then, slowly, he began to breathe.

In.

Out.

Four counts in, hold for four, release for six.

He let the world shrink to breath and heartbeat.

He pictured the twins, how tiny they would be, and wondered who they would most resemble. He pictured telling them stories, cooking for them, and being the kind of uncle who showed up with wild berries and poems. Who taught them to say grace not with folded hands but with joyful mouths?

His eyes stung.

He whispered to the ceiling, "I did it. I made it."

He made it into this. Into this moment.

Into this home. This body. This life. This love.

He sat up slowly. Picked up his old journal from the desk. Flipped to a blank page and wrote, You did well, Gabriel. You did well.

And then, three knocks at the door.

He looked up. Smiled.

"Yes?"

Jo cracked the door open, holding two mugs of tea. "Thought maybe you needed a breath."

Gabriel laughed, wiping his eyes. "You psychic now?"

Jo stepped in, handed him the mug, and sat beside him.

"No. Just know what your different pauses mean."

They sat there in the soft light, sipping tea, not fixing anything, and just taking in the peace in the air.

Gabriel leaned his head on Jo's shoulder.

"Thank you," he whispered.

Jo just squeezed his hand.

Below them, Mami started humming a lullaby.

And in that room, that house, that breath, Gabriel finally believed he could carry it all.

By morning, the house was buzzing again; coffee on the stove, sunlight kissing the worn floors, Mami humming something old and full of meaning. Gabriel woke earlier than usual, barefoot, still carrying the weight and warmth of the previous night's tea and tears.

He padded to his old room, pausing at the doorway. Jo joined him with a second cup of coffee.

"I've been thinking," Gabriel said.

"Dangerous," Jo teased, shoulder nudging his.

"No. What if this room… became the nursery?"

Jo's eyes widened, then softened with a yes that didn't need words.

They told Mami at breakfast. She clapped her hands and said. "Let's do it today."

They started by stripping the room bare, every drawer, curtain, and old book that hadn't been cracked was messier than expected, marked by dust, laughter, and unexpected tears. They found Gabriel's old poetry journals, Jo's forgotten postcards, and a year's worth of Polaroids that made Gabriel gasp and cover his face.

They painted the walls a soft, warm green. Raquel came by and brought rollers. Curtis showed up with iced coffee and a tool belt he barely knew how to use. Mami supervised from the doorway, shaking her head with affection.

The crib arrived in parts, both literally and metaphorically. Gabriel assembled it with Jo, cursing IKEA instructions and laughing the whole way. Mami stitched curtains by hand, slow and sure, her fingers dancing along the edge of the fabric like they knew secrets. She chose a soft cotton with sunflowers and tiny blue birds, murmuring in Spanish under her breath; a song half lullaby, half prayer.

As she stitched, she told stories.

"Mi mamá tenía una sala de costura en Buenos Aires," she said. "In the back of our house, past the lemon tree and the laundry lines. It was small, always smelled like starch and violets. But it was where everything important happened."

She threaded another needle and continued, her voice low and rich. "Back then, you didn't speak too loudly during the junta. But my mother's sewing room was where resistance hummed softly. Women gathered under the guise of patching uniforms or making baby clothes, but exchanged information, with hidden messages tucked into the hems. Maps etched onto the insides of fabric panels. Prayers sewn into pockets."

Raquel sat cross-legged on the floor, spellbound. "Your mom was in the resistance?"

Mami nodded. "She didn't call it that. She called it 'caring loudly in secret.'"

She paused to reposition the curtain fabric. The morning light caught the silver in her hair.

"One time," she said, "a woman came with a coat she said needed mending. My mamá opened the lining and found names. Names of the desaparecidos. Names of people who'd been taken. That coat became a ledger. A confession. A blessing."

Jo stopped painting and listened. Gabriel came in from the hallway, wiping sweat from his brow, and sat quietly.

"After she finished the coat, she added something," Mami said. "A small pouch inside. She filled it with dried yerba mate, rosemary, and a piece of obsidian. Protection. Memory. Fire."

She smiled. "She returned it to the woman and said, 'Now it's more than a coat. It's a little piece of home.'"

The room was silent.

Mami looked at the curtain in her lap. "I want these to hold the same magic. Maybe not for revolution, but for rebirth."

Jo leaned over. "They already do."

Gabriel crouched beside her. "I had no idea."

"None of you did," she said. "Because it wasn't something to boast about. It was something to breathe into the fabric of the everyday."

She touched the edge of the finished panel. "Everything she stitched had a purpose. Even the decorative things. Especially those."

The sewing machine on the table wasn't her mother's, but she touched it as if it were. "In Argentina, during the darkest years, women couldn't march. They couldn't speak out. But they could sew. Sew and sing. We used to sing old milongas with double meanings, serving as codes to identify safe houses. Songs about lost love that were really about lost people."

She added another row of stitching.

"There's power in domesticity," she said. "Because it's been underestimated. Because it survives."

Gabriel whispered, "Because it remembers."

Mami smiled. "Sí, mijo. Porque recuerda."

She handed the curtain panel to Gabriel, who held it as if it might disappear. Then she began another.

"I want these windows to be more than decoration. I want them to be witnesses. So when the twins arrive, they'll be greeted not just by color, but by legacy."

She hummed again, an old folk song that sounded like love and resistance.

Outside, the wind stirred the lemon tree.

Inside, history stitched itself into new beginnings..

Each piece added to the room came with a memory, a blanket from my first solo trip. A quilt Jo had been saving from his grandmother. A tiny framed photo of a Sunday brunch at Pan y Paz was taped to the base of the changing table.

They hung string lights along the ceiling. They're not too bright, but they're just enough to say, "We've made this soft for you."

On the second night, Gabriel sat in the center of the floor, surrounded by everyone he loved, and said, "I didn't think I could be this person."

Gabriel replied, "You didn't become someone new. You came

back to yourself."

Jo kissed the top of his head. "And you brought us with you."

The nursery was finished by the third day. It smelled like lavender and promise. The bookshelf was already half full; LGBTQIA+ fables, bilingual board books, poetry, cookbooks from their travels.

Something shifts in the air as Gabriel says, "I want to tell you about Gio."

Jo's hand finds Gabriel's beneath the table. His fingers are still and certain, bracing Gabriel. Mami tilts her head, eyes sharp and interested. I pause with my hair falling over my face.

Jo leans forward, resting his free hand on Gabriel's knee. "Gabriel showed me what hope feels like again."

Gabriel glanced at Jo, taking in the curve of his smile and the calm joy it held. Gabriel sees the night they found Gio again, months after Gabriel thought he was gone for good. See him skittish and unsure at the door, Jo's arm tight around his waist. He remembers the care and caution in his voice as he invited Gio to join them, offering trust when Gabriel had almost given up. He remembers how they learned to let their hearts unbend. Gabriel was caught between those memories and this moment, filled with the same impossible tenderness.

"He's become like a little brother," Gabriel says. "To both of us."

I reach for my tea, stealing a sip before handing it over. I brush a stray curl behind my ear, a small smile brightening my face. "A second brother we never had," she says. "Bringing sunshine into our lives."

Mami's voice brings me back to the porch, soft and deliberate. "I prayed daily for your healing, hijo," she says, hand cool and solid against my cheek. Her touch surprises me, the long-ago scent of lavender lotion flooding my senses. She uses it sparingly now, but I remember how it filled every room when we first moved to Miami, seeping from freshly unpacked boxes into my dreams. "I never expected it to come from someone so young."

Her words linger in the summer-thick air, and Gabriel thinks about those first days with Jo and Gio. Remembering how Gio crashed and coursed through the apartment, upending their careful balance and forcing each other to find a new one. Jo and Gabriel dared to plan a future with him, afraid to put words to it in case saying it out loud made it less accurate, and finding this place for him, them, and finding home.

Jo takes a sip of tea, his fingers intertwined with Gabriel's. I shift on my chair, watching him, watching me. "We didn't expect it either," Gabriel says. "But he reminded us—"

"That family can grow," Jo finishes, as if we share the thought, not just the words.

I pass the last empanada across the table, half serious and half playful. "Tell him we saved this for him."

"We did?" Mami says, her voice carrying the soft rasp of humor.

"Yes," I insist, looking at them both. I wrap the pastry in a napkin and set it by the tea pitcher.

Mami shakes her head with the mock resignation of someone used to being overruled. Gabriel sees a glimmer, a mix of pride and tenderness in her eyes. It's the same look she gave him when she saw Pan y Paz for the first time. Gabriel tells her, unsure and awkward, that the kitchen is everything he has ever dreamed of.

Gabriel remembered how she'd turned to Jo and taken his hands in hers, inspecting them the way only a mother could.

"Strong hands," she'd said, nodding as if finding what she hoped to see. "Make sure you use them to take care of my son." He had given Gabriel the most patient smile then, and his heart had done the unexpected, unfurling into new shapes.

"I want to say that family can grow in the most unexpected ways," Gabriel says, squeezing Jo's hand in thanks for the thought, for the truth of it.

The porch falls into contented hush, a quilt of night sounds covering us in familiar patterns. Mami pours more tea, the liquid a pale thread between her hands and the waiting glasses. The sky shifts from orange to indigo, pinpricks of stars like needlework over the expanse. The air is cooling around us, and we move closer together, legs touching beneath the table. Gabriel thought about how much he fought for this closeness and how far we've come to find it.

Gabriel, Mami, Jo, Darius, I, and a table between us. All of us gathered here. All of us are at home.

Later in the night, as the stars showered above us, it was as if I could see all our astrological destinies laid out in the sky. Looking over at Gabriel, then back to the stars, I thought of his star alignment, his sign. Tonight, it seemed, it was the fifth house that had to bow to him. Born under its glittering dominion, Gabriel had once been its marionette, dancing for love, performing for worth, setting fire to every room to feel seen. But somewhere between the bruises of heartbreak and the balm of braised lamb shank, he stopped being the boy who burned and became the man who cooked, loved, and stayed. He didn't escape the stage, no. He redesigned it. Now the spotlight was soft, his own, and he didn't need applause to know he mattered. The fifth house was still his, but now, he owned the paintbrush.

His story slowly repainted, one brushstroke at a time.